TAMING
THE
SCOTSMAN

TAMING THE SCOTSMAN

KINLEY MACGREGOR

WHEELER
PUBLISHING

Published in 2004 by arrangement with Avon Books, An Imprint of HarperCollins Publishers, Inc.

Wheeler Large Print Softcover.

The text of this Large Print edition is unabridged. Other aspects of the book may vary from the original edition.

Set in 16 pt. Plantin by Minnie B. Raven.

Printed in the United States on permanent paper.

Library of Congress Cataloging-in-Publication Data

MacGregor, Kinley, 1965–
    Taming the Scotsman / Kinley MacGregor.
      p. cm.
    ISBN 1-58724-595-7 (lg. print : sc : alk. paper)
    1. Highlands (Scotland) — Fiction.
  2. Large type books.   I. Title.
PS3563.A311145T36 2004
    813'.6—dc22   2003064518

For my fans, who support me and who have given me untold smiles at conferences and booksignings, and when I read my emails and letters. To the RBL Romantica and DH posters, whose presence is always a source of warmth.

For my family and friends, who make my life worthwhile. And for my editor and agent, who believe in me and are willing to give me the opportunity to introduce the world to the people who live in my heart and mind.

Thank you all! I hope each of you have all the blessings and riches you deserve. Hugs!

As the Founder/CEO of NAVH, the only national health agency solely devoted to those who, although not totally blind, have an eye disease which could lead to serious visual impairment, I am pleased to recognize Thorndike Press* as one of the leading publishers in the large print field.

Founded in 1954 in San Francisco to prepare large print textbooks for partially seeing children, NAVH became the pioneer and standard setting agency in the preparation of large type.

Today, those publishers who meet our standards carry the prestigious "Seal of Approval" indicating high quality large print. We are delighted that Thorndike Press is one of the publishers whose titles meet these standards. We are also pleased to recognize the significant contribution Thorndike Press is making in this important and growing field.

Lorraine H. Marchi, L.H.D.
Founder/CEO
NAVH

* Thorndike Press encompasses the following imprints: Thorndike, Wheeler, Walker and Large Print Press.

Prologue

Today was the anniversary of *the* day. The day that had changed Ewan MacAllister's life forever.

In one moment, he had been the naive son of a respected and feared laird.

In the next, he'd been the murderer of his own brother.

His stomach knotted by grief and guilt, Ewan stared out across the loch where its dark, choppy waves shimmered like glass, and remembered his brother Kieran's face. Remembered the day he had taken the one thing Kieran had loved more than life itself.

"Damn you, Isobail," he snarled before he downed the last of the ale in his flagon.

If not for Isobail and her evil machinations, the world in which he lived would have been an entirely different place. Ewan would have married Catie ingen Anghus. And no doubt Kieran would have married Fia of the MacDouglas clan and they would have lived out their lives as close friends.

Now his brother was lost to the blackened depths of this loch and Ewan was sworn to live out his life alone, paying penance for the fact that he had cost his brother his immortal soul.

Ewan had brought untold pain and suffering to all the people he loved and death to the brother who had meant the world to him.

It never ceased to amaze him just how easily so many lives could be destroyed by one foolish decision.

One decision he would give up his own soul to change.

Agony washed through him anew. Somewhere out there in the peaceful depths of the loch rested the body of the brother he'd been closest to. The brother who had been his best friend, his confidant.

Though Ewan loved his other brothers, it had been Kieran who had walked beside him through thick and thin. Kieran whom he had trusted with the deepest secrets of his heart.

Until the day Isobail had come between them with her lies and schemes. She had been gifted with the face of heaven and the soul of Satan's daughter.

No one had ever mattered to her, but herself.

Ewan drew a ragged sigh, his eyes stinging from his unshed tears as he recalled the moment that had shattered their youths . . .

"I love *you*, Ewan." Isobail's dark blue eyes had brimmed with tears as her long blond hair moved in the breeze.

She'd grabbed him while he was on his

way to the stables and pulled him behind the keep, into his mother's garden.

Once there, she had thrown herself into his arms and kissed him with a passion the likes of which he'd never tasted before or since.

Barely more than a lad, he'd been unable to fully understand her words. How could a woman so fair, so fine, even have a passing care for a lanky lad who could scarce walk about without banging his head into something?

Ewan knew he didn't have the handsomeness or charms of his brothers. It was a fact everyone commented on.

So how could Isobail want to be alone with him?

He'd tried to pull away, but she'd refused.

"You are promised to Kieran," he'd said.

Her viperous eyes had filled with more tears. "That is of Kieran's doing, not mine. I tried to tell him that I do not love him, but he won't listen."

Her hand had burned into his arm as she rubbed the muscles there and leaned her body against his invitingly. "Please, Ewan, you must help me. I dinna want to be bound to a man I dinna love. One who listens, but never hears a word I say. It is *you* I need. You who have won my heart with your silent power. I want a man who can care for me, protect me. One who doesn't bore me with words. Take me to England and I will be yours forevermore."

Young and foolish, he'd believed her while never knowing she'd said the very same words to Kieran to get him to take her away from Robby MacDouglas. Robby had been her father's choice of husband, but Isobail had refused to see the union met. She'd told Kieran that she loved him and that if he would help her, she would gladly be his wife.

However, the only person Isobail loved was herself.

In the quietness of the garden on that spring day, Ewan had lost his innocence in more ways than one.

Three days later, the two of them were sneaking out of the bailey and headed to England supposedly to meet up with Isobail's aunt, who would take them in.

In truth, they had been riding to meet Isobail's English lover.

Ewan would never in his life forget the sight of the arrogant man who had been waiting for them. The sight of Isobail and her lover embracing.

It was her lover's hall they had journeyed to, not her aunt's.

Her eyes had been shining with satisfaction as she imparted her devious plan to her lover, told him how she had fooled the MacAllisters into bringing her safely to his arms.

First, she'd tried to get Kieran to take her

to England, but when Kieran had decided to keep her in Scotland and marry her for himself, she'd turned her sights on Ewan, knowing he would be unable to stay there if he was to have her.

I knew he'd have no choice save to bring me. How could he stay at home while Kieran was there to hate him?

Enraged over their deception, Ewan had challenged and fought the English knight. But too young to have gleaned much skill and too uncoordinated to match the smaller man's agility, Ewan had lost the battle.

Defeated mentally and physically, he had been forced from the hall and sent on his way.

To this day the betrayal hung in Ewan's heart with the weight of a millstone.

The entire way back to Scotland, he'd vowed to make it up to Kieran. To tell his brother they were both better off without the faithlessness of Isobail.

But he'd come home to his brother's wake. Back to a home filled with grief over the fact that Kieran, unable to live without Isobail, had killed himself.

On this very day years past, his brother had come to this shore, doffed his clothes and sword, and walked out into the murky depths of the loch, where he had found an end to the pain of his broken heart.

How Ewan wished he could find his own release.

"I'm so sorry, Kieran," Ewan whispered to the waves that lapped at his booted feet. "If I could, brother, I'd gladly give you my life so that you could have yours back."

As it had so many times before, the thought of joining Kieran crossed his mind. It would be so easy to just walk out into the waves as Kieran had done and let their soothing peace end his pain, too.

To sink himself to the bottom of the loch, where he could finally make amends to Kieran . . .

Chapter 1

It took a lot of nerve to face the devil in his lair. Or in the case of Eleanor ingen Alexander, it just took a lot of desperation. Desperation that hung in her heart and throat, choking her with its urgency.

If the devil refused to help her . . .

Well, she'd walk herself to England alone then. No one would sway her from this course. No one. Not her father, not her mother.

Not even "the devil" himself.

As she neared the cave at the top of the mountain, her courage faltered. Could a man really live in a cave? That was the rumor, but until now she'd assumed it to be nothing more than a myth made up by men who were too afraid of Ewan MacAllister to face him.

After all, the MacAllisters were the most respected and feared men in all of Scotland. They were also said to be the richest. Surely such men, unlike her burly and irksome father, would have some form of refinement.

Wouldn't they?

Yet as she looked about the barren mountaintop, she saw nothing even remotely resembling a cabin or home.

Ewan MacAllister really was the barbarian of legend.

"That's just as well," she said, lifting the hem of her dark blue skirt to step around a cluster of rocks. She might be dreaming in her heart of a refined gentleman of courtly virtues to win her hand, but a barbarian was what she needed at the moment.

A barbarian with a mighty big sword.

From all she'd heard, Ewan MacAllister was just what her adventure called for.

At the top of the craggy slope, she realized that the "cave" had a wooden door that was mostly concealed by brush and dirt. Apparently Ewan had no desire for visitors.

Any other time, she would take the hint and respect his wishes, but right now, she couldn't afford to.

Her need for freedom was much greater than his for solitude.

Nora started to knock, then paused as she looked about the small cleared area.

What an interesting place he had here. The cave looked out onto the loch far below where the sunlight glistened on the water. It was a breathtaking view. Calm. Serene. No wonder the man had chosen it.

Surely a true barbarian wouldn't be able to appreciate something as refined and beautiful as this view.

It gave her hope.

Moving back to the door, she knocked on it.

No one answered.

"Hello?" she called, knocking louder. "Is anyone there?"

Still no answer.

Undaunted, she tried the door. The latch clicked, and it opened easily enough.

Inside she found an even more interesting abode. The floor was covered with plush rugs and rushes. The stone walls even held a few tapestries to blot the dampness. There was a strangely designed fireplace that had a bent flume and chimney to go out the side of the mountain instead of up through the top. A table and two chairs were set before it.

But the most interesting thing of all was the bed at the rear. Large and lush, it looked as if it belonged in some fine noble's castle, not stuck out in the midst of the woods, on top of a mountain.

Ewan MacAllister was a strange man indeed.

Why would he choose such a place and then bring with him the comforts of home?

And it was then she heard the snarling sound of the beast himself. It was a brief, eerie kind of snort, terrifying and deep.

Her heart skipped, then pounded as she realized it came from the large bed. All she could see from her position by the door was a dark lump she now assumed was a man.

He was asleep?

It was high afternoon, too early to be abed for the night and too late to be abed from the morning.

A nap perhaps?

Or was he ill?

Please, not sickness. She needed him to be hale and hearty for this venture. A sick barbarian wouldn't do at all.

"Excuse me?" she asked, stepping nearer the lump. "Lord Ewan, might I have a word with you?"

Only the snore answered her.

Well, bother this. Here she'd come all this way expecting to face an ogre and all she got was a sleeping cub. Where was the giant of legend who terrified everyone who spoke his name?

She needed that fearsome beast.

Aye, she *needed* him.

Stiffening her spine, she approached the bed, then faltered again as she saw him clearly for the first time in the dim light of the cave.

He lay on his side, spread out across the mattress as naked as the day he'd entered the world.

Not once in her life had Nora ever beheld a naked man, but she was quite certain no other man looked as fine and handsome as this one.

Especially not while he slept.

His long, muscled limbs seemed to go on forever. He was so large in stature and muscle that the bed barely accommodated him, and if he were stretched out to his full height, she was certain his arms and legs would be left dangling over the edges.

His black hair was shaggy and ill-trimmed, and draped over a face so manly and handsome that it stole her breath to look at him. He held at least a week's growth of beard on his face.

The rugged, untamed look only made him seem even more desirable. Fierce.

Barbaric.

His tanned flesh was stretched tight over muscles that were rock-hard and well defined.

Aye, this was a fine man to make her heart race and her body warm. Truly, he had no equal.

Before she could stop herself, she realized her gaze was traveling down to the center of that delectably male body to his . . .

Her face flamed.

Och now, she couldn't be having any of this. She was a decent maid. Not some hoyden to be staring at a man's piece.

Although . . .

Nora cocked her head as she studied it. It was an interesting piece. Rather large as it lay nestled in the short, dark curls. It seemed oddly harmless lying there, and she had a sudden urge to reach out and touch it.

Eleanor ingen Alexander, where is your mind?

In the sty obviously. Mired with earthy, lust-filled curiosity.

Though she'd never seen a man naked before, she most certainly knew what naked men did to naked women and what could happen to a woman who allowed a man to do that to her.

It was certainly a maid's downfall.

Her face burning even more, she quickly grabbed the fur covers on the bed and tossed them over him.

There now, all better.

Well, not *all* better. There was still the sight of his broad, gleaming shoulders and those long, masculine legs . . .

Nora!

Oh very well, she'd look no more.

At least not *there*.

But she couldn't quite seem to keep her gaze from drifting over him again. There wasn't really anything wrong with looking at a man's legs. Was there?

As she contemplated the sinfulness of it, he shifted and the covers took a dangerous tilt.

"We can't be having any of that," she said aloud, pulling the cover back over him.

As her fingers accidentally brushed his hard, rippled stomach, one large, powerful hand seized her wrist and held it immobile.

Gasping, she looked up into a pair of the

bluest eyes she'd ever beheld. Eyes that were rimmed in red and filled with rage as they narrowed on her with malice.

"Who the bloody hell are you and what are you doing here?"

His voice was deep and threatening, and when awake he was as fearsome as the rumors she'd heard.

"I'm . . ." Her mind went blank as she became aware of the fact that her hand rested on warm skin and over a muscle so hard and taut that it made her ache with a sudden throb.

Her mouth went dry as a foreign, demanding fire consumed her.

He was a fine-looking man, indeed.

"Woman, you'd best be answering me."

The angry accusation of his tone grated against her tolerance. Indignant at it, she jerked her hand away from his and straightened. "And just who are you to be taking that tone with me? Have you no manners at all?"

Ewan blinked in disbelief. She was taking him to task? This woman who had invaded his home and disturbed his nice ale-induced slumber?

Amazed at her audacity, he again blinked his scratchy eyes to clear his blurry vision while his head throbbed a painful staccato beat. With her mouth closed, she was pleasing enough to look at.

Even though she wore a long blue and white brat pulled up over her head, he could see she had thick, golden blond hair that reminded him of sunshine. Her medium-sized amber eyes were shaped like a cat's and they turned up just a hint at the corners.

Impish. That was the only word to describe her fey beauty, and yet there was a proud dignity to her that told him she was well bred and not some country lass come to wreak havoc with him.

But why would such a woman be here in his cave?

Alone.

"Who am I?" he answered her question slowly. "I happen to be the man who owns this place and one who doesn't take well to unannounced, unknown visitors. Now given the fact you've intruded into my domain, the least you can do is enlighten me as to who you are and why you're intruding."

That took some of the bluster out of her as she looked away from him and muttered. "Well, aye, I did do that." She turned her gaze back to his and lifted her chin as she recovered her courage, and when she spoke, her words were full of conviction. "But I'm here for a good reason."

"It'd better be a *damned* good reason."

"Here now," she said as she actually waved a chastising finger at him, "no need to curse at me. This is already awkward enough, what with your being naked and all . . . ."

He arched a brow at her words. He'd forgotten that one piece of this, but since she brought it up, he was instantly aware of the fact that nothing but a fur covered him.

". . . but that's no need to be discourteous."

He snorted at that. "I was born discourteous."

"So they say. However, discourteous or not, I have need of your services."

He arched his other brow as a bit of amusement went through him, and he taunted her before he could stop himself. "My *naked* services?"

A high blush rose to her cheeks, making her eyes appear more green than gold. "Most certainly not. I'd much rather have you clothed, but if 'tis your custom to walk about bare, well then, I suppose to each his own."

For the first time in years he was actually amused. She was a cheeky, bold lass. Unlike anyone he'd ever met before.

Of course, he'd never before met an unknown well-born woman while he was lying naked in his bed.

And somewhere deep inside was the question of whether she would be so bold where it counted most . . . between his fur covers.

His shaft stirred instantly at the thought and grew more rigid as he swept his gaze over her body. Aye, she was ample enough to be well worth the savoring. Lush hips and breasts. Probably no more than a year or two younger than he, she would make a fine morsel to nibble.

One that would probably last out the night until they were both well sated and spent.

Aye, she had a nice rump. One a man could grab on to and —

"My lord," she said firmly, like a tutor addressing an errant, daydreaming child. The tone instantly intruded on his meandering thoughts about her "attributes." "I am here to procure your services as an escort."

He frowned at her words. "My what?"

"I need a man to accompany me to England."

Nay, his mind roared as he remembered all too well what had happened the last time a woman had said those words to him.

That was the last thing he needed said to him today of all days. Most especially out of the mouth of a beautiful *blond* woman.

She took a step back at his snarl.

"I beg your pardon?" he growled.

She swallowed. "I need a man to take me to my aunt's home in England."

It was all Ewan could do to stay in his bed and not tear down the walls.

Surely the Fates were mocking him with this. How could this happen to one man twice in the same lifetime?

"Why?" he asked.

Unaware of the fury roiling inside him, she cleared her throat. "I am engaged to be wed to a man I cannot stomach, and I need you to escort me in safety to my aunt's home so that I won't have to marry the toad."

Ewan cursed foully at that. It echoed off the stone walls around them. "Are you daft?"

"Most definitely not."

"Then why would you come to me?"

"Because you are the most feared man in Scotland. No one in my father's clan or my betrothed's would dare stop you from taking me."

"Aye, well, you can forget all about that happening, love. There's no power on this earth or beyond that could make me take you to England. Now hie yourself out of here and —"

She stiffened. "I can't."

"You mean you won't."

"Nay," she said, twisting her hands in the fabric of her brat. "I mean I can't go back there."

"Whyever not?"

"Because I've already left a note saying that I ran off with you."

Chapter 2

By his face, Nora could tell she had just uttered the most horrific words imaginable to the man. His skin tone was a strange, mottled mixture of fury, disgust, and disbelief.

"What the hell do you mean you left a note?"

Judging by the wrathful gleam in his icy blue eyes, she had most definitely said the wrong thing.

Suddenly, Nora was terrified, and that didn't happen often. Indeed, her father oft said she had been born without a single fear in her body.

But right now her heart hammered with panic at the sight of his barely leashed wrath. Ewan MacAllister was no small man, and she had no idea just how dangerous he might prove when riled.

"I had no choice," she explained, hoping to offset his temper at least a small degree.

"Woman, we all have choices." Ewan came off the bed and winced as if a fierce pain had shot through his head.

The fur fell away from his naked body as he buried the heel of his hand against his left eye and cursed again.

Nora gasped and spun about to give him her back, even though a tiny, wicked part of her wanted to stare at all that lush strength and tawny skin.

He was truly a fierce man.

One of brawny, unrefined power and handsomeness.

She could hear him cursing even more and grabbing his clothes, then pulling them on, and all the while she felt Ewan's glower. It was hot, powerful and terrifying, and it set her to trembling.

"How could you have done such an lack-witted, cursed thing?" he snarled. "Whatever got into your mind that made you pick *me* to say you ran off with?"

"Please," she said, her voice soft and pleading. "I can't marry Ryan MacAren. He is egotistical and arrogant. He smells of bad hygiene and eggs —" She shuddered at the memory of that one. "He likes to eat raw eggs, which is a disgusting habit to say the least, and now that I think on it, it is probably his most endearing one. I would sooner die than wed him."

Ewan growled again. "The last time a woman said those words to me, I believed her, and it caused a feud for my clan that resulted in the deaths of untold men and women on both sides of it. It cost my brother his life and his soul, and it sent my father to his grave as well. Now I ask you, why should I give a witch's damn about what happens to you when I don't even know you at all?"

Nora was baffled by his words. "Someone else ran from Ryan MacAren and caused a feud for the MacAllisters?"

He came around her to glare. A vein throbbed in his temple as he narrowed his eyes ominously. "Are you trying to anger me more?"

"Nay. I'm not trying to anger you at all. I am only trying to gain your help. I can pay you, if that's your concern."

"I have no need of your money."

Ewan had never in his life met a woman like her. How dare she come in here and ask him such a thing?

Surely she had no more sense than a leek pea. What kind of woman would traipse alone into a man's home and ask him, a total stranger, to lead her astray of her parents?

And as he stared at her, he wondered just how much like Isobail she really was.

Just how far would she go to gain his help . . .

He gave her a hot, lustful once-over and let his gaze linger meaningfully on her breasts. "Is there anything else you would offer me?"

She blinked at him once as if not understanding, but as he watched, her amber eyes sparked.

She gasped, then raked a repugnant stare

over him that duplicated his own. There was no guile or artifice about her. She was truly offended by his question.

"Och now," she said, curling her lip, "you are foul to even make such a suggestion to a well-bred lady. How dare you! Well, never you mind. I'll be finding my own way to England and not be in your presence another moment."

He was surprised by her words and her indignant reaction.

Huffily she gathered her skirts into her hands and gave him one more sneer for good measure. "You are a crude, ale-smelling beastie, and I have no use for such a man. Better I should go alone to my aunt's than have to deal with the likes of you. I should have never come here."

Now she had that thought?

Ewan caught her arm as she started past him. "How did you get here?"

She glared at his hand on her arm. "I rode a horse until I reached your mountain and then I walked."

"Is that how you intend to get to England?"

"Aye. I'll crawl there on my hands and knees if needs be."

"You'll never make it alone."

She gave him a hard, determined stare. "Then I shall die trying."

He saw red again. "The bloody hell you

will. I'm taking you home to your clan."

"Never."

His jaw twitched. In all his life he had never had a woman infuriate him so. Women were either too terrified or too lust-filled in his presence to do much more than nod or giggle. But this one . . . this one made his blood boil.

"You think I won't?" he asked her.

She snatched her arm free of his grasp. "I think you don't know who my clan is. You have no idea who I am, and you can't take me back to my father unless I tell you, which I most certainly will not do."

She had him there.

But not for long. "You *will* tell me."

"Ha!" she snapped, lifting her chin defiantly.

Ewan clenched his hands into fists. What did a man do with such a woman?

"Why of all the men in Scotland did you come to me?" he asked.

"Because you and your brothers are the only men I know who scare Ryan. I knew Sin and Braden MacAllister would never leave their wives to take me to England, and Lochlan, being laird, would never consent to help me for fear of running afoul of my father and his clan. That left you, who has no other tie to anyone. I thought that if I told my father that I had eloped with you, no one would dare come after me."

Ewan muttered under his breath about women and their mindless machinations.

This was a nightmare all over again. So close to the events with Isobail and yet so oddly different.

How could this be happening to him again? Especially on this particular day that marked the death of his brother. "You told them you eloped with me?" he asked.

"Well, what else could I do?"

"You could have done as you were told."

She shook her head. "That is the one thing I canna do. Nor *will* I."

"Why?"

"Because I will not allow myself to be some useless adornment."

Ewan frowned at her unexpected words. Although why he even reacted to that, he didn't know. She seemed to throw his keel every time she opened her mouth.

"I am not some nothing to be ignored and patted on the head and tolerated like a pet dog," she continued. " 'Tis bad enough my father thinks me lack-witted, but to be married to such a man . . . Never."

What a bizarre concern for a woman. Who'd ever heard of such? A woman's place was to do as she was told and to bend her will to that of her father and then to the husband her father picked for her.

God help them all if a woman ever took it into her mind to think for herself.

He, for one, would never again help a woman defy her family's wishes.

"For this you are willing to risk your life?" he asked.

"If someone planned to shut you away and ignore you, to listen but never hear a word you spoke, would you tolerate it?" She looked about his cave and appeared to change her mind. "Well, mayhap *you* would, but I will not. I have a mind of my own and I wish to use it."

Ewan shook his head in disbelief. "Wherever did you get these ideas?"

She ignored him. "You've made it quite clear that you've no wish to help me. So be it. I'll trouble you no more. Now step aside and let me be on my way. I've a long journey ahead and —"

"You're not leaving."

"I beg your pardon?"

"You heard me. I'm not about to allow you to take a journey that at best would result in your ravishment, at worst your death."

"I'm no concern of yours."

"Lady," he said, his voice gruff and menacing, "the moment you put my name on a piece of parchment designating me as your betrothed, you became my concern. What think you would happen if you were harmed? Your father, whoever he is, would demand my head for allowing you to be hurt. According to your own words we are bound to each other."

She cringed as if she hadn't thought quite that far ahead. "They might not believe it," she said hopefully. She nodded her head as if she had just convinced herself of her reasoning. "After all, we've never met before. Come to think of it, they shouldn't believe it at all."

"But they will," he said morosely.

"How do you know?"

"Trust me, my luck would have it no other way."

Ewan growled deep in his throat again. She seemed to have that effect on a lot of men when they spoke with her. Though why everyone became exasperated with her, she was never quite sure.

Nora watched as he began gathering his things. "What are you doing?"

"I'm getting ready to take you to my brother's."

"Why?"

"Because you can't very well stay here with me."

She braced her hands on her hips. "I don't wish to go to your brother's. I must get to my aunt."

"In England."

"Aye."

Ewan paused to look at her. "And who, pray tell, is this precious aunt you would have me deliver you to?"

Nora hesitated. That knowledge could quite easily hurt her more than help. She always had to be careful of whom she told that to — the repercussions could be quite dire.

"If I tell you, you must swear on your soul that you won't take me back to my father."

"Fine. I swear on whatever portion of soul I possess that I won't take you to your father."

She took a deep breath and hoped he would abide by those words. "My aunt is Eleanor of Aquitaine."

Ewan laughed incredulously at her declaration.

Och now, what a load of blather that was. He'd never heard anything more preposterous.

This woman, whoever she was, was a fine piece of work to make such a grand claim. "Queen Eleanor of England is your aunt?"

"Aye."

Oh, the lass was a daft one, for sure. There was nothing more to be done about it. Her being niece to the queen of England was complete and utter madness. "Then I am the son of William the Conqueror."

" 'Tis nice to meet you, William Rufus."

Ewan raked a hand through his hair, though what he really wanted to do was wrap it around her neck and squeeze.

Whatever was he to do with her?

He didn't believe her for a single moment.

If the niece of Eleanor of Aquitaine was any-where in Scotland, everyone would know.

"And your name, lass?"

"Eleanor, named for my aunt, but they call me Nora."

"And your clan?"

"That I won't tell you."

For the first time, Ewan understood some of Lochlan's frustration when his older brother had been dealing with Maggie during the last days of their feud with the MacDouglas clan. At least then Lochlan had had Braden to come in and save the day, and tame the wench. There was no one around to help him with this vexation.

What did a man do with a woman who wouldn't heed reason?

Was it too much to ask for some divine in-tervention?

Obviously so.

Ewan wasn't sure how to proceed, but then dealing with women was the specialty of his brothers, not him.

"Very well then, Eleanor —"

"Nora."

Nora cringed at the murderous look he gave her.

"You know," she said quietly, "I truly didn't mean to be a bother to you. I just want to go to my aunt's. Eleanor always said that I could come to her any time I needed to."

"Did she now?"

"Aye."

"And did she say anything else?"

"To let no man, save the Lord, our God, dictate my behavior."

Ewan hesitated. Now that sounded like the queen of legend; however, it didn't mean anything other than the fact this woman had learned of her. There was no way she could be a princess or whatever it was Eleanor's niece would be.

This lass was as Scots as he was.

And the sooner he removed her from his life, the happier he would be.

With that thought in mind, he extinguished his fire and gathered a few makeshift food-stuffs and plaids.

Nora watched as Ewan made ready to leave. Part of her was tempted to run, but she held no doubt he could catch her. Those long legs of his could take one step to her three.

Perhaps Lochlan could be bribed or per-suaded to force Ewan to take her to England, or maybe one of his other men. She had to get out of this country before her father missed her and led a search.

She'd pleaded women's troubles and made her bed up to look as if she slept. She hoped it would be a few hours before her mother came to check on her and discovered the note.

It might be enough time.

You should never have left that note!

Aye, but she hadn't wanted her father to worry overmuch. She'd thought that mentioning Ewan's name would both scare and soothe her father into leaving her be or at least hesitating before he sought her.

It hadn't sounded so daft when her maid had helped her come up with the plan.

Och, this was a bad idea all around now that she thought it over again. But she'd been desperate, and as her mother said, desperate people do desperate things. Not to mention her maid had encouraged her to seek out Ewan.

Surely such a man as a MacAllister wouldn't leave a lady in such dire distress. 'Tis said they have each sworn to protect all those down-trodden, and I can think of no one more down-trodden than a lady married to Lord Ryan. Seek him out, my lady, and whatever you do, don't let him sway you from this course.

And so here she was on top of a mountain with a man who looked as if he'd rather have his head pried apart than tolerate her company for another moment.

Nora watched Ewan move about angrily. He was a fearsome beastie, and yet she wasn't truly afraid of him. There was a deep sadness to his eyes and an air of ill humor. Still, other than being gruff, he didn't appear mean or abusive.

At least he listened to her.

Somewhat, anyway.

He moved to stand beside her, and she had to crane her neck to look up at him. "Whatever did they feed you to make you grow so large?"

An amused gleam came to his glacial eyes. "A great deal of *breast* milk."

Nora gasped at his response. "You take great delight in shocking people, don't you?"

His softened features made him appear almost boyish. Charming. But it didn't last long before his face settled back into the frown she was getting used to. "What I delight in is people leaving me alone. I find that by being shocking it often causes them to flee my presence posthaste."

"I offered to leave."

He growled at her. "Come, we might as well get started. The sooner I get you to Lochlan, the sooner I can come back here."

"And mope?"

He stiffened at that. "I'm not moping."

"Oh, forgive me. See, where I come from an upside-down smile means you're frowning, and if you're frowning while withdrawn from everyone and everything, it means you're moping. I guess here in your cave, the world is backward and a frown means you're happy."

"Do you always talk this much?"

"Aye, especially when people, usually men,

36

try to ignore me."

He gave her a droll stare. "What a wonderful trait to possess."

She ignored his sarcasm. "I personally think so. My aunt calls me charming."

"Your Aunt Eleanor?"

"Aye."

"And when, pray tell, did you journey to England to meet with her?"

"Oh, never. My mother doesn't travel well, so Eleanor has come to us several times over the years to visit and catch up."

"And no one else in Scotland knows of this?"

"My father always knows, as do our servants, but Eleanor prefers to travel in disguise. Seems something happened once when she was traveling as queen, and now she makes sure no one knows who she is or when she travels."

"I see."

He said the words, but she could tell he didn't mean them. He thought she was insane. Well, she had been called worse. Mayhap if he thought her a bit light in the head, he might be swayed to turn his back while she went on her way.

It was a thought . . .

He led her from the cave.

"Have you ever been to England?" she asked as she hastened her steps to keep up with his long, dangerous stride. "My mother says London is a dirty place that is hot in the summer and very crowded."

Ewan groaned aloud as he secured the door to his home. This was going to be a long trip if she insisted on prattling the whole way there. Already his head felt as though it would splinter.

He turned and found her so close to him that he almost ran her over.

She blushed rather prettily, then moved aside. "Will we be off then?"

Grimacing, he rubbed his forehead with his hand.

"Have you an ache in your head?"

He paused and opened one eye to look at her. "Aye."

"Here," she said, taking his arm and leading him to sit on a rock off to the side. "Sit down and let me help."

Mistrustful, he grimaced. "What can you do?"

"You'd be amazed. My father says 'tis a gift the good Lord gave me to help alleviate the damage I cause."

Ewan frowned even more at her words as he sat down. "Is your father always so harsh with you?"

"Nay, he's a good man. I just tend to unnerve him from time to time."

He gave a short snort at that, not doubting it in the least. This woman could try the patience of Job himself.

As soon as he was seated, she ran her hands through his hair, massaging his scalp.

Och now, that felt rather nice. Her hands were warm and gentle, and her fingers deftly soothed the pain from his head as she tugged lightly at his hair.

Before long, he found himself greatly relaxed and much calmer. The tight band of pain loosened.

A man could get used to this. And for the first time he noticed the pleasant scent of her. She smelled of fresh lilacs and warm sunshine, a scent that was as fetching as the lady herself.

She was a pretty little maid. Her brat had fallen down around her shoulders to form a shawl while she tended him. Her long blond hair fair glistened, and her figure was trim and ample enough to be well worth a good tupping.

His body reacted instantly to the thought of her underneath him. To the thought of him tasting her slightly parted lips . . .

Ewan sucked his breath in sharply as he hardened against his will.

"Here now," he said, rising to his feet. "Enough of this. We have a trip to make."

"Is your head any better?"

"Aye," he said gruffly. It most definitely was. However, it was his other region that now pained him.

Clearing his throat, he headed for the small

trail that would lead them down the mountain to the stable where his horse was kept.

Nora followed after him, all the while noticing the ease with which he moved, the manly grace. He was tall and strong and as surefooted as any man she'd ever seen.

When he wasn't snarling at her, he was actually quite handsome, even with his thick whiskers covering his face.

His curly black hair needed a combing, and for some reason she couldn't fathom, she wanted to offer to brush her fingers through it so that she could remove the becoming tangles.

He reminded her of some great, hulking bear, what with his massive form, snarling tones and gruffness.

It was obvious that he and the word "refinement" were complete and utter strangers, and yet there was something about this rugged, tormented man she found strangely captivating, and she wondered if he'd always been so morose.

Surely as a lad, he'd been laughing and carefree.

Hadn't he?

"Have you always been so large?" she asked.

He cast an evil glare over his shoulder. "Aye. I came from my mother's womb at full height. The shock of it almost killed her."

She grimaced at his humor. "Do you always walk so fast? I can barely keep up with your strides. I feel like a small child running after a parent."

When she stumbled on the rocks, Ewan quickly caught her and set her back on her feet.

To her chagrin, her hands went flat against the strength of his arms, and she felt the incredible power of his body. The man was a wall of well-toned muscles. One that made her breath catch in her throat and her body erupt into heat.

Against her will, an image of his nude form spread out invitingly across his bed went through her mind.

Aye, she knew all too well what primal masculine charms were concealed by his saffron shirt and trewes.

All six-foot-six strength of it.

His was a body surely made for sinning.

"Take care, my lady," he said sharply. "I have no wish to take you home mangled."

In spite of his rough words, there was a gentleness in his touch that belied his tone. Her ogre wasn't the fierce beastie he let on to be. She was rather sure of it.

"Why do you wish to live out here alone?" she asked as he withdrew from her and took up his lead again.

"I like my solitude."

"But doesn't it get lonely?"

He hesitated. "Nay."

She learned something about him then. His nose wrinkled ever so slightly when he lied.

"Don't you miss being with your brothers?"

A deep, dark sadness fell over his face, and his entire body tensed. "My lady, would you please hold your tongue for a bit? I'm not used to conversing, and I find myself quite worn out by it."

"I shall refrain if you will answer one more question."

"And that is?"

"Why does everyone say you killed your brother?"

Chapter 3

"Because I *did* kill my brother."

If Nora lived a thousand years, she would never forget the look on Ewan's face as he said those anguished words to her. She saw his grief. His pain.

His wasn't the face of a man who had killed his brother. At least not on purpose.

It was the face of a man who was tormented by the loss. One who would do anything to have his brother back.

"What happened?"

His blue eyes turned arctic as he moved away from her. "What do you care? You didn't know him. Hell's toes, you barely know me and I've no wish to speak of it."

She would respect that. It was more than obvious that he felt deeply about his brother and whatever had happened to him.

Over the years, she'd heard a number of stories about the death of Kieran MacAllister. Some claimed Ewan had cut his brother's throat while he slept. Others said he'd cut out his heart.

Some were much more lewd.

The only thing the rumors had in common was that Ewan had killed Kieran.

Personally, she didn't believe those tales for one reason and one reason only. Had Ewan MacAllister taken the life of his older brother, his other brothers wouldn't be so close to him now. Nor would they rally to his defense when others spoke harshly of him.

Everyone with an ounce of Scots in them knew the one law that governed the MacAllister clan. To threaten one brother was to threaten them all.

A kinship such as theirs would never tolerate, let alone protect, Ewan if he were guilty of killing Kieran.

And so she'd bet her life on her reasoning.

Luckily, so far she'd been right.

Ewan led her to a small stable that she hadn't noticed on her arrival. Hidden behind a copse of trees, it had a good-sized corral that was made up of the mountain on all but one side of it.

She glanced around with a frown. She'd left her maid and one of her father's retainers waiting close by, along with her mare.

Now only her horse was still present.

The other two people and horses were nowhere to be seen.

"Agnes? David?" she called out, looking about for them.

"What are you doing?" Ewan asked.

Nora frowned as she continued to look about. "My maid and one of my father's men were here. I left them to travel alone to your . . ." She paused before she said something to offend him, then finished with "home."

He looked at her incredulously. "Your father's man allowed that?"

"Well, aye. He didn't question it when I said I would go up to your cave alone. He said they'd wait right here until I returned." Fear and concern knotted her stomach. "You don't think anything happened to them, do you?"

Before he could answer, she caught sight of a folded piece of parchment tied to her saddle by a red ribbon.

Curious, she went over to it and pulled it free. She opened the letter and read it.

Nora stared at the words in disbelief.

"What is it?" Ewan asked, coming over to stand by her side.

"David says they have abandoned me," she said quietly.

How could they have done such a thing?

Nora read the words aloud. "It says that since they delivered me into your capable hands, they decided it would be best for them to return home before someone missed them and thought they were part of my conspiracy."

Ewan let out a disgusted sigh. " 'Tis a good thing I was here then, otherwise you would have been left to your own defenses. Were I your father, I'd have some of that

45

man's skin for his carelessness. Such a dereliction warrants a beating and then some."

Spoken like a less than refined gentleman. True, David should have ascertained her welfare before leaving; still, it didn't warrant a harsh beating.

David had always been a faithful servant to both her and her father. It didn't make sense that he would leave without verifying her well-being.

Why had he done such a thing?

Turning his back to her, Ewan whistled for his horse, and to her amazement, the beast obeyed.

It trotted over to him like an old friend.

He clucked his tongue at the horse and patted it gently on the nose. "Hi there, laddie," he said softly. "You ready for a ride?"

The horse nickered, then butted Ewan's shoulder affectionately.

Without a word to her, Ewan released his horse and made his way into the small barn.

She followed behind him curiously.

Inside the makeshift storage area, she saw the hay and feed for the horse. Everything was very neat and well kept, much as his home had been.

Ewan pulled a bridle from its peg on the wall and grabbed the heavy saddle up as if it weighed nothing at all. Her eyes widened at the sight of him as he carried it out the door. The fabric of his shirt contoured against every deep crevice of the muscles on his back and ribs. Every masculine bulge was practically laid bare to her hungry gaze.

Her knees went weak.

Ewan was a heavenly feast for the eyes, no doubt whatsoever. His muscles fair rippled with every move he made, and though his hair was much too long, she found the texture of it strangely beckoning.

She remembered only too well what it had felt like to run her fingers through those thick, black waves.

And his eyelashes . . .

Surely no man should have a set so long. They made a perfect frame for his crystal blue eyes.

He was what her mother called a heavenly form of masculine perfection.

Nora remained perfectly silent while he saddled his mount. She found her throat far too dry to speak.

Especially when he bent over to fasten the saddle around the horse's belly.

It was the first time in her life she'd ever noticed a man's backside. His dark brown trewes were tight over his rear and showed her his manly proportions. Of course, it didn't help that she had already seen that backside bare and knew firsthand just how well shaped it was.

Very disturbing.

But not nearly as much as the peculiar desire she had to walk up to him and run her hand along those lean hips, then up his back and over his chest.

Nora!

Where were these thoughts coming from? Her mother would die of shock, and she herself was mortified by the wayward drift of her attentions.

What was it about Ewan that made her long to do things with him that would have her spending the rest of her life in penance for them?

She'd always fashioned herself to be a moral and decent lady. Circumspect in all things.

Until now, she'd never really tasted decadent lust.

But she tasted it now.

It was hot and demanding.

Frightening.

And all too alluring.

Ewan led his horse to hers and inspected her mare. An involuntary shiver ran over her as she noted the care he took with the animal. The way his long, tapered fingers stroked and soothed her horse.

Nay, he wasn't a completely evil ogre. Such a man wouldn't care for animals the way he did. And a true ogre would never have so tender a touch.

He turned toward her with a frown. "Do

you intend to come over here and mount your horse, or are you wanting to stare at my backside for the rest of the day?"

Heat scalded her cheeks, though from anger at his words or embarrassment from the fact that she was doing just that, she wasn't sure.

"You, sir, have the manners of a stump."

He gave her a droll stare. "Since I'm as tall as a tree, that would be rather fitting, don't you think?"

His humor caught her off-guard. Interesting that he could laugh at what, in all honesty, had been a very rude comment on her part. She really shouldn't have said that. It wasn't something she would normally do, but something about this man rather brought out the worst of her.

Most likely, it was the fact that he really did have the manners of a stump.

She went to her horse, then turned to look at him expectantly.

He moved to his own mount without so much as a backward glance at her.

"Well?" she asked when it became completely obvious that he had no intention of returning to her side.

He looked at her blankly, as if he had no idea what she wanted from him. "Well what?"

How dense could the man be? Surely he had more common decency than this?

49

"Are you not going to help me mount?" she asked.

"Can you not do it yourself?"

She was aghast. Did the man not have a mother? A sister? Anyone around him who was female?

"Well, no. I need your help."

He used his reins to scratch his bearded cheek as he stared at her speculatively. "Need my help . . . what?"

"To mount."

He snorted at that. Dropping the reins, he folded his arms over his chest and pierced her with those icy eyes of his. "If you be needing my help to mount, it seems, my lady, that you are forgetting the one important word in that sentence."

Nora was stunned by his demand. The bear who lived in a cave was lecturing *her* on manners?

Was this some kind of jest?

"I'm waiting," he said impatiently.

She glared at him, and that arrogant stance that demanded manners from her and yet required none from him.

"Fine then," she said stubbornly, refusing to give him the satisfaction of correcting her, "I shall do it myself."

Or so she thought.

What she quickly learned after trying to mount was that her mare was wont to move away every time she started to climb onto the horse's back.

She tried several times, and several times the horse danced away from her.

"Ow!" Nora snapped as her foot was wrenched by the stirrup and she again found herself standing by the horse's side while the cursed beast stared at her with mirthful eyes.

"Having a wee bit of a problem there?" Ewan asked.

"Nay," she hastened to assure him as she gathered her skirt around her to prepare for another try. "No problem at all."

If she could just get the beast to hold still.

Nora tried again.

This time, her horse stepped away at the worst possible moment.

Unbalanced, she fell sprawling into the dust with her skirts flying up high over her legs, exposing her to his view. Och now! She was humiliated over this.

Ewan bolted to her side and forced her prancing mare away from her. "Are you harmed, lass?"

She shoved her skirts down to cover herself. "Nothing more than my dignity, I assure you."

To her surprise, he helped her to her feet and gently brushed the dirt from her skirts.

"I dinna mean for my ill humor to cause you hurt, Nora. Here . . ." He picked her up as if she weighed nothing at all, and set her on the back of her horse.

Completely dumbstruck by the turnaround of his actions, she watched in silence as he walked to his own horse. He slung one long leg over his mount with an ease that truly made her envious. Without a single care, he positioned himself on the horse's back and leaned forward to take the dangling reins he'd dropped when he dashed to her aid.

Why did his horse stand there so patiently while hers felt the need to prance about and embarrass her?

But what amazed her most was the way Ewan looked on top of his horse as he controlled the powerful, spirited steed with ease. He sat confidently in his saddle with a raw masculine aura that brought heat to her cheeks and a strange pounding to her chest.

Even ill-kept and half drunk, he was an incredibly handsome man, and she couldn't help but wonder what he would look like with a bath, a shave and fresh clothes.

Truly, he would be devastating.

Perhaps his condition was a godsend after all. Dressed as he was, it was much easier for her to remember that he was nothing like the type of man she fancied.

That he was as ill-refined as any man could possibly be.

He lacked manners and couth.

But what he lacked in personality, he more than made up for in looks . . .

Nora!

She shook herself mentally. Whatever was the matter with her? She was acting like her mother's maid, who was ever quick to chase after any passably handsome man, with no regard for the man's heart or the consequences of her actions.

Nora always looked at what a man was on the inside. A pretty package might be beautiful to behold, but if it contained an asp, it was better cast aside than cradled to one's bosom.

She'd lived her life always by that motto and no one, not even Ewan MacAllister, was going to change her.

Without a glance back at her, Ewan clucked his tongue at his mount and spurred it forward.

Once more, Nora was incredulous at his actions as he and the horse tore across the craggy land where any step could send both man and horse flying into peril.

Why, they'd be lucky if the two of them didn't break their necks!

"Well, if you be thinking that I intend to run after you at that careless pace, you've another think coming, Ewan MacAllister," she said, even though she knew he couldn't hear her.

He might be Lord High-and-Mighty with a horse, but she wasn't so foolish with her life. She actually wanted to get to England in one piece.

So she urged her mare forward and trotted much more carefully through the mossy landscape.

When she reached the edge of the meadow, Ewan was stopped and waiting for her with one hand fisted on his hip. His horse strained restlessly against the bit, wanting to run some more, but Ewan held it under control.

By his face, she could tell the man was greatly peeved at her.

"Gathering wool, are we?" he asked in a sharp tone.

"Nay," she said primly, "merely practicing irritating you, and by the looks of your face, I'd say I'm doing a rather remarkable job of it. My mother always says that any effort worth pursuing is worth pursuing well."

Growling, he scratched at his beard and eyed her fiercely. She wondered if the man even knew how to smile, if he realized just how fierce a specter he looked.

"You're a spoiled lass, aren't you?"

"Aye," she said, tilting her head impishly. "My father says 'tis one of my more *endearing* qualities."

He grunted at that, then turned his horse about and led her into the thick forest.

This time his pace was much more reasonable. So much so that she had little trouble keeping up with him.

Now that they were in closer proximity,

Nora began asking the questions she'd wanted to ask earlier. "How long will it take us to reach your brother's castle? We are on MacAllister land, are we not?"

"Aye," he said, his gaze focused on the area before them. "But we're on the outer reaches of it. I can usually make the ride in a day and a half, but if you insist on this pace, it will probably take us a year or more to reach it."

She scoffed at him. "Do you always race about like a madman, then?"

He didn't answer.

Nora waited for almost a minute.

He didn't acknowledge her in the least. He acted as if she didn't exist at all.

"Excuse me," she said irritably. "I asked you a question, Ewan MacAllister."

Again he didn't respond.

Nora was appalled. "Do you always make it a habit to ignore questions?"

He expelled a long-suffering sigh. "My lady, if you will travel in silence, I will give you anything you ask."

"Will you take me to London?"

"Nay."

She clenched her teeth. So be it. If he wouldn't do as she requested, then she wouldn't do as he requested.

"Fine weather out, is it not?" Nora looked about the forest. She spurred her horse forward so that she could ride apace of Ewan.

"Quite refreshing and warm. I rather like this time of year. It was always my favorite. Why, I remember being a young girl. My mother and I would . . ."

Ewan groaned as he realized the woman intended to chatter until he either killed her or gave in to her.

His ears fair buzzed with her words, and though her voice was quite dulcet and beguiling, it would be even more so if heard sparingly.

His head throbbed from the ale he had consumed. The bright sunlight made his eyes burn and his stomach sour. He'd planned on spending the rest of this wretched day in blissful stupor, lying abed.

Now he was off to Lochlan's castle, where he would have to face his mother and brother. See their own grief over the death he had caused.

To this day, he found it hard to look his mother in the eye. Though she had never said a single word against him, he knew, as she did, where the blame for Kieran's death lay.

Squarely on his shoulders.

His gut tightened. It seemed like only yesterday that he and Kieran had played at battle. That the two of them had dreamed and bragged of the men they would someday be.

"Are you all right?" Nora's question intruded on his thoughts.

"I am fine."

"You don't look fine. You look sad and upset. Is my company truly so distasteful to you?"

It was on his tongue to tell her aye, but the lie lodged in his throat. There was no need to be deliberately cruel to her. She couldn't help it if she wasn't entirely sane. Mayhap there was some cruelty in her past that had caused her delusions.

Having lost his dreams so painfully, he would never rip them away from another.

"Nay, my lady. I don't find you distasteful."

"Just irritating."

"Your words, not mine."

She smiled at him then. It was a warm, soft smile that made her amber eyes glow. "So you find me charming?"

He felt a strange urge to whimper at her insistence. "Are you incapable of silence?"

"Are you incapable of speech?"

"Aye. Completely and utterly."

"Well, then you speak incredibly well for a mute. I once knew a mute. He lived in the local village and used to make the most divine shoes. They were so soft that you felt as if your feet were cushioned by pillows."

Ewan did whimper as she continued with her tale of the cobbler and the village where he lived.

This must be his penance.

Surely the devil had sent this woman to him on this day to be his torment. There was no other explanation possible.

She was his anchor. His millstone.

It would have been kinder to have him hanged, drawn and quartered.

For hours they traveled at a leisurely pace that was far more frustrating than productive. And all the while she prattled on endlessly about everything imaginable until he feared his ears would bleed from the stress.

As night approached, Ewan looked about for a place to sleep. Someplace where he could put a wide distance between the two of them before he yielded to the urge to throttle her.

He found them a small clearing beside a stream that could provide them with fresh water.

"We're stopping here?" she asked as he reined his horse in. "To sleep until morning?"

"Aye," he said gruffly, "unless it's your wont to ride through the night." Which he was more than willing to do. Anything to get her away from him as soon as possible so that he could return to his home and be at peace again.

She bit her bottom lip as she looked about with pinched features. "Is there not some-place we could find a bed?"

"Do you see a bed?"

She narrowed her eyes at him. "Is there no village nearby?"

"Aye, a few hours away, and the way you travel, more like half a day away."

Nora stiffened. "The way I travel? What do you mean by that?"

Ewan let out a tired breath. Was the woman blind not to know the answer to that? Or was she merely trying to aggravate him more?

"How many times did we have to stop for you to attend your needs, my lady? Better still, how many times did I have to circle back to your side because you were off daydreaming instead of keeping up with me? I swear a —"

"Do not swear at me. 'Tis rude."

Ewan snapped his mouth shut and held his tongue from saying what he really thought. If she thought *that* was rude, he could certainly educate her on truly rude.

He dismounted and led his horse toward the stream so that it could drink.

Glancing back, he saw the look of horror on her face as she contemplated a night spent on the cold ground.

And with that image came another. That of his gentle mother and sisters-in-law.

Each one a lady who deserved only the best.

As irritating as Nora was, she was someone's child, and she wasn't used to such hardship. No doubt she had never slept on anything save feather ticks and pillows.

Weary and tired, he remounted his horse and headed back toward her.

"Very well," he said. "If we travel back a bit the way we came, Lenalor isn't that far away."

"Lenalor?"

"It's a small village where we can eat a hot meal and you can sleep in comfort."

Relief brightened her soft amber eyes. "How long will it take us to reach it?"

"An hour, mayhap a little longer."

"Is it a large village? I've never heard of Lenalor before. What will we find there?"

Ewan raked his hand through his hair as she began barraging him with questions again. The lady was ever curious and never silent.

"You're not answering me again, are you?" she asked after several minutes.

"You ask too many questions. I can barely draw breath to answer one before you give me three more."

"Then I shall ask them more slowly."

"I'd rather you didn't."

"Why?"

"Because then I'd feel obligated to answer them."

To his surprise, she laughed. It was a sweet sound, not high-pitched or silly. Rather it was deep and pleasant.

"Poor Ewan, ever vexed by a maid's simple tongue. My father oft says that if he could harness the unfailing energy of my mouth and feed it to his troops, he would never have to worry over any army defeating them in battle. He says an hour of my chatter would keep an army battling for at least three or four days."

Ewan looked back at her over his shoulder. "Those are harsh words."

"Nay, not at all. My father loves me, and well I know it. I do talk too much. 'Tis a fault I've had all my life. My mother claims it's because I had no other sibling, and since she wanted to have a large family the good Lord gave her me. I might be a single child, but I make enough noise for several dozen."

Ewan snorted at that.

"Was that a laugh?"

"Nay, it was a noise of agreement."

"Mmm," she said as she stared at him. "You know, I'm thinking that must be why you're quiet."

"What do you mean?"

"You have so many brothers, I imagine it was rather difficult for you to be heard over them."

"Believe me, I can make myself heard over them if needs be."

She came to ride by his side. "I don't know," she said doubtfully. "Your voice is so

61

deep that I doubt you could get much out of it in way of a shout."

Nora lowered her voice to a deep pitch that sent a strange shiver down his spine. "See how when I talk like this, it's far too deep." She raised her voice back to its normal level. "Nay, no real bellow would be possible with that. Poor you, to be so cursed."

"Poor me, indeed," he said under his breath, wondering why he was unimaginably amused by her.

There was something refreshing about her now that he thought about it. She was rather brash and stood up to him in a way no one other than his brothers ever had.

Most women were intimidated by his height and scowl. He'd scarce had to do more than turn a glance to a maid to send her flying off in the opposite direction, or worse, have her start giggling at him.

He hated giggling.

Nora never giggled.

Her laugh was pleasant. Soothing.

Then she began to hum.

Ewan reined his horse in and stared at her.

She paused and looked up at him with large eyes. "Why are you scowling at me now?"

"You are interminably pleasant. How can you sit there and be so happy over nothing at all?"

"It certainly beats being sad over nothing at all. Don't you agree?"

He stiffened at her implication. "I happen to like being sad over nothing at all. I find it suits me."

"A smile would suit you better. My mother always says that a smile is dressing for the face."

"And I always say the face, much like the body, is best left naked."

Her cheeks pinkened at his words. "Do you always speak so freely?"

"I thought you said I don't speak at all."

Her face fair glowed with impish delight. She was enjoying their verbal sparring, and though he hated to admit it, there was a part of him that liked it, too.

"You're certainly an interesting dichotomy," she admitted. "I will give you that. A paragon of contradictions."

"How so?"

"Well, you live in a cave, which suggests a rugged demeanor, and at the same time you made sure that you brought the comforts from home. You act beastly to people and you treat beasts with care. What say you to that?"

"I say that you have spent entirely too much time contemplating me."

Just as he had spent entirely too much time contemplating her and the way the breeze played through her blond hair that peeped out from under her brat. The way the curve of her lips looked so moist and inviting.

Lips that would probably be as soft as a rose's petals.

Lips that would taste like heaven . . .

He shook himself from that mental direction. The last time he had thought such foolishness, he had paid well for it.

And so had Kieran.

"Do you like living alone?" she asked suddenly. "I'm not sure if I would like it or not."

Before he could respond, she added. "Of course, I talk so much you're probably thinking that I could carry on a conversation with myself for so long that like as not I'd never miss anyone else."

He smiled in spite of himself.

Nora gasped. "Was that a smile?"

He cleared his throat. "Was what a smile?"

"That strange curvature of your lips. You know, the one where the corners are actually going up instead of down."

It was all he could do not to smile again. "I know not what you mean."

It didn't work.

She sat back with a satisfied look on her beautiful face. "You have a most pleasant smile, my lord. Perhaps 'tis best to keep your smiles hidden. The rarity of them will make them all the more valuable. So I shall cherish that one until I gain another from you."

She was the strangest woman he had ever met. Quite daft, point of fact.

She continued to chatter, and he found himself listening to her in spite of himself. Listening to the cadence of her voice, the soft lulling quality of it.

There was something soothing about the sound and the fact that she didn't really expect to converse with him, but was content just to prattle away on her own.

But what disturbed him most was the craving she awoke inside him.

He purposefully kept himself away from women. He'd been lied to enough to last out his lifetime, and he'd vowed long ago to let no other woman into his heart.

So he had kept all women at a distance. Both physically and mentally.

He hadn't been lured by any of their kind since Isobail. But something about Nora made him yearn again.

He wanted to kiss her.

To *savor* her.

Worst of all, he wanted to hold her in his arms and let her sate the loneliness that lived inside him.

What strange thoughts were these? He needed no comfort. He'd proven that. He deserved no comfort after what he'd done.

Still, he took an odd pleasure in being in Nora's company.

And before he even realized it, they reached Lenalor.

At least here he could seek a modicum of peace from the lady at his side and the disturbing thoughts in his mind that she evoked.

"What a quaint place," Nora said as they entered the small village. It was long after dark, and most of the people were inside for the night. Firelight could be seen from the cracks around doors and through the open windows they passed.

"Not particularly large," Nora continued, "but still wholesome and serviceable enough."

Ewan held his silence as they approached the brewer's house, which was at the end of the line of cottages that made up the road that led through the village.

Old Aenos the brewer and he had a love-hate relationship. Aenos loved to see the only man he'd ever known who could drink him under the table, and he hated whenever Ewan had to leave.

Ewan stopped his horse and dismounted before Aenos's door. He knocked on it.

"I be closed for the night," the old man snarled from the other side. "So whoever you be, you better well . . ." His voice trailed off as he swung open the door to see Ewan.

Aenos's face and demeanor lightened immediately.

"Ewan!" He laughed, clapping him on the

back. "Finished off my ale so soon, eh? Well, come in, my lord. I've plenty more to keep you happy."

Ewan had started to step inside when he realized Nora was not beside him. He turned around to find her still on her horse, looking down at the ground skeptically.

Growling low in his throat, he excused himself from Aenos and walked over to her. "Jumping wouldn't kill you."

"Nay, but it might break my leg. Sprain my ankle. At the very least, soil my gown. Are you always so discourteous as to leave a lady to her own means?"

"I'm not used to being in a lady's company without my brothers being present." Ewan clenched his teeth as soon as the words were out of his mouth. He couldn't believe he'd said that to her.

"What do you mean by that?" she asked.

"Nothing." He helped her down from her horse and did his best not to notice just how pleasant she felt in his arms.

How good her body felt sliding down along his . . .

It was all he could do to not lean forward and breathe in the sweet, feminine scent of her. To let that pleasant smell wash over him and make him drunk all over again.

He'd no sooner set her down before him than old Sorcha, Aenos's wife, came over to greet them. Part of him hated to see her joining them, but the rational side of him was grateful for the distraction.

Her long gray hair fell in braids down the sides of her face as she clutched a plaid shawl about her shoulders. Her gray eyes were happy and bright, just like the woman herself.

Ewan had known her all his life and oft-times thought of her as another mother. He loved the old woman dearly.

"My lord." The older woman beamed. "Aenos didn't tell me you brought company with you this time, and a lady no less. Have you finally gone and settled down?"

"Nay, Sorcha. I'm only taking her to my brother."

He left Nora to Sorcha's care and led the horses around the cottage to deliver them up to Aenos's apprentice, who also doubled as a stable hand.

Nora watched him leave and shook her head. "His manners are appalling," she said under her breath. She turned back to the older woman. "I'm called Nora."

The woman gave her a chiding smile. "Don't be so hard on the lad, my lady. He's a bit gruff, but he has a good heart."

"He keeps it well hidden."

The woman took her arm as if she'd known her all her life, and led her inside the small cottage. "Shall I answer your question for you?"

"What question?"

"The one you posed to him just now about what he meant by not being around a lady without his brothers."

"Aye, please."

"Have you ever met any of his brothers?"

"Nay."

"Well, I've met them all. Wiped both ends of most of them back when I was a maid for his mother. They are a spirited bunch of lads to be sure. But Lord Ewan was always quieter than the others, and whenever a lady came near, his brothers would fair knock each other down in an effort to win the lady's notice. I can't tell you the times I saw him attempt to speak to a woman only to have Braden or Kieran elbow him aside. After a time, he quit trying to compete with them and simply ambled off to tend his own needs and ignore the others."

That *was* interesting.

"Are his brothers as handsome as he?"

"Some think they are more so. But I think each one is handsome in his own way. The youngest, Braden, holds many of the same features as Ewan and is unearthly handsome, but is rather arrogant about it. Lochlan reminds me of a golden angel, all fair, graceful and refined. The eldest of them, Sin, is like a fallen angel, dark in his ways and yet extremely compelling. And Kieran, God rest his soul, was what every woman dreams of, I think. He had black hair and eyes so pale they looked almost colorless."

Sorcha sighed wistfully. "Oh, those eyes of his. They smiled even when he was serious. He was a charming rogue who dallied with more women even than Braden. I tell you, the world is not as happy a place as it was when he was in it."

Sorcha glanced behind them as if looking for Ewan, then leaned forward and whispered to her. "You do know what day today is, do you not?"

"Tuesday?"

Sorcha shook her head. "Nay, my lady. 'Tis the anniversary of Kieran's death. This is the very day his brother Lochlan went out to find the lad and found his sword and plaid lying on the banks of the loch."

Nora went cold at her words. "Ewan drowned his brother?"

Sorcha pulled back with a scowl. "Whatever makes you say that?"

"I've heard rumors that Ewan killed his brother."

"Nay, my lady. Kieran killed himself because Ewan ran off with the lady they both loved. I was there that very day when Kieran had learned Ewan and Isobail were gone. He couldn't believe that he had lost his lady to his brother. Heartsick, he'd told his family that he needed some time alone. Ewan was probably halfway to London by the time

Kieran took his own life."

Nora frowned at that last bit. "Halfway to London?"

"Aye, they were going to the lady's aunt. She was supposed to shelter them. Only 'twas a lie the lady told Ewan so that he would take her off to England to meet with her lover. The poor wee lad was devastated when she left him."

Nora felt ill at the news. No wonder the man had looked so angry when she had posed her suggestion to him.

"Oh, Sorcha, I am such a fool."

"How so?"

"I asked Ewan to take me to London so that I could stay with my aunt and avoid marrying a man I loathe."

Sorcha gaped.

"I didn't know," she hastened to assure the woman. Oh, but she felt terrible over this. "I can't believe I said it today of all days, no less. At least now I know why he looked as if he wanted to strangle me."

No wonder the poor man had been lying drunk in his bed. He'd probably been doing his best to forget the pain he had caused his brother.

Nora wished she could undo what she'd done. She wished she could take back this day and have plotted her course on any day save this one.

If only she'd known . . .

71

Sorcha cleared her throat as Ewan headed back toward them. His eyes were still rimmed in red, but clearer than they'd been when he'd first started this trip.

He walked with his shoulders back, a proud man. Still, the sad torment in his eyes betrayed the inner pain he felt.

Pain she had unknowingly added to.

He'd started past them when Nora called out to him. "Ewan?"

He paused to look at her.

"Might I have a word with you?"

Sorcha excused herself as Ewan came to stand beside her.

"Do you need something?" he asked gruffly.

"I . . ." Nora swallowed as she tried to think of what she should say to him.

I'm sorry seemed somehow paltry given what she'd done to him this day, the memories she'd unknowingly dredged up.

"Thank you," she said quietly. "I really appreciate your doing this favor for me even though you didn't have to. It was very kind of you."

She raised up on her tiptoes and laid a quick kiss on his cheek before heading toward the cottage.

Ewan was dumbstruck by her actions.

She'd thanked him?

She'd *kissed* him.

He didn't know which one stunned him

more, and for his life he couldn't understand what had prompted either action.

The lass was an odd one to be sure. Peculiar and strange. And yet on some level she was rather charming, especially when her mouth was closed.

Bemused by her, he followed the women inside the cottage.

Aenos was already seated at the wooden table in the middle of the main room, pouring large goblets of ale.

Without taking a seat in one of the five chairs, Ewan grabbed his goblet and downed it in one gulp, then belched loudly.

As he set the goblet down to be refilled, he caught Nora's horrified face as she sat herself in the chair next to Aenos.

"Why, I don't think I've ever seen a man swallow the whole of his cup with one breath," she said, her tone chiding. "If you keep that up, you'll be drunk in a matter of minutes."

He scoffed at her warning as he pulled a chair out for himself and sat down. "Trust me, it'll take more than a few minutes."

He nodded to Aenos, who poured the goblet full.

Sorcha made them trenchers of roasted ham with leeks and onions.

As was his custom, Ewan ignored the food and continued to drink. He also did his best to ignore the lady who sat across from him.

Something that proved to be impossible. All he could see was the firelight playing in the golden highlights of her hair. The way the shadows played across her creamy skin.

The delicate grace of her hands as she used them to cut her food and eat.

Nora was pure elegance.

And it made him ache with desire for her.

She didn't say anything else about his drinking, but chattered with Sorcha.

" 'Tis so kind of you to feed us, good wife. I'm sorry we arrived unannounced."

Sorcha waved her words away. "We're used to it. Ewan comes to us all the time like this."

Nora looked at him expectantly. "Then why did you pass by the village?"

"I wanted to get you to Lochlan as soon as possible."

"Then why did you double back?"

Because a lady so fine deserves better than to sleep on soggy ground with me for company.

That was something he had no intention of explaining to her. "Because I wanted to."

Ewan poured more ale and downed it, then poured more. He took the goblet and pitcher and made for the door.

Frowning, Nora watched him leave.

"Aenos, go after him," Sorcha said. "I don't want him sleeping in the barn again. He caught a cold and was sick for days the last time he did that."

74

Aenos nodded and got up to follow him.

After Aenos left, Nora turned to Sorcha. "Sorcha, why is Lord Ewan so —"

"Gruff?"

"Surly and drunken was what I wanted to say, but gruff works as well."

"Guilt, my lady, is hard on a man. Every day he lives that his brother doesn't is a day he feels he owes to Kieran."

"What do you mean?"

Sorcha traced a circle on the table for a minute as if debating whether she should answer. When she spoke, her voice was scarce more than a whisper, as if she were imparting a secret to her. "Well, one night when the lad was drunk, he said something that has stuck in my mind. He said that he didn't deserve comfort while his brother was lying at the bottom of a cold loch because he was a fool."

Nora frowned at that. "But his cave is furnished in luxury."

"Aye, the doing of his mother once she saw how he was living up there in the hills with nothing at all for comfort. Not even a blanket to warm him. The lady couldn't stand the thought of him in such misery, so she led an army of helpers and threatened to come every day if he removed any of it."

Nora smiled at his mother's kindness. "So he intends to waste away his life because his brother is dead?"

"It appears so."

Nora sat back as she thought that over. Why would he throw away his life because his brother was weak?

"Well, what foolishness is that?" she asked.

"My lady, you don't understand how close they were."

"Perhaps not, but does he honestly think that his drinking and such would make his brother happy?"

It didn't make any sense at all that he would think that or act the way he did.

Before Nora could think better of it, she got up and went outside to find Ewan.

He was sitting on a log at the rear of the cottage drinking with Aenos.

The instant he saw her, he cursed. "Why are you out here?"

She didn't answer. Instead, she took the goblet from his hand and poured it out.

His face flushed with anger. "What are you doing?"

The answer was so obvious that she didn't bother explaining. Instead, she grabbed the pitcher and headed back toward the house.

Nora didn't get far before Ewan caught her.

"Give me that," he said, trying to take it from her hands.

"Nay," she said firmly.

His face was aghast. "Nay?"

"Nay."

Ewan reached for it again.

Nora twisted and tried to get past him, but somehow in the process she ended up dousing both of them and stumbling.

So intent on regaining his ale, Ewan didn't think to catch either one of them. They landed on the ground, limbs entwined with Nora on top of him.

His body reacted instantly to the feel of her softness squirming against him.

For a moment, he couldn't move. All he could do was feel her breasts against his chest, her legs against his, her breath falling on his face.

It had been so long since he last held a woman, so long since he had seen a woman as fair as this one who didn't belong to one of his brothers.

Longing pierced him as he focused his gaze on her parted lips.

Taste her.

It was all he could do not to yield to the anguished need he felt for her. To the heated fury of his groin that begged for a wee taste of her body.

Aye, she was all fire and beauty. And he wanted her in a way most mad.

Nora couldn't breathe as she stared down into Ewan's perfect blue eyes. Never in her life had she been this close to a man.

Who knew one would be so hard, so . . . well, masculine.

She felt a peculiar urge to rub herself

against him, to feel his hardness with the whole of her body.

His eyes were dark, dangerous as he watched her in silence.

"Here, my lady," Aenos said as he joined them. "Let me help you up."

Ewan cursed again, and as Aenos helped her up she saw their clothes, and she realized why he'd done that. They were both drenched by ale.

Aenos snorted. "Have no fear, lad. There be plenty more of that to be sure."

Ewan got up slowly.

"He doesn't need to be drinking any more ale," Nora said, turning to Aenos. "He needs a good bath and a night of rest."

"And who are you to be lecturing me on what I can and canna drink?"

She thought about that for a moment, then seized on the one thing he couldn't argue with. "Your responsibility."

Ewan's face went from anger to shock in the span of a heartbeat. "Beg pardon?"

"I'm your responsibility," she told him, "and you can't be watching after me while you're knee-deep into your cups. I happen to be quite a handful and could get into any number of fixes while you're off unconscious. So you see, it is my place to lecture you on how much ale you consume."

She watched as the muscle in his jaw worked furiously.

He glanced to the old man beside him. "Aenos, fetch me an ax."

Aenos headed off at his command.

Those words made her nervous. Especially since they were said with a mixture of anger and determination. "An ax? Why do you need an ax?"

His eyes blazed. "I'm going to take care of *my* responsibility so that it plagues me no more."

She gulped audibly. "Take care of me how?"

"I'm going to cut your head off and bury your body in the back."

She stepped away from him, unsure whether he meant that. His face was stern and serious enough.

"That is a jest, correct?"

"Mayhap. But if you don't leave me be, woman, you're going to find out firsthand why I choose to live alone."

Aenos returned with the ax.

Ewan grabbed it from him, cast her a menacing glare and handed Aenos the empty pitcher. "Take her inside to finish her meal, Aenos. I'll be back later."

"Where are you going?" Nora asked.

He didn't answer. He merely headed off into the woods.

"Leave him be for a bit," Aenos whispered. "He's only going to work out some of his anger."

"How?"

"He chops wood. I've enough of it now to fuel the whole village through the harshest of winters. But it calms him down, so I never say anything. Come, my lady, let's get you inside so that you can get dried off."

Nora followed him back to Sorcha inside their worn but cozy cottage.

"Where is Ewan?" Sorcha asked while she was cleaning Ewan's trencher.

Aenos pulled his cap off and replaced it on the hook by the door. "The woodpile."

Sorcha sighed. "Poor lad. At the rate he's going we'll be able to build a castle."

Nora retook her seat. "Is he always so angry?"

"He's a man in pain, my lady," Sorcha said quietly as she returned to the table to keep Nora company. "He's forgotten how to live without it. Forgotten how to find joy of any sort."

"Remember when he was a boy?" Aenos asked, retaking his own seat.

"Aye." Sorcha smiled as she wiped a cleaning cloth over her area of the table. "He was such a happy lad. He used to get up and stagger down the stairs asking, 'Where's my Kieran?' "

She smiled at Nora and explained her comment, "He thought he owned his brother. And Kieran, bless his heart, very seldom ran out of patience with him. I don't think I ever saw one without the other."

"Until they fell in love with the same woman," Nora breathed.

"Aye. Isobail was an evil lass," Aenos said. "Turning them against each other so that she could get what she wanted. I know the devil's saving a special corner of hell for her."

"Aenos!" Sorcha gasped. "Watch your tongue before the lady."

"Sorry," he muttered. "But 'tis truth."

Nora ate in silence as she thought about the lonely man outside in the woods.

What would it be like to live with such guilt?

She couldn't imagine it.

Once she finished her meal and had changed her clothes, she left them and headed outside again to find Ewan. There was a small path that led from the back of the cottage into the woods.

It didn't take long to find him. She could hear his chopping even from a distance.

What she didn't expect was to find him shirtless. His body was covered in a fine sheen that fair glowed in the moonlight.

He was beautiful.

Manly.

Powerful.

And as soon as he saw her, he did what she expected. He cursed. It seemed to be the only greeting he could give her.

"Unless you come bearing more ale, I suggest you head back inside."

"And if I come bearing an apology?"

He didn't even pause as he swung the ax. "I'm in no mood to hear it."

"Be that as it may, I am in the mood to give it. I just wanted to tell you that I'm sorry I dragged you into my problems when it is obvious yours are much worse."

He tugged the ax free of the stump, then buried it into the wood again. "What do you know of my problems?"

"Truly, nothing. You just seem incredibly sad and angry. I should have left you passed out in your cave."

He struck the wood again. "Aye, you should have."

Nora watched him with fascinated interest as he picked up the logs he'd made and carried them to the large pile. Sorcha and Aenos were right. It was quite a mountain of lumber.

And he was quite a mountain of delectable male flesh. A man whose body rippled with every move he made.

Ewan wiped his face with his arm, then retrieved the ax from the ground and headed for another tree.

She swallowed at the strength and sight of him working. The muscles of his back rippled and flexed, making her body strangely warm and needful.

"Tell me," she said, "does it help? Does ale really alleviate your feelings?"

"Why do you want to know?"

"In the event I don't make it to England and am forced to marry Ryan, I was just wondering if that would be the way to ease the misery of the life I'm sure he'll give me."

With three strikes, he felled the tree.

He waited until it was down before he spoke again. "Have you ever met this man you are betrothed to?"

"Aye, many times."

"Is he truly insufferable, then?"

She shivered at the thought of Ryan. They had never gotten along, and in truth, she couldn't believe he wanted to wed her given their mutual distaste.

"You can't imagine. He is beastly. He looks at me and sees nothing but my purse. I speak and he turns away." She shook her head. "How I wish I were a man. If I were, I would never waste my life hiding away."

"Judge not lest ye be judged."

"I know, but still it makes no sense. You are in complete control of your life and yet you do nothing with it. I, on the other hand, must do as I am told. I can't just leave whenever I choose."

"Is that not what you've done?"

"Aye, and at what cost? My maid and servant will like as not be punished for it, and you would hand me back over to my father in an instant if I told you who he was."

Ewan thought about that. He'd never given

much thought to what it would be like to be a woman. He'd always taken his freedom for granted.

She was right; he answered to no one.

He was his own man with no ties to anyone except his family.

Ewan paused and looked at her. "If you were free, what would you do?"

She shrugged prettily. "I know not. Travel perhaps. I've always wanted to see Aquitaine. My mother has such marvelous stories about the acres of vineyards there. She says there's not a more beautiful place on this earth. Or perhaps I would go to Rome. Make a pilgrimage. Have you ever been to the Holy Land?"

"Nay."

Her face fell. "Oh. My aunt went. She had a marvelous time there."

She unpinned a brooch from her dress, then moved forward to show it to him. "She gave me this. She said she bought it from a crusader who was selling items so that he could gain enough money to return home."

Ewan studied the piece. It was a knight on horseback who bore a cross on his shield, and was indeed a pilgrim's badge.

He tightened his grip on it.

Was it possible that she really could be who and what she claimed?

Still, he couldn't shake the feeling that it couldn't be. For all her sincerity, it wasn't possible for the niece of the most powerful woman in Christendom to have shown up in his cave without escort. Eleanor's niece would be a woman of unquestionable value.

Under careful guard at all times.

She would never be allowed to just leave her father's house on so foolish a quest. Not without every member of the guard being raised.

He handed it back to her.

Her fingers brushed his, sending an unexpected jolt through him.

She was so soft and she smelled so feminine and warm. Closing his eyes, he inhaled her scent.

She was so tender.

Truly a morsel worth savoring.

Nora trembled at the look on his face. She'd been kissed only once before. It had been quick and rather slimy. The event was so distasteful that she had never wanted to repeat it, and yet as she stood there alone with Ewan, sharing her wishes with him, she felt a strange desire to taste his lips.

He bent his head down.

Instinctively she rose up on her tiptoes.

He reached out with one large hand and tipped her chin up toward him. In one heartbeat, he lowered his head and took possession of her mouth.

Nora moaned at the intimate contact and at the taste of him mixed with ale. His tongue brushed hers, making her entire body quiver.

Of their own accord her arms rose up and wrapped themselves around his bare shoulders so that she could feel his muscles bunch and flex underneath her hands.

He was sweaty and hot, and she should be revolted by his smell, but she wasn't. He truly didn't stink. It was a pleasant manly scent, and the sensation of his wet skin only made her ache more for him.

Gracious, she'd never felt the like. No wonder some women turned wanton.

Who knew touching a man could be so pleasurable?

Ewan growled deep in his throat as he tasted the sweet honey of her mouth. It had been so long since he last kissed a fair maid.

So long since a woman's hands had brushed through his hair.

He had forgotten the pleasure, and yet as he kissed her the thought was in his mind that no other woman he'd sampled had ever tasted this good.

It was followed by another thought . . .

While he was kissing her, she wasn't speaking.

He laughed at the thought.

Nora stiffened, then pulled back. "Are you laughing at me, sir?"

"Nay, love," he said honestly, smiling even though he wanted to cease as he brushed her swollen bottom lip with his thumb. "It was but a passing thought that made me laugh."

Her eyes narrowed as if she didn't believe him. "And what thought was that?"

"That you can't talk and kiss at the same time."

Her face turned bright pink. "You are a knave."

"Aye, to the core of my rotted soul."

Her gaze turned gentle, warm. "It really isn't proper for me to be out here with you like this."

Her gaze ran over his body, making him harden in lustful need to touch more of her. To touch *all* of her. "My mother would be quite scandalized."

He dropped his hand from her chin. "Your father would be furious."

"Aye, he would indeed. No doubt he'd want your head."

Aye, and not the one on his shoulders. "No doubt."

She cleared her throat and turned around. She took three steps, then stopped and looked back at him over her shoulder. "Oh, and Ewan?"

"Aye?"

"You kiss very nicely."

Bemused, Ewan watched her leave.

You kiss very nicely. The words rang in his head and brought an odd wave of arrogant pride to him.

Why that was so, he couldn't imagine. All he knew was that he had an overwhelming urge to follow after her, scoop her up in his arms and see if she was so bold and outspoken in the privacy of his bed.

And on the heels of that thought came another, much more painful one.

He would never know.

A man who had caused the death of his brother and best friend didn't deserve a woman like her.

He deserved nothing at all.

And nothing was all he would ever have. He owed that much to Kieran.

Chapter 4

Catarina paused by the fire as she listened to the three men plotting their attack against Ewan MacAllister while a fourth man leaned back against the wheel of the wagon, watching them.

Pagan had his arms crossed over his chest as he sat with his long legs stretched out before him, ankles crossed. His long, dark gold hair spilled over his shoulders and chest. It had a reddish cast to it from the firelight that played in the sharp, handsome angles of his face.

He was truly a handsome warrior. Tall. Well-muscled. Serious to a terrifying level. He had the deep blue eyes of a predator who never missed a single detail.

Whenever he looked at Catarina, she felt the profound urge to cross herself.

No one was really sure where he came from. He refused to speak of his past or his homeland, which must be far away since he had an exotic accent none of them could identify.

Their only clue about his past was his unnatural ability with a sword. It was obvious he had been trained and trained well, but they didn't even know if he was a knight or a former squire.

Not to mention, Pagan wasn't really his name. It was a nickname Lysander and others had given him long ago in the Holy Land for his wild fierceness and for the fact that he feared no one. Not even the Heavenly Father Himself.

Or so Pagan said. For a man who claimed he had no soul or respect for divine justice, he was never found without a small crucifix around his neck.

He hadn't been in their company long. Only a few weeks. He'd joined them in England while they'd been on their way north to Scotland. Catarina hadn't been sure if they could trust him and that deadly aura that clung to him like a second skin, but Lysander and Pagan went far back, and Lysander had spoken up on his behalf.

So after a little debate, Pagan had joined their group. Part of them, and yet he always kept himself apart.

Pagan passed a look to her as she continued to stand there watching the men, and it was only then Catarina realized he was as amused by the other men's plotting as she was. One corner of his mouth twisted up wryly so that he could share with her his own condemnation of their discussion.

Viktor, who was the closest thing to a father she had ever known, held an old, large, tattered bag in his left hand. It was a bag she had repaired earlier that day. His gray hair stuck out in the front as if he'd been tugging at it while trying to prove his point. "I say we attack him from behind."

Viktor looked to his right and handed the bag to the man beside him. "Bavel, take this sack. We toss it over his head and conk him right on the noggin."

Bavel nodded in agreement. Not much taller than she, Bavel was the musician of their clan. At a score and a half in age, he was only three years older than she, with black hair and flashing black eyes. He was a handsome man who had always been like a brother to her.

"I can use my hammer and we can have him in the wagon in a matter of minutes," Lysander added. A tall, fierce warrior, Lysander had been sent to keep watch over her and to be the strong arm should they need one.

"Or the lot of you could kill him," Cat said, joining their discussion.

She looked at each man in turn. Viktor's tired gray eyes held an uncommon spark to them, while Lysander's green ones glinted in anticipation.

Bavel looked away, shamefaced.

Pagan gave a deep, rich laugh that drew scowls from the others.

Lysander kicked at Pagan's booted feet, but

before he could make contact, Pagan moved them quickly away as if anticipating the "friendly" attack.

It was eerie how fast Pagan could move and how well he knew the minds and intents of others, sometimes even before they did.

"What do you know of it, woman?" Lysander asked irritably, turning his attention back to her. " 'Tis men's business you're interrupting."

"Oh aye," she said, laughing bitterly. "Murder most often is, but if you'll recall we were paid to *abduct* Ewan MacAllister, not kill him. Think you, what would happen if we return with his corpse?"

Pagan subtly nodded his head as if impressed by her speech. Without a word, he watched the others to see how they would respond.

"Have you a better plan?" Viktor asked. Unlike his other two coconspirators, he respected her ability to think.

Cat nodded. "I say we drug him."

"A devious woman's trick." Lysander spat. "I say we be forthright like men."

She scoffed. "You'll kill him if you do. A man like him won't come with you peacefully. If you attack him, he'll attack you."

Lysander made a rude noise at her. "Come, let us be about this. Cat, you make the wagon ready for him."

"Pagan?" she asked, looking to the man

who still appeared amused by their debate. "What say you?"

His voice was rough and deep, like thunder, as it resonated with his foreign accent. "I say you should never involve yourself in the machinations of others unless invited. Throats have been slit for far less."

"Will you join us, then?" Lysander asked.

Pagan shook his head. "I hold no grudge against this man and have no wish to fight him. I leave the entire matter to the three of you."

Lysander gave him a curt nod.

Catarina threw her hands up, unwilling to argue further. "When Ewan MacAllister ends up dead and his brothers demand the lives of the lot of you, I want you to remember who had the voice of reason."

As Viktor started off with them, Lysander made him stay behind. "You make too much noise, Viktor. It'd be best if you leave this to Bavel and me."

Reluctantly, Viktor agreed.

He ambled back toward the fire where Cat still stood with her hands on her hips as she watched the other two imbeciles head off.

"They are such fools," she said under her breath.

"Now, Cat, don't be so angry because they didn't listen to you."

"I'm not angry. I'm perfectly calm. See."

He laughed at that, then he and Pagan

helped her clean up their dinner remains. Catarina washed their cups and platters while Viktor fed the scraps to their horses.

Pagan returned to sit by the wagon, where he remained totally impassive and silent.

After a short while, Bavel and Lysander returned, empty-handed. Both of them had lost a good deal of color in their cheeks.

"Well?" Viktor asked, his voice a cross between fear and hope.

"Have you seen the size of the man?" Bavel gasped. "He's even taller than Pagan."

Cat looked at said man who stood at least a head taller than any other man she'd ever seen.

Even Lysander's face was pale, and Cat had never known anything to daunt the ex-soldier. A veteran fighter of the Crusades, Lysander had always had fearless nerves.

Until now.

"I don't want to be hitting this man, to be sure," Lysander agreed. "Like as not, it will only upset him."

Pagan laughed at that.

"How big can he be?" Viktor asked.

Lysander stretched his arm over his head and stood on his tiptoes. "He's a giant. No one said anything about kidnapping a giant."

Bavel nodded furiously. "We'll need a bigger wagon to hold him."

Cat exchanged an amused look with Pagan, who continued to watch them in silence.

Viktor stroked his gray beard as he considered their words. "I was told he drank much. Was he not in his cups?"

Lysander shrugged. "All I know is he had an ax and I watched him cut down a tree twice the size of me with only three strokes. I wasn't about to get between him and that ax to figure out if he was drunk or not. And if he could do that drunk . . . Well, I'm thinking he's a mighty fine terror."

Suddenly, all three men looked to Pagan, who arched a brow at their attention.

"You won't be involving me in this madness. If you want him, you'll have to get him on your own."

In unison their gazes moved on to her.

"Oh," Catarina said snidely. "Now why you be staring at me, huh?"

Lysander cleared his throat. He looked at the others, then back to her. "What's your idea, woman?"

"So *now* you be facing me for ideas, eh? What makes you think a simple, brainless woman like myself would have any idea on how to accomplish *men's* work? Why, I feel faint just trying to think any thought at all."

Lysander curled his lips.

"Please," Bavel said, moving over to stand by her. "You've no idea what we've just seen. If you be having any more ideas, I'm willing to listen." He shot a look at Lysander over his shoulder. "And if he insults you again, it'll be his noggin we conk."

Nora woke up early, even before the brewer and his wife did. As quietly as she could, she left the small cottage to attend to her needs.

It was barely after dawn, with the light just creeping through the village. This was one of her favorite times of the day. She almost always woke up before anyone else, and she treasured the times where she was alone in the world.

But she wasn't alone, she realized as she neared the small stream that ran behind the cottage.

Ewan had beaten her awake and to her spot.

She froze the instant she saw him in the early morning misty light. His black hair slicked back from his sculpted face, he was waist-deep in the water, holding a knife to his throat as he shaved himself.

Her gaze feasted on the sight of his tanned flesh. On the way the waves of the water lapped against his bare, tawny skin, caressing and teasing it to a fine sheen.

She traced the line of his muscles with her eyes, watching the way his body bunched and flexed with every move he made.

Aye, Ewan MacAllister was the finest-looking man she'd ever beheld.

Always sheltered at home, Nora had never

known such desire for a man, but she felt it now. Felt it in every part of her body. Her heart that raced, her lungs that struggled to breathe, her legs that threatened to buckle.

What was it about this unrefined ruffian that he appealed to her so? He wasn't the kind of man to woo her with poetry. Nor the kind of man who would sit for hours with her while she listened to a bard sing.

Like as not, he'd be like her father, ever impatient with a minstrel. She couldn't count the times her father had forced her mother up to their room rather than sit and listen to a bard's tale.

Her father was ever quick to bellow for her mother and never content to sit and listen to others.

Her mother, God bless her soul, was ever patient and caring as a wife should be. Whenever her father wanted to retire for the night, her mother went, even if she was in the midst of something else.

But Nora wanted more than that.

She didn't want to be the dutiful wife who lost herself to her husband's bidding. She wanted to live her life on her own terms.

When she closed her eyes, she saw her perfect man. A man of culture and thought who would read with her and compose poetry and songs.

Not one who stormed off to attack trees with an ax every time he became angry.

But as she stared at Ewan's bare form, she had to admit that attacking trees had certainly done fine things for his body. It had given him powerful shoulders that bulged with strength. Thick, muscular thighs that were dusted with dark, curly hair, and a chest that rippled with masculine beauty.

Suddenly he turned around and caught sight of her standing in the middle of a circle of trees.

Nora froze, unable to move.

Unable to breathe.

Time seemed to have stopped as they stared at each other. But what struck her most was just how gorgeous his face was when clean-shaven. The graceful lines of it . . .

If not for his size and manly presence, he might even have been called pretty.

But there was nothing pretty or feminine about the man before her.

He was raw masculinity incarnate.

"Did you need something, lass?" he asked.

The deep tenor of his voice shivered through her. Nora swallowed and tried to speak, only to find herself strangely mute.

"Is something amiss?" he asked, taking a step toward her.

Nora squeaked at the thought of his coming out of the water. If she was this affected by nothing more than his bare chest and back, she shuddered at what the sight of him awake and completely unadorned would do to her.

When he'd been naked in his bed yesterday, he hadn't seemed this . . .

Large!

"I'm fine," she said, spinning around and running back toward the cottage.

Ewan smiled as he watched her haste.

So the lass had caught him bathing . . .

He smiled even more widely as his body reacted instantly to the thought of her staring at him. She had a bold, unflinching gaze. One that hadn't caused her to blush or giggle.

She had stared at him like a woman who knew her mind and her desires.

The thought made his body jerk awake with desire. Made his blood turn to lava.

Imagine taking a woman such as her to his bed . . .

The thought was quickly followed by another. He would never know her. Not like that. Even without his promise to Kieran, there was the small matter that she was promised to another.

He'd taken a woman from a man once before. He would never make that mistake again.

Isobail had assured Kieran that her betrothed, Robby MacDouglas, didn't care for her, just as she had convinced Ewan that his brother didn't love her. In the end both

Robby and Kieran had been willing to sacrifice their lives for the viperous bitch. While Kieran had chosen to die, Robby had fought a feud that had almost destroyed both the MacAllister and the MacDouglas clans.

No woman was worth that.

Nora belonged to Ryan.

No matter what Ewan felt for her, he would honor her as if she were already the man's wife, his own desires be damned.

Nora spent the rest of the morning avoiding Ewan. Something that proved extremely difficult once they left the brewer's house and were again on their way toward Lochlan's castle.

"You are so strangely quiet, lass, that you've got me fearing for your health. Are you sure you're all right?"

"Quite well," she hastened to assure him. He'd asked that question entirely too many times.

The last thing she intended to tell him was that *he* was what was the matter with her. Who knew that the absence of his beard would make such a significant change to his face?

He no longer looked quite so off-putting or beastly. There was an elegant grace now to his features. An air of powerful predator.

Why would any man with a face so breathtaking seek to bury it under hair? Surely there should be a law to prohibit such a crime.

And those broad shoulders of his . . .

They were decadent. Powerful. They rolled with his movements, making her hot and needful as she imagined brushing her hand over his smooth skin.

Touching his ebony hair again.

All day long she'd been trying to banish the images of him that she had in her head.

The sight of him naked and sprawled in his bed. The sound of his deep laugh.

The way he'd tasted last night when they kissed.

And most of all, the sight of him this morning in the stream.

Aye, but it was hard to focus on anything else while she was plagued by such wanton things.

At least he hadn't drunk any ale this morning, nor had he accepted Aenos's offer to take it with him when they left. It appeared he did intend to remain sober while they were together.

That was most definitely a good thing.

They passed the morning quietly until they happened upon a peddler who was coming down the road toward them. The man's wagon was heaped with cloth, boxes and kegs. A small, muscled brown horse pulled the loaded wagon while the man walked before it, holding on to the horse's bridle.

He was a short, pudgy man with kind brown eyes, who smiled and tipped his cap to them.

Nora's heart quickened at the sight of his wares.

"May we stop?" she asked Ewan.

"Why?"

"I wish to look. Please?"

Ewan reluctantly stopped the peddler for her and helped her from her horse. He did his best not to be short with her again, but it wasn't easy.

The lady was much a magpie whose head was turned by any item she found passingly attractive or interesting. But at least today she hadn't made him stop while she dawdled with flowers.

He expected her to grab one of the costly furs that was draped over the back of the wagon.

Instead she approached the side where the peddler had four lutes tied.

She ran her hand over them as if they were the most precious objects on earth.

A chill stole down his spine as he watched her gentle caress and wondered what her hand would feel like gliding down his spine . . .

"Oh, these are beautiful," she gasped.

"My lady likes the lute?" the peddler asked.

"Aye."

Ewan scoffed at her enthusiasm, even though her bright face enchanted him. "They are only lutes, Nora. They're not even particularly good ones."

She scowled at him. "What do you know of them?"

Her face softened as she looked back at the cheap willowwood lutes. "They are beautiful, aren't they?" she asked the peddler.

Ewan shook his head at her as she plucked one of the strings.

The peddler pulled one of the lutes from the wagon and handed it to her. "Would you like to hold it?"

"Oh aye. Thank you so much." Nora's face beamed brightly, much like the sun itself. She was a beguiling creature. Filled with as much merriment as he was with ill humor.

"Have you played much?" the peddler asked her.

"Nay. My father said I played like a maid wringing a cat's neck. So one night after I went to bed, he used my lute for kindling." Nora cradled the lute in her lap and strummed an ill-fated chord.

The discordant sound made everyone cringe.

Her father was right. It did indeed sound like someone wringing a cat's neck.

"Let me have that," Ewan said, pulling it from her hands before she tortured them further.

Nora started to protest until he took the lute in his own hands and quickly tuned it.

Stunned, she cocked her head and watched the expert way Ewan held and strummed the instrument.

Why, he didn't even need a pitch pipe to tune it like the minstrels she had seen in her father's home.

"You play?" she asked rhetorically.

He answered by playing "Bad Roy's Anthem."

Nora gaped at his expertise. Who knew the big, giant bear would be so talented?

She'd never heard anyone play better. His large hands made the chords with an ease that bespoke years of tender practice. Fierce and strong hands that had also chopped and piled up wood the night before.

Hands that belonged to a man wholly unrefined.

Wholly unrefined and yet strangely delectable. Even more delectable now that she'd heard his skill.

He handed it back to her.

She smiled up at him as she tested the strings with her hands.

"How much for it?" he asked the peddler.

Nora paused at his words.

"Five pounds, my lord."

Ewan didn't even quibble. He pulled the money out and handed it over to the peddler. "Have you extra strings?"

"Aye, my lord."

"I'll a take two sets of those."

Her heart hammered at his kindness. Why would he gift her with such a thing? He barely knew her, and she had forced herself rather rudely into his life.

He should hate her for what she'd done to him.

Instead he gave her a present. One she had pined for every day since her father had destroyed her original lute.

Once Ewan had paid the peddler for the strings, the man took his leave of them.

Nora stood in the center of the road, looking up at Ewan in awe. At that moment, he was the sweetest man she'd ever known.

She wanted to weep from her happiness and gratitude that he had bought this for her.

It was all she could do not to kiss him for it.

"Why did you purchase this for me?" she asked, her voice filled with her joyful tears.

Ewan swallowed at her question. He still wasn't sure why he had done it. Other than that the look on her face when she had seen it had struck him in the gut like a fist. It was obvious that the cheap lute would bring her untold hours of happiness, and for some reason that didn't bear pondering, the thought of her being happy made his day brighter.

Unable to speak a word of that, he shrugged and headed back toward his horse.

"Wait!"

He turned at her call.

"Can we not stop for a bit and you show me how to play it? Just a little?"

"Nora, we've still got —"

Her face fell.

So did his stomach.

"Very well," he relented. What was a few more minutes when added on to the others they had already wasted?

Besides, he rather liked traveling with her. She was a fetching maid and did distract him from the past.

At least for a bit.

She bestowed a smile at him that dazzled his senses.

She rushed toward a fallen log and took a seat on it while he grabbed the horses' reins and led them to an area where they could rest and graze.

Nora sat with the lute in her lap, held at an awkward angle. Seeking to correct her, Ewan put his arms around her to show her how to hold it and was immediately assailed with the fresh, sweet scent of her blond hair. With the softness of her hands on his. With the way she felt like heaven in his arms.

Deep-seated need tore through him, making him so hard for her that he ached with it. He breathed in her scent, letting it wash over him as her hands touched his.

Och, but the woman felt too good in his embrace.

And she had tasted even better . . .

Nora was all too aware of Ewan's arms around her. Of his breath falling against her neck.

Of the way his strong hands led hers to the frets and strings to show her how to play.

She savored the warmth of him as dreams of her fictitious courtier evaporated. Gone was the image of her blond minstrel, and in his place, she saw only the face of a man with tormented blue eyes.

A man who could make beautiful music with his hands.

Ewan clenched his teeth as he fought the urge to bury his face into the crook of her neck. He lost all track of time as he sat there with her practically in his lap, as he ran her hands through a series of chords to teach her an easy song.

"Do you know the words to the song?" she asked.

"I do."

"Will you teach me that too?"

"Nay, Nora. You've no wish to hear me sing, I assure you. I've been told a frog's hoarse croak is infinitely superior to my bellowing."

"I don't believe it. I wish to hear you sing."

Ewan cringed at the idea. He'd spent far too many years with his brothers' brutal mockery to have any delusions about his talent.

But as he stared at her and the expectant look she held, Ewan couldn't resist her plea. "Only if you swear not to laugh at me."

Nora looked up over her shoulder to see the sincerity in his eyes. Who would have thought a man like him would be afraid of someone mocking him?

Who would even dare? Better to mock the devil than a man like Ewan MacAllister.

"I promise not to laugh."

He sang a few words and quickly proved that he was right. He sounded dreadful.

But she didn't laugh.

She only smiled at him until she'd learned enough of the song to sing it herself.

"You have a lovely voice, my lady," he said, his tone gentle and tender.

She couldn't remember the last time a compliment had warmed her so much. "Thank you."

Ewan listened to her and let the sound of her voice soothe him.

Before he realized it, he was lacing his fingers through her hair.

She didn't protest.

"Who are you really, Nora?" he asked quietly as he stroked her scalp and fought the urge to bury his lips against her exposed neck.

No doubt her skin would taste like honey, and the salty taste of it would only make him crave her more.

"I can't tell you that, Ewan. You'll summon my father if I do."

Ewan traced his fingers from her hair, down her soft, delicate cheek. He'd never felt skin so soft and smooth.

He'd been so long without a woman. So long without the peaceful release of a tender body close to his that it ached to be close to her now.

And yet he couldn't bring himself to move away. She compelled him in a way he'd never experienced before.

It was on the tip of his tongue to ask her if she would let him make love to her. But he knew better. Bold though she might be, she was a gentle-born lady.

A maiden whose innocence reached deep inside him.

She'd never known a man's touch. Never known the beauty that came from that one moment when two people were naked and entwined, both taking comfort in each other as they reached the ultimate in human pleasure.

Isobail had been the one who had shown him that for the first time. There for a little while, he had felt as if he were something other than the forgotten MacAllister.

Braden was the handsome one. Lochlan the

smartest. Kieran had been the charmer, and he . . .

He'd been the quiet one.

The one his father would look at and shake his head while mumbling under his breath. *"There's no telling what will become of that one, Aisleen. Mayhap we should just oblate him for the priesthood and let them deal with his sullenness."*

"Och now, keep your voice down before he hears you. Ewan is a good lad and he'll be a fine man."

"He's weak. Do you not see how he bows down before his brothers. Even Braden, who is younger. It's embarrassing. He might as well have been born a daughter. At least then I could understand why he wants to stay hidden in his room. He's no match for the others. He will never be."

His father's condemnation had always burned deep in his soul. He'd never been afraid of his brothers. He'd just never seen the use in fighting with them over every little thing. There was only so much fighting a man could do.

Unlike his brothers, he'd always valued solitude and quietness over a fist in the face.

Mayhap he should have been a monk after all.

But as he watched the lady practice her song, he realized that the priesthood for him would have been a tragic mistake. There was no way he'd be able to keep those vows.

Nora leaned back in his arms, startling him instantly.

"How old were you when you learned to play?" she asked.

"Ten and two."

She rested her head against his shoulder and tilted her head so that she could look up at him. "What made you decide to learn?"

He shrugged.

She rolled her eyes at him. "I wish you would answer a question once in a while, Ewan. What are you afraid of?"

"I'm not afraid."

"Then why won't you tell me?"

He sighed as he remembered his childhood. The place he'd been relegated to in his family. He seldom ever ventured that far into the past. There was truly nothing much there worth remembering.

But for some reason, he found himself answering her question. "The lute belonged to my brother, Kieran. He'd bought it so that he could write a poem for the lass who held his heart that particular week. He'd attempted to play it, then found himself in love with another lass and left the lute in his room to gather dust. I snuck it out one day while he was off frolicking and taught myself to play it."

"Really?"

He nodded.

"Why? And don't you dare shrug again."

His lips twitched at her commanding tone. "I don't know. It just seemed wasteful to have it there with no one to care for it."

Her lips curved up at his words. "Do you like music?"

"It's all right. I'd rather make my own, though, than listen to someone else."

"Oh," she said, stiffening in his lap, "I'm sorry if my singing bothered you."

"Nay, Nora. I like the sound of your voice." Ewan cringed inwardly as those words left his lips. It was a confession he'd rather not have made to her. No doubt, she would now make even more free with her talking.

But his words relaxed her, and she returned to leaning against him, looking up at his face with her gentle amber eyes inviting him to take liberties he dared not take.

Nora knew she should move away from him, and yet she couldn't bring herself to do it. This was so peaceful being in the circle of his arms. If she were at home, or around any other person, she wouldn't dare do such a thing.

Still, it felt so right to be where she was, looking up at him and the way the sunlight glinted against his dark hair. No man could ever be more handsome.

"Even when I talk too much?" she couldn't resist adding.

He glanced at her, then glanced away. "We

should probably start back on our journey. I'd like to be at the castle before dark."

Reluctantly, Nora got up.

Ewan helped her back on her horse and then handed her the lute. He mounted his own horse.

Nora rode behind him while she held the lute carefully in her arms like a precious babe. The last thing she wanted was to have it damaged in any way.

"How long do you think it will take me to learn to play?" she asked.

"I suppose it depends on how much you practice."

"Should I practice every day? How much do you practice? How long did it take before you were any good? You said you taught yourself, so how did you learn without anyone to teach you?"

Ewan winced as her questions assailed him, but deep down inside he was relieved. In truth, he had been concerned by her earlier quietness.

Now she was back to her normal, chattering self.

They rode for several hours before they neared the meadow where he normally rested his horse when he made this trip alone.

Today his favorite spot under the large oak tree was already occupied. Damn. He'd have to find them a new place to settle down for a rest.

Ewan was leading her away from the small group of people who were eating when an older man waved to them.

"Greetings, my lord. Would you and your lady care to pass the midday meal with us? We've plenty to share."

Ewan sized them up. It was an older man, three younger ones, and a woman. With the exception of a blond man who watched them with deviltry in his eyes, they appeared harmless enough. Either peddlers or gypsies of some sort judging by their covered wagon and clothes.

The woman had hair as black as jet and eyes that were slanted like a cat's. The older man had the same dark skin, but his hair was all gray.

His gaze went back to the blond man who gave him a nod and a smile and appeared to be amused now, not threatening.

Nay, there would be no harm in resting with them.

"What say you, Nora?"

She offered him a broad smile. "I think it would be pleasant to pass a meal with someone who will do more than grunt at my questions."

He grimaced at her.

"Or give me that look," she added.

Ewan accepted the invitation. He helped Nora down and noted the way she continued to clutch the lute to her as if it were un-

114

speakably precious. It was all he could do not to smile at her actions.

How could anyone derive so much pleasure from so cheap a gift?

The youngest of the men came forward to help him tend the horses. His skin was almost as dark as a Saracen and his black hair was curly and thick. He wore a green shirt with a red sash knotted at his waist.

"My name is Bavel," he said, extending his arm.

Ewan inclined his head and shook the man's proffered arm. "Ewan MacAllister."

Bavel indicated the older man who had waved them over. "That is our Uncle Viktor, and my cousins Lysander and Catarina. The blond man is another traveler we picked up who goes by the name of Pagan."

Ewan nodded at each of them in turn while Catarina quickly befriended Nora.

"What brings you to MacAllister lands?" Ewan asked Bavel as the man moved to rub down Nora's mare.

"Just passing through."

"Are you peddlers?"

"Entertainers. There's a fair in Arrowsbough that we're headed to."

Ewan fell silent as he fed and watered his horse. Nora's easy laughter and chattering filled his ears as she and the others talked.

"Have you traveled all your life?" she asked Catarina.

"Aye, since the moment I was born."

"Where have you been?"

"Everywhere."

Nora took a sip of wine before she continued her inquisition. "Have you ever been to Aquitaine?"

"I was born just to the south of it."

"Nay, truly?"

"Truly."

Nora's face turned dreamy and soft, making Ewan's body react instantly. He would love to put that look on her face after a night spent sating his aching loins.

"Oh, I would love to travel about," Nora said, her voice thick and heady. "You're so fortunate to have an uncle who allows you to join him."

"Aye, I am indeed."

After a few minutes Bavel leaned forward. "Does your lady ever run short of questions?"

"Nay, she does not."

Bavel pulled back from him and muttered. "No wonder you drink."

Ewan stiffened at the words that had been whispered under Bavel's breath. Words he barely heard. "I beg your pardon?"

Bavel cleared his throat. "I said I would be drinking if I had to travel with such a woman."

Ewan frowned. Had he heard the man wrongly?

"Ewan!" Nora called. "You must come

taste this stew. 'Tis marvelous fare. The best I've ever found."

Catarina beamed in satisfaction. " 'Tis a recipe my mother taught me."

"Does your mother not travel with you?" Nora asked.

"Nay, she is in Anjou with my father."

Nora's eyes glowed with appreciation. "And they let you come to Scotland with your uncle? Alone?"

Catarina shrugged. "My mother is quite understanding of my need for freedom."

Nora sat back on her heels as if the thought was more than she could fathom. "I can't imagine a mother such as that. My parents would have the vapors should I . . ." She paused and looked up as Ewan joined them. "I'm sure they are having vapors at this very moment."

Without thought, Ewan reached out and touched her hand comfortingly. "We'll send word to them as soon as we reach Lochlan's castle."

"You are eloping?" Catarina asked.

Ewan almost choked at that question.

"Nay," Nora hastened to assure her. "Ewan is merely being kind enough to help me escape a dreadful situation."

Ewan sat next to Viktor, who handed him a cup of ale and then a bowl of stew. Nora sat to his right and continued to eat and chat with Catarina.

"So what brought you to Scotland?" she asked Catarina.

"We heard how beautiful it was here," Viktor answered. "So we decided to come see for ourselves."

Nora swallowed her bite of food. "Are you planning on going home soon?"

"Perhaps."

By the time Ewan finished his stew, his head had started buzzing. At first he thought he might have developed a headache from Nora's endless curiosity, but the world around him was moving.

"Are you all right?" Nora asked.

"I feel strange."

Nora frowned as she watched Ewan. He looked a bit pale as he swayed.

When he started to rise, he fell back to his knees.

She swallowed in fear. "Ewan?"

Lysander and Bavel caught him between them an instant before he passed out.

Nora's heart pounded even more at the sight of her fierce guardian unconscious.

Whatever could have happened to him?

"Ewan?" she asked, rubbing his stubbled cheek. "Are you ill?"

Catarina stepped forward and pulled her back from the men. "It'll be all right, my lady. Viktor is a wonder with healing. We'll get him into the wagon and tend him."

"But —"

"We'll take care of him," Catarina assured her. "Where were the two of you bound?"

"The MacAllister's castle."

"Well, that's no problem," she assured her. "We were headed that way ourselves. We'll let the two of you ride in the wagon where you can watch over your man and we'll get you there in no time at all. Isn't that right, Viktor?"

"Aye. We'll get you both home, mark my words."

Nora smiled at the kindness. It really was good of them to be so willing to help.

And come to think of it, it was a good thing they had stopped. What would she have done had Ewan taken ill and she'd been alone with him?

"Thank you," she said to Catarina.

Lysander and Pagan helped Ewan into the wagon while Nora stayed outside with Catarina. Viktor went inside to help tend Ewan and to see what he could do.

Nora waited several minutes before the men came back outside to join her.

Viktor patted her gently on the arm. "He'll be fine after a little rest. You may ride inside with him if you wish."

Nora crossed the short distance to the wagon's steps.

With a curious look to Viktor, Bavel helped her inside.

Nora went to check on Ewan, then froze as

she caught sight of him.

He'd been tied up and gagged.

What . . . ?

A chill went down her spine.

Och now, this wasn't any good at all. There was no reason for Ewan to be trussed up.

She turned around at the same moment Viktor shut the door to the wagon behind her.

Her sight dulling, she went to the door, only to learn it had been locked from outside.

"Catarina? Viktor?" she demanded angrily. "What is the meaning of this?"

"All will be well, my lady," Catarina said from the other side of the door. "Don't panic. You'll just be our guests a little longer than you had planned."

She heard Lysander scoffing at Catarina's words. "Just tell the lass she's been kidnapped, Cat. It's not as if she's not going to find that out anyway."

Nora gaped at his words.

Kidnapped?

Och, this was a fine mess now, wasn't it? Out of the pot and straight into the fire she'd landed.

And all because Ryan MacAren was a devil!

The wagon lurched as Viktor climbed up on it. She heard the others mounting and tying her mare and Ewan's stallion to the wagon.

Kidnapped. The word rang in her head as she turned back toward Ewan.

Her irritable companion would be even more so once he awoke and learned of this new fix.

It was all her fault, she was sure of it. No doubt the group had recognized her as the niece of the queen of England and had sought to use her for ransom.

Now what was she going to do?

Chapter 5

Ewan came awake to a pounding in his skull so fierce that for a moment he wondered if he'd been kicked by his own horse. But as he tried to move and realized his hands and legs were tied, he began to suspect something much worse than that.

Blinking his eyes open, he found Nora sitting beside him. Her face pale in the dim light of the wagon, she was staring at the door as if wishing she could splinter it with her thoughts.

The wagon lurched, slamming his ribs hard into the floor. Ewan ground his teeth against the pain.

"Where are we?" he growled.

His question startled her. She jumped and turned around to face him. Relief was etched into her delicate features as she met his heated gaze. "You're awake."

"Aye. Why am I tied? Did you do this?" he asked, even though he knew the very idea was preposterous.

Then again, with her, almost anything was possible.

She looked offended by that. "It was our friends. I think they drugged you during the meal, then they brought you inside and trussed you up."

"And what were you doing while they did this to me?"

"I thought you were ill." He noted the way she avoided answering his question.

"Didn't you find it strange that they sought to tie an ill man?"

She shifted about as if agitated. "I didn't know about that until I got inside the wagon myself and saw you lying on the floor of it."

"Then what did you do?"

"I tried to leave."

"Then?"

She held up a small piece of cloth that had been lying beside him. "I ungagged you."

That was not what he wanted to hear. Surely she had done something other than blithely submit to their capture.

"How wonderfully considerate of you. Did you not think to remove the rest of my bindings?"

"Aye, but they are too tight. I would need a dagger to loosen them."

Ewan took a deep breath and tried not to be angry at her. After all, there were four men out there, and had she fought them, she most likely would have been hurt. At least this way, she was unharmed and able to help.

It was his own fault he'd let his guard down and been duped. There was no need to take his anger out on Nora.

"Look inside my right boot."

She arched a brow at that. "You have a dagger on you?"

"Aye. Always."

She reached for his knee and felt along his shin.

"The inside of my leg, Nora."

She hesitated as if dreading to touch him in so personal a manner. Her face blushing, she did as he told her.

Ewan held his breath as her cool hand brushed against his inner calf. Her fingers felt wonderful as they carefully slid inside the leather, seeking his dagger that was hidden in a specially designed sheath.

Her touch was like silk against his skin, and it raised chills all over him.

Not to mention other things.

"Pull it out slowly," he cautioned as she found it. "I've no wish to be maimed."

She did, and her slow, careful movements only made him harden more as desire burned through him. It was all he could do not to moan at the sensation.

What he wouldn't give to have her soft, delicate hands on his back while he held her beneath him.

She bit her lip, making his body jerk with pleasure.

Once she had the dagger free, she cut the ropes that bound his hands.

Ewan let out a deep breath as he relaxed a

degree and fought the urge to touch himself to help alleviate some of the discomfort from his erection. At the rate he was going, he was beginning to feel like Priapus, and if he didn't find a way to ease his body, he was sure his health would be compromised by his unspent lust.

He took the dagger from her hand, cut the bonds on his feet, then returned it to his boot. "How long have I been unconscious?"

"It's hard to say, but it feels like quite a few hours. We've been traveling at a steady pace the whole time."

"Any idea why we've been taken?"

She shifted uncomfortably.

His stomach drew tight. "What did you do, Nora?"

"Nothing," she said defensively. "I can't help being who I am anymore than you can."

"What do you mean?"

She sighed and stared down at her hands as she wrung them in her lap. "I think they must have recognized me. They did say they had been through Aquitaine and England. 'Tis quite possible they ran across Eleanor and —"

His temper exploded. "Would you stop with the Eleanor nonsense? I need you to be sane for a moment."

She stiffened and glared at him. "I beg your pardon? What makes you think I would lie about something like that?"

"Because my brother is an advisor to King Henry, and if his niece was here in Scotland, Sin would have mentioned it."

She looked even haughtier than she had before and pinned him with a disbelieving stare of her own. "Well, if your brother is so close to Henry, then why has he not heard of *me?*"

He was baffled by her logic. "What?"

"Mayhap your brother is not as close to Henry as he would lead you to believe. After all, what Scotsman would Henry trust near him? He has a very strong disliking for anyone born north of Hadrian's Wall."

This was ridiculous. Why would she not see reality? He needed her sane if they were to escape.

"That's utter nonsense," he snapped in his brother's defense. "I have seen Henry embrace Sin myself."

She made a rude noise at him. "I don't believe you," she said, her eyes narrowing to sharp amber points. "I know my uncle well. He embraces no one. Not even his sons."

Ewan ran his hands over his face. The woman was beyond sanity. For whatever reason, she firmly believed herself related to Eleanor.

Arguing with her would get him nowhere.

Which left him with the one burning question. Why had they really been abducted?

What did the gypsies hope to get out of this?

126

Lochlan would sooner die than ever part with coin for Ewan's life. His brother would expect him to get himself out of this mess, and well he would.

There was no other reason to abduct him.

Mayhap Nora was the reason for it, after all. Like as not, her father was someone important, and he would probably pay a king's ransom for his daughter's return. Any decent father would, and though the lass was delusional, she was rather endearing at times.

"Where do you think they are taking us?" she asked.

"I have no idea. Did they say anything to you?"

"They said they would take us to Lochlan's castle. But I don't think that's where we're headed."

"Truly now?"

She stiffened at his sarcasm. "You don't have to mock me."

Ewan leaned his head back against the wagon's wall behind him and closed his eyes. How had he gotten himself into this? All he'd wanted was to drown out his pain with some ale.

He should be at home in his bed, oblivious to the world. Instead he was trapped in a rickety wagon with a woman who had no comprehension of the virtue of silence.

"Where do you think they'll take us?" Nora asked. "You think they have a cell waiting for us? Perhaps it's some noble's castle. But who would dare to keep a MacAllister in their lair? I wonder if they'll cut off your ear or mine as proof that they have us. My father oft tells the story of his grandfather whose hand was taken as proof of his capture by his enemies when they held him for ransom."

She held her hand up and studied it in the dim light. "I should hate to lose my hand. I'm sure you feel the same way. A man's hand is a necessary thing. I wonder what else they might take . . ."

"Mayhap they'll take your tongue as proof."

She frowned at him. "My tongue? How would that prove anything? I should imagine one tongue would look the same as any other."

"Aye, but the mere fact they cut it out would tell him that they did indeed hold you and not some other."

She glared at him, but at least it bought him a small reprieve.

Unfortunately, it didn't last long before she started in again asking him all manner of questions about where they were headed and what awaited them.

As the minutes ticked by slowly, Ewan began to hope it was his ears they took after all.

He wanted to listen to the people outside the wagon for clues, but all he heard was

Nora's endless conjectures.

She'd been right. She did make enough chatter for a whole family of people.

And even though it should anger him, he found himself conversing with her a bit. She was a creative and intelligent lass whose imagination knew no bounds as she ran through various scenarios of what could happen to them.

"You know," she said as she picked at her brat. "They say there are dragons in the hills. Mayhap they'll take us there to feed one. I never really believed in dragons, but this peddler came once to our home and he had a bite wound. It was this big." She held her arms out to a good size. "And he had it on his arm. He said a dragon had bitten him as a young man."

"How old were you when he told this story?"

"Ten and two."

"Perhaps he made it up to entertain you."

"Perhaps, but he looked terribly sincere about it. Do you think there are dragons? I should like to meet one if there are . . ."

Ewan shook his head at her while she continued on with her stories. The lady loved to talk as much as he loathed it.

At last the wagon stopped and so did Nora's prattle. She cocked her head to listen.

Ewan heard the muffled voices from outside.

"Think he be awake by now?" Ewan wasn't sure which of the men spoke.

"He should be," Catarina answered. "I only gave him a bit of the root, and considering his size, it should have worn off a while back."

"Poor man," another one said. "Imagine being locked in the back with the woman's tongue. No doubt he'll be wanting all our heads for it."

Nora gaped indignantly.

"I think we should keep him unconscious." That was definitely Lysander's voice. "He'll be more than angry at us and I've no wish to taste his wrath."

"That would defeat the purpose, now wouldn't it?" Catarina asked. "Nay, we have to be getting the man up at some point."

Ewan scowled at that. What did they mean?

"Let's open it then, and see if he's up." It was the first man again.

Then a small slit was opened in the back of the wagon and a pair of black eyes peeped in.

It was Bavel.

"He's loose," Bavel said. "The lady must have untied him."

"I thought you said you tied him well," Catarina inserted testily.

"I did."

Bavel was moved out of the way and

Catarina's blue eyes stared inside. "Hand me your ropes," she demanded.

"Why?" Ewan asked.

"Well, if you be wanting out of there to attend to your business, you'd be best doing as you're told."

"Just let them out, Cat," Viktor said.

She refused. "Not until I see those ropes. I want to know how they got them off him."

Ewan pulled Nora back as she started to comply. "You've no need to see the ropes, lass. Let us out."

"Ha!"

Ewan ground his teeth. What was it with this day that he was cursed with women who didn't know their places?

Nora shrugged off his hold and handed one of the ropes to Catarina through the slot.

"What are you doing?" Ewan asked her through his clenched teeth.

"Getting us out," she hissed back.

"See," Catarina said triumphantly. "The rope's been cut. They have a dagger in there. Had you opened the door, one of us would most likely be dead now."

"Hand over the dagger!" Lysander snarled.

Ewan scoffed at the thought.

Hand over his only weapon? Never.

"Nay."

"Then the two of you can just stay in there," Catarina said.

"There's one wee problem," Nora said. "I really need to leave the wagon."

"Why?" Viktor asked.

"I have to . . . umm . . . I just need to leave the wagon. Very soon."

Ewan cursed as he caught her meaning. Leave it to a woman to have no control over her body.

Catarina was the one who answered. "Then you'd best be making your man hand over his dagger."

Nora looked up at him imploringly.

"Nora, I can't give them my dagger. If I do that, we're defenseless."

"Ewan, I have to leave the wagon. I can't wait much longer."

The slot opened and a metal chamber pot was slid through it. "Never let it be said we lack mercy," Catarina said.

"Oh, but you can't be serious," Nora said as she eyed it with distaste. "I'll not be using that with him in here with me. 'Tis indecent!"

"I won't look."

Nora was aghast at Ewan's words. The man was truly a barbarian to even suggest she do such a thing while they were in such tight quarters.

Not to mention they were unmarried. Unbetrothed.

Unsuitable.

He was mad!

"Nay! I'll not be using that. You hand over that dagger right now, Ewan MacAllister, or I swear I shall talk until your ears bleed."

He grimaced at the threat.

She could see the indecision in his eyes.

"Ewan, please," she tried again. "I truly have to go outside."

Growling under his breath, he removed the dagger from his boot again and handed it hilt first through the slot to the gypsies.

"Are you happy now?" he asked, his tone surly.

"Aye. Thrilled." She turned back toward Catarina, "Now may I be let out?"

The door opened slowly to show Lysander and Bavel holding swords angled at them.

Viktor and Pagan stood back. Viktor looked nervous, while Pagan looked as if he were withholding laughter.

Nora descended the wagon and watched the armed men carefully.

Both men had their attention trained on Ewan, who stood assessing them as well. He was coiled like a snake, ready to strike, and both men knew it.

Nora bit her bottom lip as she weighed what she should do. Oh bother that, she knew what she needed to do. It was the only way to keep Ewan from attacking them and killing one of the fools.

Stumbling against Lysander, she caught his wrist that held the sword and gave a sharp twist with her hand.

The sword came free as she used her unexpected weight to unbalance him. She pulled her skirt up and wrapped it around her left hand, then turned to confront Bavel, whose face paled considerably as he looked about trying to decide if he should fight her or not.

Ewan was beside her in an instant. "Give me the sword."

She stiffened at his implication. "You know, I am quite capable of fighting him. My aunt sent a tutor to me when I was scarce more than a child, and at her behest I studied for years, even though it made my father livid that she would dare acquire such without his approval."

"The sword, Nora. Now."

She made a face at him as she handed him the sword hilt first. There was no use in arguing with him while they needed to escape. That wasted time, and the distraction would only get them taken again.

"Get him, Bavel," Lysander said as he came to his feet. The two men clashed swords.

Nora watched in awe of Ewan's skill. For a bear, he was quite nimble. He moved like fluid. Graceful. Powerful. He was quite a handsome sight.

It was quite apparent who the better swordsman was. She doubted if anyone could best Ewan's skill.

Then Bavel did the unexpected. He ducked beneath one of Ewan's parries, spun on his heel, and handed the sword off to Catarina.

Nora gaped at his actions.

Catarina tested the sword's balance, then moved in to engage Ewan, who backed up in disbelief.

"Afraid of a woman?" Catarina asked.

Ewan shook his head. "I'll break your arm if I hit your sword."

"Try me." She swung, but Ewan didn't even attempt to parry.

Instead he ducked and twirled away from her.

"Ewan!" Nora cried, holding her hand out for the weapon. If he wasn't willing to fight for their freedom, she most definitely was.

Nora didn't really expect him to return the sword to her, but he did.

She inclined her head at him in thanks, then turned to face Catarina. "Shall we?"

Catarina's eyes glowed. "Let's."

Ewan stood back with the men as he watched the women fight. He'd never in his life seen the like. They fought like two champions.

At first Ewan had almost not handed the sword off to her, but he'd been completely unwilling to hurt Catarina by fighting her. Now he realized he had made a very wise choice in trusting Nora.

"Amazing, eh?" Viktor said, coming to

stand beside him. "Catarina is one of the finest swordsmen you'll ever see."

Ewan frowned as he looked at the four men beside him, all of whom were watching the women.

He should be fighting the men, but he couldn't quite manage it while the women were at it. They were fascinating. Not once in his life had he ever seen two women fight with swords.

"Cat was trained by King Phillip himself," Viktor said. "He always said she had the skill of ten men."

Ewan agreed. "I'm impressed. She fights well."

"As does your lady," Bavel added. "Truly she is Cat's equal."

Aye, she was.

"How is it King Phillip trained a gypsy lass to fight?" Ewan asked Viktor.

Viktor and Bavel exchanged uneasy glances. "He's a friend of the family. Sort of. He's known Cat all her life."

Hmmm . . . how very odd.

"Shouldn't *we* be fighting?" Lysander asked.

Ewan unfolded his arms and turned toward the men. "Most likely. Shall we?"

The three related gypsies gave one another nervous looks while Pagan laughed and shook his head as if to decline the fight.

Viktor and Bavel took a step back.

"I for one have no wish to spill blood this day," Pagan said. "What say we allow the women to determine the outcome?"

"Aye," Lysander agreed. "Whoever wins gets . . ." He paused as if a thought had just occurred to him. "Well, if we let them go we won't get paid, now will we?"

Viktor sighed. "Most likely not."

"Get paid for what?" Ewan asked.

"We were hired to abduct you," Bavel said.

"Why?"

They shrugged. "We were told to ride you and the lady about for a few days and then leave the two of you alone to find your way home."

"Why?" Ewan repeated.

Again they all shrugged. Except for Pagan, and Ewan had a feeling he knew more about this than he was telling.

But that could wait.

Ewan whistled at the women. "Ladies, please rest your weapons."

The women did.

Ewan turned back toward Viktor. "Now tell me again who paid you?"

"No one has paid us yet. We was just told to get you out and then go pick up our money."

Ewan was completely baffled by their unexpected words. "Who is going to pay you? Did you not see the man who hired you?"

"Well, aye. But we never saw him before,"

Bavel said. "He just showed up while we were visiting —"

Lysander cleared his throat and stepped on Bavel's foot.

Bavel cursed and pushed the man away from him. "I wasn't going to tell him that."

"Tell me what?"

"That we were visiting Cat's godmother."

"Bavel!" Viktor took his hat from his head and hit Bavel with it.

"Ow!" Bavel snapped. "That hurt."

Viktor hit him again.

Ewan moved to stand between them and to keep Viktor from any further assaults. "Gentlemen, please. Who you were visiting doesn't concern me. The man who hired you does. What exactly did he say to you?"

Catarina came forward and handed her sword back to Bavel. There was a calculating gleam in her eye that Ewan didn't quite trust. "He said he would pay us twenty silver marks if we were to grab you and ride you about for a while. Once we go to Drixel, he'll be waiting to pay us."

"I thought Viktor said it was to ride me and Nora around."

"Viktor was mistaken. We were paid to abduct *you* and you alone."

Ewan frowned at that. That wasn't what he'd heard while he and Nora had been inside the wagon.

The gypsies were lying to him, but he

didn't know about which part.

Could they have another reason for abducting them?

"Do you know why he wanted you to kidnap me?" Ewan asked.

"He said he wasn't going to harm you," Viktor said. "I made a point of asking him that. I didn't want to take part in killing anyone. He just said that he needed for you to be gone for a short time, and that once we had you a few days away from your home, we could let you go."

"But you didn't abduct me from my home."

Viktor squirmed at that. "We were going to, but when we got there we saw the lady and her man and maid. So we waited until they left and then you left, and then we followed the two of you to the village, hoping to capture you last night."

He passed a shamefaced look to Lysander and Bavel. "Since we weren't able to get you last night, it was Cat's idea that we head out a little early and wait for you in the meadow to capture you this afternoon."

Ewan's scowl deepened. How had he missed something as important as five people following them? It wasn't like him not to have a sixth sense for such things.

No one had ever caught him off-guard before.

Of course, he had been drunk and then

hung over the entire way to Lenalor. Mayhap Nora was right; he needed to stay sober a little more often.

Ewan rubbed the back of his neck as he considered what he should do about the gypsies and the man who had ordered him taken.

Who would dare such a thing and why?

He needed to know if he had such an enemy.

"What did this man look like?" he asked.

"About this tall." Lysander held his hand up to indicate the man would be around five-six or so. Far too short to be one of his brothers.

Who then?

Who other than one of them would say such, let alone pay for it? It didn't make a bit of sense.

"Is he planning on meeting you in Drixel?"

Viktor nodded. "That was the plan."

Ewan turned to Nora. "Would you mind if we traveled with them for a bit longer?"

By her face, he could see she was torn. But when she spoke, her brave words surprised him. "I'm always up to a bit of adventure."

"Then you're not mad at us?" Bavel asked hopefully.

Ewan cast him a menacing eye. "I'm not particularly amused by the throbbing in my skull, but if the five of you can refrain from drugging me again, I think I can manage to forgive you."

Viktor clapped him on the back. "You're a good man, Ewan MacAllister. Bavel, get the ale."

Ewan shook his head as the three men went to the wagon to search out the ale and Pagan stayed behind with him, Catarina, and Nora.

"I can't believe I'm traveling with gypsies," Ewan said.

Pagan smirked. "I say that to myself every day and yet here I am."

Nora smiled at Ewan. "I can't believe you're not angry at them."

He turned to find Nora standing beside him, looking up at him with an appreciative glint in her amber eyes. The light on her face made her skin look even softer, more touchable. More delectable.

He fought the urge to smile at her. "Had they been more accomplished at the task, I might have been. But all things considered, they seem rather harmless. I'll just make sure to drink no ale until they've sampled it first."

"You're a wise man," Pagan said under his breath.

Ewan arched a brow at Nora as he remembered her earlier urgency to leave the wagon. "I thought you had to attend to some personal business?"

"I do." She handed him the sword, then ambled off toward the trees.

Ewan watched her. She walked like some

regal queen with the most delicate sway to her hips that made him ache to sample her. She was a fetching wench, and it was hard to believe a lady so refined was able to handle a sword almost as well as a man.

Nora was ever full of surprises, and to his deepest chagrin, ever appealing.

Why was he so amused by her?

For that matter, why was he amused by the gypsies?

Such a thing was not really in his nature. He'd always been the surly one. Always found the dark side in everything and happily wallowed in his moroseness.

He should be angry and vengeful. Instead he was actually looking forward to the two-day trip to the north.

"Are you sure the two of you aren't married?" Bavel asked as he returned with the ale.

Ewan was taken aback by the question. "Why do you ask?"

"You can barely stand to speak to each other, and yet when the lady walks off you look as if you can already taste her. Smacks of marriage to me."

"Aye," Viktor agreed as he brought the cups.

Ewan scratched his head at their logic. "Nay, not married." He was merely lusting.

For him there would never be such a thing, and oddly enough, he began to wonder whom Nora would be married to. If this Ryan she was running from would be kind to her.

Would this unknown man see in her all the things Ewan saw, or would he lose patience with her and her incessant prattling?

She deserved a husband who could appreciate her unique charms. She was actually quite pleasing once a man got used to her ways . . .

Nora paused in the woods as she gathered a few flowers to make a garland and a sweet-smelling bouquet. She'd always had a fondness for fresh flowers. The colors and the smell of them . . .

It was so beautiful out here.

She lost track of time as she frolicked in the woods daydreaming and pretending to be a fairy queen who could banish Ryan out of existence and get her safely to Eleanor.

She was completely lost in her own thoughts.

Until she heard a loud bellow.

"Nora!"

She jumped at the fierce sound of Ewan's voice. It was loud enough to shake the earth. She had been wrong earlier. Even though his voice was deep and low, he was capable of quite a loud noise when the urge took him.

She could even hear him tromping through the woods like some big, lumbering bear.

"I'm over here," she said as she caught sight of his white shirt.

He turned and glared at her.

"What did I do now?" she asked.

"Have you any idea how long you've been gone?"

She smiled. "You were worried?"

His scowl deepened. "There are all sorts of wild animals and bandits in the woods. Any of them could have found you and done you any kind of harm."

"You were worried?" she repeated.

He looked about uncomfortably. "You shouldn't wander off," he snapped gruffly.

"You *were* worried."

He growled at her.

She smiled more widely. "You know, my lord, you're not nearly so fearsome when you're *worried*."

He scoffed at her. "Why is it so important to you that I admit that I'm concerned?"

"It's not. I just like to nettle you with it because the idea of it seems so distasteful to you. Perhaps I should be offended?"

To her surprise, he reached out with his large hand and brushed a strand of stray blond hair from her face. The gentle touch was so out of character for him that it raised chills on her body and made her heart ache in tenderness.

He was a decent man when he wanted to be.

"I was worried," he admitted finally.

She fought the urge to close her eyes and savor his light touch. How could a man so large be so gentle?

"It was nice of you to come after me."

He grunted and lowered his hand away from her cheek. "What kept you?"

"I was picking flowers." She showed him her collection.

He curled his lip. "And you think that handful of weeds was worth risking your life and well-being?"

She pouted as she ran her hand over the wild flowers that released their sweet scent into the air. She inhaled them and let the smell remind her of her childhood days when she and her mother had spent hours alone gathering them and tending her mother's garden.

She cradled them to her breast. "My mother has oft told me that men have sacrificed their lives and kingdoms for a woman's smile, so why not risk the ire of a bear for a bouquet?"

"Most men are fools."

She paused at his words and the pain she heard his voice. Remembering what Sorcha had said about his betrayal, she felt sorry for the man who had forsworn beauty in his life. "You don't think beauty is worth sacrificing for?"

"Nay. I do not." His sincere blue eyes scorched her.

He meant that.

"But surely you didn't always feel that way?"

"I learn from my mistakes."

Her stomach tightened at what he said. She couldn't imagine such a life.

"And you've been without beauty ever since," she said wistfully. "I'm sorry for that, Ewan. Everyone needs some beauty in his life."

Ewan wondered for a moment if she were mocking him, but one look into her guileless amber eyes and he knew she wasn't.

She could never relate to the kind of pain he lived with. To her, the world was a kind, happy place filled with only goodness and light.

How he wished he could live so ignorantly.

"I can't imagine living a life where nothing gives me pleasure," she said softly. "It would take a strong man to live as you have. To get up every morning and carry on when all you can see is the gloom and misery of the world."

"I'm not strong," Ewan confessed. He wondered why he said that. It wasn't like him to be open with anyone. But there was something about Nora that comforted him. Something about her that made him want to share things with her. "I was a weak-minded fool who believed a lying termagant. There's no strength in what I do now or what I did in the past."

He took her back through the woods, toward the gypsies' camp.

"I disagree," she said as she walked beside him. "A weak man wouldn't still be alive."

"A strong man would be able to look his mother in the face." Ewan couldn't believe those words had left his lips. Never before had he confided that secret to anyone.

Nora paused and took his hand into hers.

Ewan stared at her tiny hand, at the long, graceful fingers that were laced with his own. His hand was almost twice the size of hers. Her skin was pale, soft, while his was tanned and callused.

There was no softness in his life.

No grace or beauty.

In truth, there was nothing in his life at all.

"This is not the hand of a weak man," she said as she gave a light squeeze to his fingers. "You could have left me to my own ends and yet you didn't. Even though my situation caused you pain, you came with me rather than see me hurt. What is weak in that?"

Ewan didn't know what to say. No woman had ever said such a thing to him. No one had ever before defended him.

She made him feel almost heroic.

How did she do it?

Lifting her hand to his lips, he kissed it gently and inhaled the soft, fragrant scent of her skin. She smelled of the flowers she held in her other hand, of the earth and of the woman. It was a heady combination. One that cut through him and made his entire body burn.

In that moment, she was beautiful to him. Not just in her looks, but in her being.

She was the beauty he wished he had. The beauty he would love to spend the rest of his life staring at and holding close to his heart.

But she could never be his.

She belonged to someone else.

"Thank you," he whispered, lowering her hand.

"For what?"

"Making me feel better."

She smiled at him, and he felt an invisible fist slam into his gut.

How he wished he could keep her with him like this forever. But it wasn't meant to be. She was promised to someone else, and like as not she had a father who was probably beside himself with panic at her disappearance.

If he were a decent man, Ewan would head off to Lochlan's castle with her now and let his brother find her father so that she could go home and relieve the man's worry.

Instead, he was going to spend the next few days with their untoward hosts. Not just because he wanted to find out why he'd been taken, but because he wanted to spend more time with this woman.

148

It didn't make sense.

Nora was everything he should hate. She was bold and stubborn. Vexing.

But most of all, she was enticing, and it had been so long since anyone had enticed him. An eternity since he'd felt the molten heat of passion or desire.

He wanted her.

With every ounce of masculinity he possessed, he wanted to take her in his arms and claim her body with his. To peel the clothes from her and explore every inch of her bare skin with his mouth.

To fan her hair out across his pillows and watch her face contort with pleasure as she came beneath him.

Yet it would never be.

She was a virtuous maid.

And he would move heaven and earth to keep her that way.

Nora held her tongue as Ewan led her back to camp. He must have washed his face right before he came to seek her. His black curly hair was slicked back from his face and sleek. His shoulders were broad, and yet he didn't appear as fearsome to her now as he had before.

She was growing accustomed to his brooding features and scowls. He was a strange combination of gentleman and beast. An intoxicating blending of dangerous predator and protector.

His touch was so gentle that it amazed her. He showed a kindness with her that she would never have thought him capable of.

And in the back of her mind, she wondered what he would be like as a husband.

Would he listen, or would he be like the others of his kind and shut her out merely because she had been born the wrong gender?

Nora, what are you thinking?

The man is wholly unsuitable.

Truly he was. Big, hulking.

With kind blue eyes that glittered with tormented pain.

She shook her head to clear it of the thought as she rejoined the gypsies.

Viktor and Bavel were sitting in front of the fire, smoking from pipes and drinking ale as they chatted together. Lysander was off to the side of them, lying down with his arms crossed over his chest, and appeared to be dozing, while Catarina was making dinner. Pagan sat beside the fire, whittling a small piece of wood with a curved dagger.

It was a strangely cozy scene.

Catarina waved her over while Ewan left her to join the men around the fire.

"So he found you," she said as Nora drew near.

"Aye."

"He was worried about you."

"That's what he said."

"Nay, my lady," she said, her eyes burning her with a deep sincerity. "I don't think you really understand what I mean. He was *extremely* concerned for your welfare. Have you not noticed the way he looks at you?"

Nay, she hadn't really paid much attention. "What way is that?"

"Like a beggar before a banquet. He has hungry eyes where you are concerned."

Nora scoffed at the idea. Ewan barely noticed her, and when he did, he seemed always to be peeved by her very presence. "You are mistaken."

"He watches every move you make."

Nora glanced around to where Ewan sat with Viktor and Bavel. True to Catarina's words, his intense gaze was on her, but as soon as he realized she was looking, he averted his eyes.

"See," Catarina said.

"You make too much of it."

"Perhaps. But what do you make of it?"

"I make nothing of it."

"Nothing?" she asked incredulously. "Then you've no wish to claim him as your own?"

Nora was slightly aghast at the thought, though to be honest, she wasn't as aghast as she would have been the day she met him.

"Nay, never," she said quickly. "I'm bound to my aunt's in England. Ewan is . . . Well, I'm sure he'd like to return home and forget the day he ever awoke to find me in his cave."

Catarina cast a speculative look to him. "He would make a fine husband to some lucky woman. He's a handsome one, to be sure."

"Aye, he is."

"Strong. Quite charming, I think."

Nora frowned at her gushing praise. Just what did she mean by that?

"Not too charming," Nora said as she helped stir their stew. "Rather moody and quiet, to be truthful. He can be rather rude when the mood strikes."

"They say still waters run deep . . ."

Nora paused as she watched Catarina's face while the woman looked to where Ewan sat with the others. The woman's beautiful features were dreamy and glowing.

Speculative, one might even say.

Nora didn't care for the look of her at all. "What are you thinking?"

"Just that if you're not interested in him, perhaps I should give it a try. I haven't found any man to equal one like him. He is one of a kind, and I happen to be fascinated by his earthy ways and rugged bearing."

Nora's heart sank at the thought of Catarina and Ewan embracing. Of the thought of Catarina doing *anything* with Ewan.

"The thought bothers you, doesn't it?" Catarina asked as she looked back and caught her gaping stare.

Nora closed her mouth and started to lie, but couldn't quite manage one. It bothered her much more than it should, and it made her want to do nasty things to Catarina for even hinting she was interested in Ewan.

Catarina smiled. "Tell me, Nora, have you ever heard of the works of Rowena de Vitry?"

Nora was thrilled to find another person who knew and loved bardic tales. "Aye! The Lady of Love is one of my favorite troubadours."

"Then you are familiar with the 'Romance de Silence'?"

"Nay, is it new?"

"Fairly." Catarina added the vegetables she had been cutting, then took the ladle from Nora and stirred them into the pot.

Catarina tapped the ladle twice against the pot, then set it aside. "It's the story of a woman in love with a man she sees every year at a fair. She watches him as he grows to love another, and as the years pass, she sees him with his wife, his children and such until he is an old man. On his deathbed, she goes to him and tells him of her love. That she has been dreaming of him since he was ten and eight and she just a bright-eyed maiden. That because of him she never married and never knew any happiness except in her dreams, where she could pretend he was hers."

Nora's throat tightened in sympathetic pain. It was a tribute to Rowena's wonderful imagination that she had written such a tragic tale. "How sad."

Catarina wiped her hands on her skirt. "Aye, but the saddest part of all is that right before he dies, he confesses to her that he always loved her as well. That he would go to the fair every year just so that he could watch her from afar, but since she refused to even meet his gaze, he assumed she felt nothing for him. So the two of them spent the whole of their lives aching for what they could have had, had they just talked to one another."

"How tragic."

"Aye, and you're not following where I'm going at all, are you?"

"What do you mean?"

Catarina nodded at Ewan. "Don't you think it odd that you feel jealous when I speak of wooing him?"

Nora stiffened at what she was implying.

"Nay," she lied.

Catarina laughed. "You like him, admit it."

"I do not," she said primly, picking up the ladle and returning to stir the stew. She didn't dare admit her feelings aloud to anyone. She could barely acknowledge them to herself. "He is entirely not the type of man who interests me."

Catarina looked aghast. "My lady, you set

your sights too high. What more could you ask for in a man?"

"Refinement. A man who is decorous and mannerly. One who is —"

"Boring."

Nora gave her a peeved look. "How so?"

"Have you ever been around such men? They're mewling. Fussing over their hair, their clothes. They're more woman than man."

Catarina indicated Ewan with her head. "Give me a man who isn't afraid to get a little dirt on his hands any day. Think you your gentleman would have gone after you because you tarried in the forest? He would have feared for his own life and given no thought to yours.

"Do you think such a fanciful, prim man would have laughed off what we did to him? Or would he have demanded our lives for daring to muss his hair and clothes? Ewan has been a very good sport, all things considered. Any other man would have Viktor's head for what we've done. Instead Lord Ewan travels with us as a friend and equal."

"He is a bit odd, which confirms what I'm saying."

Catarina shook her head. "Sometimes, my lady, a person needs to look at someone only with her heart and not with her eyes."

Nora glanced over to where Ewan sat. The other men were joking and laughing. He sat with his face stern, his eyes troubled.

How she wished she could make him laugh. "He's always so sad."

Catarina concurred. "You know, my mother has a saying. A jovial man can be happy with anyone, but when a sad one laughs, he treasures the one who brings him the sunshine."

Nora thought about her words. There was truth to that. No one should live with the guilt Ewan did, especially when he hadn't been at fault.

Kieran had made the choice to end his life. Ewan had done nothing more than make the mistake of believing a lying tongue.

Nora had no real designs on Ewan romantically. No matter how appealing he was or how well he kissed. At the end of the day, he wasn't what she wanted for a husband. But she wouldn't mind helping him if she could.

No one deserved to be relegated to a cave without family or friend.

She had a few days with him. Mayhap a little reprieve would help him see that life was better when one participated in it.

Chapter 6

"What are you doing?" Ewan asked as Nora came up to him with a peculiar impish look on her face. The look was so out of character that it made the hair on the back of his neck rise.

She handed him her lute. "You said you would teach me to play. I would like another lesson."

He took the instrument from her hand while she sat down next to him.

Close to him.

He tried not to notice the happy glint in her eyes. The way tendrils of her blond hair fell around her face as she lowered her brat to watch him.

She possessed a great beauty. Beauty that made him burn for her.

Even now he could taste her innocent kiss, remember the sensation of her warm breath on his face.

The way she had looked when she had told him that he kissed well . . .

It set fire to his blood. His heart pounded, and he felt oddly dazed, as if her presence alone intoxicated him. Made him light-headed and happy.

No woman had ever made him feel like this.

Not even Isobail.

Isobail had only aroused his body. At the time he'd been too young and inexperienced to understand the difference between love and lust.

What he felt for Nora was entirely different. He actually liked the lass. Liked spending time with her, listening to her unique ideas and endless stories.

On some deep inner level, she soothed him.

He took her left hand and moved her fingers into position as he showed her the first three chords to his mother's favorite ballad.

"You're very good at teaching," Bavel said from across the fire.

"Yes, he is," Nora agreed.

Unused to praise, Ewan cleared his throat and showed her another bar. "A teacher is only as good as his student."

She smiled up at him.

Enchanted, Ewan couldn't take his eyes off her face. Her skin was so smooth and perfect. Her eyes were clear and bright. Her lips, red and plump, were made for long, hot kisses. For driving a man wild with desire.

And she was definitely doing that to him now. He felt reckless and somehow free. Wanting her no matter the rational arguments.

Her presence took him past sanity and reason.

It took him straight into the realm of fantasy where anything was possible. Where there was no past to torment him. No future to fear.

There were only the two of them, and nothing else mattered.

He had to get away from her. Quickly, before any more of his will crumbled.

Moving back so that he was no longer near her and the danger she posed, Ewan nodded at her progress. "Just keep practicing those chords and I'll teach you more later."

While she strummed, Bavel went to fetch his own lute.

"You play your three chords, Nora," he said as he returned to his seat.

As she did so, Bavel composed music to go with hers.

Catarina came forward, clapping her hands in time to their song.

Ewan sat back, listening and watching.

Nora's amber eyes danced with happiness, and her cheeks were flushed. No doubt she was enjoying her small part in the harmony. The heightened color looked good in her face, making Ewan wonder what she would look like while fired with passion.

He ground his teeth and looked away, unable to think those thoughts. Unwilling to let his mind ponder the delicacy he knew she would be.

Closing his eyes, he swore he could already taste the salty-sweet flavor of her skin. Feel her warm and welcoming in his arms . . .

What would it be like to lie with her?

Nora smiled at Bavel as she played. She'd never had a night like this one in her entire life. She was making music. Real music!

Ewan sat across from her, his presence electrifying while Catarina began to dance to the music they made. Pagan stayed to the side, his eyes never wavering from Catarina.

Lysander produced a drum that he used to mark the beats of Catarina's movements. Nora was impressed with Catarina's exotic and wild dance until she happened to glance over at Ewan, who watched the woman as if transfixed by her.

He reminded her of a hungry wolf watching over a hen it wanted to gobble up.

For the first time in her life, she felt a vicious stab of jealousy.

How dare Ewan look at Catarina like that! Like he wanted to kiss her or do something more.

He wasn't supposed to look at *her*.

Nor was he supposed to make Nora feel hot and nervous when he sat too near her. Yet he did all those things and more.

Needing to distract him from Catarina, Nora handed Ewan her lute. "Would you like to play?"

He shook his head. "Nay."

"Oh, come now," Viktor said. "Play a song if you're able."

"No, really," Ewan insisted. "I've never played before an audience."

"I should like to hear you play," Catarina said, her voice low and sultry.

Nora frowned at the suggestive tone.

"Very well then," Ewan said, setting the lute in his lap.

Now Nora truly was upset. He wouldn't play when she asked him to, but he played for Catarina?

He was an evil man!

The men began to play a fast-paced tune, one that allowed Catarina to dance like Salome. Only it wasn't Ewan's head the woman was after, Nora was sure of that.

Och now, how could Catarina be like this after their discussion? The woman was a Judas. A tall, dark-haired, beautiful Judas who might tempt Ewan away from . . .

Me.

The single syllable hung in her mind.

It was true. She liked Ewan. More than she should, and the thought of him with Catarina was enough to make her want to do something vicious to the woman.

But he didn't belong to her. He wasn't hers to control, and she had no right to tell him whom he could and couldn't stare after.

Whom he could desire . . .

Ewan could never be hers.

161

He wasn't what she wanted for a spouse.

Why, he'd be just like her father, belching about the table, always off and practicing with his sword. Gathering his friends around for boisterous nights of boasting and drinking while they told and retold the same boring stories over and over again.

She'd spent her life watching her graceful, dainty mother being dogged by her much larger father, who would scarce let the poor woman out of his sight. He was always making loud demands for her mother's time. Wanting her to partake of his less than refined activities, such as watching him fight.

She couldn't count the times her father had whisked her mother up in his arms and carried her to their chambers while her mother protested, telling him she had duties to attend to.

And did he listen?

Nay, never.

While her mother preferred to speak softly, her father bellowed. Her mother loved poetry and music; her father liked caber tossing and stag hunting.

Nora had never seen two more mismatched people in her life. And while her father was a good man with a caring heart, he and her mother had nothing in common.

Why, they scarce spoke to each other. Her father demanded and her mother nodded.

Nora wanted more out of her husband

than that. She dreamed of a man who could talk to her about science. One who could keep up his side of the conversation and not get irritable because she was asking too many questions.

There was nothing wrong with questions. But her endless inquisitiveness oft made her father lose his patience and order her from the hall.

I love you, Nora child, but one more word from you, lass, and I swear my humble brain will boil over until I'm as empty-pated as old Seamus. Now get to your room and give me peace afore I lock you in there for the rest of eternity.

Nora winced at the words she had heard countless times.

Ewan was her father all over, she was sure of it. The only difference was their appearance. Her father was short and blond, not gargantuan and dark.

But inside, they might as well be the same man.

Yet as she watched Ewan play, she noted something odd about him. His eyes were brighter than they had been before. The corners of his lips turned up, almost as if to smile.

He loved music as much as her father despised it.

That was a little common ground between them. Something the two of them shared.

Och, lass, what are you thinking?

You tie yourself to a man such as he, and you'll *be gone forever.*

Marriage was good only for the man. The woman lost all sense of herself. She became lady to his lordship. Forever docile to him. Forever deferring to him.

She would become her mother.

She didn't want that. She wanted her own life, just like her Aunt Eleanor.

Eleanor answered to no man. She did as she pleased and lived her life to the fullest. She alone made Henry, king of England, bend to her will.

Aunt Eleanor was her ideal.

Aye, Nora not only wanted to be named for her aunt, she wanted to be her. Powerful. Decisive.

A woman in charge of her own destiny.

Catarina twirled around the fire, then held her hand out to Nora. "Care to dance?"

Nora hesitated for only an instant. "Show me how?"

Catarina pulled her to her feet, then raised her skirt up so that Nora could watch her feet.

Nora followed her carefully while the men played.

"You look as if you have French blood in you, little Nora," Viktor said as he smiled at her attempts to duplicate Catarina's movements.

Nora returned his smile, pleased by his

praise. But she knew she was no match for Catarina, who moved as if she were one with the music.

Catarina led her around in a twirling bit of dance.

Nora glanced to Ewan, then swallowed. He wasn't looking at Catarina anymore, he was staring at *her.*

With searing heat.

With hunger.

With need.

It made her burn. Imagine him looking at her like that. She wouldn't have thought it possible.

Yet he did.

And that look . . .

It made her feel womanly and beautiful. For the first time in her life, she understood passion and desire.

Ewan was magnetic and powerful, and his need for her was so intense that it was virtually tangible.

Unaware of why Nora had stopped moving, Catarina grabbed her hands and whirled her around again. And even though she danced, Nora's gaze continually went back to Ewan and the heat of his celestial eyes that burned through her.

After they had finished the dance and music, Catarina and Nora cleaned up the mess from supper. The men packed away the instruments and made pallets for everyone.

Catarina was putting away the pot when she met Nora's bemused stare.

"For a woman not interested in Ewan, my lady, you certainly looked ready to kill me over the fact he was paying attention to my dance earlier."

Nora's face flushed but she wasn't willing to let anyone know just how much she really did desire Ewan MacAllister. "I most certainly did not."

Catarina laughed. "You can't hide the truth from me, Nora. I saw your heart. It was plainly written in your eyes."

She wrinkled her nose at the woman. "I think you just like to play matchmaker, don't you?"

"Only when I see two people who belong together."

Nora scoffed. "I do not belong with Ewan MacAllister. Believe me."

"Whatever you say." But her tone carried the full weight of Catarina's doubt.

Nora left her to return to the others. Bavel, Viktor, Pagan and Lysander had withdrawn to bed. Only Ewan remained. He sat alone before the fire, staring idly into the flames and drinking from a large goblet.

Ewan didn't appear drunk, but a cloud of sadness engulfed him.

Nora dropped her gaze to the lute at his feet. "Are you all right, my lord?"

He grunted.

She waved her hand in front of his face.

At first he paid her no heed until finally he blinked and looked up at her.

"Are you planning on going to bed soon?"

"I know not," he said quietly. "Mayhap in a bit."

She took a seat beside him, wanting to banish the sadness she saw inside him. Wanting to add a little humor to his night. "Did you ever look up at the sky as a child?"

He frowned. "Not really."

Nora leaned back on her hands and looked up at the bright sky where millions of stars twinkled down at them. "My mother used to tell me that every star in the heavens has a story attached to it."

She pointed to a star just south of Ursa Minor. "That one there she told me was once an ancient Greek soldier named Abrides. She said he was a noble Spartan commander whose wife had died. Distraught, he looked up at the heavens and demanded vengeance on the one responsible.

"The queen of the sky" — she pointed to a collection of stars a little way over that looked like a lady — "told him that in death there is no satisfaction. Only pain will find you. So he asked her when the pain would lessen. The queen told him never. The pain is what shows us how much we loved them. If you truly love someone, then the pain of their loss will always be in your heart."

He gave her a hard stare. "Why are you telling me this?"

She returned his stare, hoping to make him see past his guilt. "I'm telling you this because if you loved Kieran so much that you still ache like this after his passing, then he must have known how you felt before he died."

"Aye, and he died because I betrayed him."

"Nay," she said. "He died because he wasn't capable of living with the pain you have."

A tic worked in his jaw as he turned away from her. "This is not comforting me."

She put her hand on his arm and felt his biceps flex. Her poor Ewan. Would he ever find a way to forgive himself for something he'd had no part in?

How she wished she could make him lay aside his guilt and find happiness once more.

"The queen looked at Abrides," she began again, "and asked him who he would have her kill for his wife's death.

" 'Kill me,' he said. 'For it was my want of a son that cost her her life. Had I been content as I should have with her alone, she would be with me now.'

"The queen shook her head in sorrow and said to him, 'We all must die. Nothing can ever change that. But it is how we live when we are here that matters most. I will not kill you,' she said, 'because your death will not set things right. Only by living can you do that.' "

"Living doesn't make things right," Ewan said, his deep voice scarce more than a whisper.

"Perhaps. But do you really think your brother would want you dead?"

"If he were alive, I am quite sure he would kill me."

Nora gave a small, sad smile at that, not believing it for a second. "Beat you perhaps, but not kill you. I think had Kieran had the strength to live, he would have found someone worthy of his love, and now the two of you would be laughing over the foolishness of his infatuation with Isobail."

Anger flashed in his eyes, turning them a stormy blue. "You've no right to speak about my brother. You didn't know him and you don't understand —"

"I do understand, Ewan."

She reached out and touched his face, turning his chin until he looked at her. She wanted him to see the truth. Desperately. "I know exactly what it's like to love someone with the whole of one's heart and then to have to smile as that person goes off to marry someone else. I know how much it hurts. I know how much I wanted to die when it happened to me, and every time I think about the fact that had I married him, I wouldn't be facing a life with Ryan now, I

169

could scream with the frustration of it."

His eyes snapped fire at her as if the words were hurtful to him. "Who were you in love with?"

Nora moved back a bit as her memories tore through her. "Michel de Troyes."

Even after all this time, just saying his name tugged at her heart. "He came to my father's castle three summers back and was the most incredible man you can imagine. Handsome. Charming. Well educated. He made me laugh until my sides ached. I thought he felt the same way for me until I learned that my mother's lady-in-waiting had been meeting with him. In the end, I had to smile and wish them well while inside I wanted to tear every shred of Joan's hair from her head."

Ewan's gaze studied her face. "Did he know how you felt about him?"

"Aye. As you well know, I tend to rattle on about everything, and I confessed my feelings. After I had embarrassed myself, he told me about the two of them."

"At least he was honest with you."

"Aye, but the hurt was no less severe for it."

He patted her hand, his eyes searching. "Do you love him still?"

"Aye, to a degree. I think there is a part of me that will always love him. But I don't think we would have had a happy marriage. I was young and he enchanted me."

"And Ryan?"

She shuddered. "I shall spend the whole of my life lamenting *him*."

"I am sorry for that. But how do you know this man doesn't love you?"

Nora laughed bitterly. "How could he? Ryan knows nothing of me even though we grew up as neighbors and he visited often. All he ever did was drop frogs down my back and pull my braids. He is a beast. A complete and utter beast. All he knows of me is that I am my father's heir and that I carry the weight of his fortune in my dowry. 'Tis all he cares for. I could be a pox-ridden mule and he would be glad to have me."

"I doubt that."

"Doubt all you like. It is truth and well I know it."

She leaned forward until their noses almost touched. "So you see, you are the stronger man, Ewan. You are still here. You came home when another man wouldn't have had the courage to face his family after running away with Isobail and then being abandoned by her. At the time, you thought your brother would be there to laugh at you or beat you, and yet like a man, you returned to take your punishment."

He drew a deep breath and looked away from her. "I appreciate what you're trying to do, my lady. But nothing will ever make this right. It was my actions that caused his death and no other."

Nora tapped him on the shoulder twice to emphasize her point. "Think for a moment, Ewan. Had you not run off with Isobail, do you honestly believe she would have stayed with Kieran and married him? Nay, she would not. She would have run off anyway to meet her lover, and he would still be dead because she was gone."

By his face, she could tell the thought had never crossed his mind before. "But *I* betrayed him."

"Isobail betrayed him, and he betrayed all of you by killing himself. What he did was his fault, not yours. He died because he couldn't live without Isobail, who would have gone to England regardless of who escorted her. Had it not been you, I am certain she would have found another man to lie to and deceive. Either way, Kieran would have perished."

Ewan sat there in silence as he contemplated her words. He knew she was right and there were many nights when he lay awake cursing and hating Kieran for what he'd done. Hating his brother for leaving him behind to feel this pain and guilt.

But it didn't stop what he felt in his heart.

It was there that he saw the brother he'd known. The boy who had helped him make mischief on Braden and Lochlan. The man who had taken him aside and introduced him to drinking and gaming.

There was seldom a happy memory of his childhood and youth in which Kieran wasn't a large part.

He had respected and loved Kieran. And he had paid his brother back by stealing away with his woman in the dark of night.

Ewan growled at the fierce pain stabbing his gut and heart. Unable to stand the weight of it, he got up and headed for the woods to be alone.

He wanted to run away from it. He wished he could just bury the past and forget all that had happened.

But there was no escaping it.

No matter what Ewan did, it was always there. Hurting. Aching. Demanding and bleak. It accused him of being wrong and told him how worthless he was. How he had wronged his entire family.

Drinking was the only way to reduce the pain of it.

Drinking was all he had now.

"Ewan?"

"Leave me alone, Nora," he growled without pausing. "I need to be by myself."

"Ewan," she repeated, her voice more insistent.

He turned to face her.

She came to stand before him, her face pale and concerned in the moonlight. "I think you're a good man, and if Kieran was half the man you are, then 'tis a shame he's no longer here. Isobail was a great fool if she failed to see that."

Her words reached out to him in a way nothing had in a long, long time.

She moved toward him, slowly, like a wraith in the night's mist.

"Don't touch me, Nora," he breathed as she reached to touch his face.

"Why?"

"If you touch me, I'll kiss you, and if I kiss you right now, I'm not sure I'll have the strength to pull back and be satisfied with just the taste of your lips."

Nora trembled at his whispered words.

By the light in his eyes, she could see the truth of it. He wanted her.

Part of her wanted his touch, and part of her was terrified of it. She was terrified of what she felt for him.

Here there were no lies. No hiding.

She could lie to Catarina, but not to herself.

Nora had never been with a man, and until now she'd never really felt anything more than a passing curiosity about a man's touch.

But for some reason, she was more than just curious about Ewan.

What would it feel like to hold a man like him?

One who was wild, untamed?

174

One who could make her quiver with nothing more than the sound of his deep, rich voice?

Would he be gentle with her or would he mount her like an animal whose only desire was to sate himself?

Touch him and see . . .

She stood in indecision. The air between them was rife with desire. Rife with need and hunger. Both of them wanted it.

All she had to do was reach out and take it.

She stepped back.

He released a relieved breath. "Go back to camp, lass," he said. "I'll return shortly."

Nora watched him get up and leave.

Heartsick over what had happened and over the fact that she was a coward, Nora made her way back to camp, where Catarina was waiting.

"Are you all right?" Catarina asked.

"Honestly, I'm not sure." Nora glanced back in the direction of where Ewan had been. "I can't understand what it is about Ewan that lures me so. It's rather baffling."

"No mystery there. He's a fair one, to be sure. Strong and handsome as any."

"I've been around many handsome men in my life, but none of them . . ." Nora couldn't bring herself to say it.

Catarina arched a brow. "None of them what?"

"Nothing," she said hurriedly. "I am being foolish." Nora excused herself to go sleep on her makeshift pallet that Ewan had readied for her by the fire.

The ground was cold and uncomfortable, but she did her best not to notice that, while her mind replayed everything that had happened between her and Ewan since the moment they met.

Catarina went to bed and Nora listened as the three men related to Cat snored rather loudly. She had a feeling Pagan slept lightly, if he slept at all. There was something about him that seemed vigilant even while he rested.

For hours she watched the stars cross the sky all the while Ewan didn't return.

Ewan lost track of time while he lay in a small clearing, staring up at the sky. He should go back to camp, but he had no desire to be there, where he would be forced to stare at something he couldn't have.

Still he could taste Nora. Her scent permeated his head and left him craving her like a starving beggar.

All he'd ever wanted in his life was to find a woman who could look at him as women looked at his brothers. Not to have a woman glance at him, then watch as her gaze slid over to one of the others and stayed there.

That was half of why he'd been so taken in

by Isobail's lies. He'd thought that maybe, just once, he wouldn't have to compete for someone's affections. That a woman could love him and not lust for his brothers instead.

And it had been a lie.

No doubt Nora would be the same. She'd see Lochlan and fall all over herself to gain his notice. What woman wouldn't? His brother was tall, but unlike him, not freakishly so. And Lochlan had the golden fair looks that made most maids swoon.

Best of all, Lochlan was laird.

Ewan sighed. What did he have to offer a woman?

Nothing.

He had money of his own from lands his father had left him, but they were nowhere near the riches of his brothers' holdings. It was more than enough to keep him and a wife quite comfortable, but he wouldn't be able to be lavish with her.

And yet as he lay there, he knew it would never be enough to interest a woman. Especially not a woman like Nora. She was refined and graceful. A true gentlewoman.

She probably belonged to a wealthy lord who had spoiled her immensely. Her clothes and mare were the finest he'd ever seen, and 'twas obvious she had been well schooled.

She was refined. Delicate. Graceful.

Wonderful.

Such women were beyond his reach. They belonged to men like Lochlan who were refined in grace, form and tongue. Not to a man who was so tall he had to bend almost double just to enter a room. One whose form was so long that he couldn't even fit his legs under a table comfortably.

"Ewan?"

He jumped in startled alarm at Nora's voice coming out of the darkness.

"What are you doing here?" he said, his voice gruff.

"I couldn't sleep."

He sat up as she neared him. She wore only a thin shift and held a plaid wrapped around her shoulders. She'd braided her blond hair, and it fell over one shoulder, all the way down to her hips. She was a vision in the bright moonlight.

One that stole his breath.

"You should have stayed in the camp, Nora. 'Tis dangerous for you to be out in the woods alone."

"I knew you were out here."

"Aye, but what if you'd gotten lost?"

"You would find me."

"What if I couldn't?"

"You would find me," she repeated. She knelt down beside him, her face bright by the light of the full moon. "I have a feeling that if you set your mind to it, you could move a mountain if needs be. Never mind find one lost woman in the woods."

He felt an urge to smile at her. How did she do this? How could her mere presence lighten his heart?

Ewan studied the curve of her jaw and wondered what it would be like to trace the beauty of it with his tongue. To taste her creamy skin with his lips.

To hear her moans of pleasure in his ears.

Against his will, his gaze fell to the drawstring of her chemise. It would be all too easy to reach out and pull the laces that held it closed.

Better yet, to pull it free with his teeth . . .

Blood rushed through his veins like fire, making him hard and throbbing for her. He wanted to taste her. Wanted to drown himself in her scent and warmth until he forgot all about everything except her and how she made him feel.

It would be heaven.

Nora couldn't breathe as she saw the heated look in Ewan's light eyes. There was no ice in them tonight. They burned with need.

She wasn't sure why she'd come to him. She'd felt a strange urging, and it amazed her that he wasn't drinking. He appeared perfectly sober and quiet.

"What were you doing out here?" she asked.

To her further astonishment, he answered. "I was looking up at the stars."

She glanced up at the sky.

"And I was thinking about what you said earlier. About how each one held a story."

She smiled at his unexpected words. "Do you know the stories?"

"Nay. I only know the one you told me. Would you tell me more of them?"

Nora trembled at his request. Something told her that he would normally never say such a thing to anyone.

He was reaching out to her, and it made her feel special.

"Well, my lord, you know how much I cherish the sound of my own voice . . ."

He gave a halfhearted laugh at that, then lay back on the ground as he had been when she first saw him.

Thrilled at the sound of his laughter, she lay down beside him and grunted as she tried to find a comfortable position.

"Here." Ewan pulled her closer to him so that she could lay her head on his shoulder.

Nora's heart pounded as he cuddled her to his side. She'd never had a man hold her like this. Her head was pillowed on his shoulder while his arm was wrapped about her waist with his hand resting on her stomach.

It was intimate and touching, and made her feel very strange. The rich, masculine scent of him invaded her senses, warming every part of her.

She was acutely aware of the strength of him. Of his hard muscles sheltering her. Her body exploded with heat and an aching throb she didn't understand.

Clearing her throat, she pointed up at the constellation of Orion. "Do you know of Orion the Hunter?"

"Nay."

She moved her hand over them, showing him Orion's belt, head, arms and legs. "Can you see the outline of him?"

"Aye, I see it."

"Well, long ago in ancient Greece, Orion was a mighty hunter. Born the son of Poseidon and Euryale, he searched the world for his one true love . . ."

Ewan listened in silence as she told him how Orion tried for years to win the hand of Merope and to gain the approval of her father for their marriage. And how Orion had become so tired of the wait that he forced himself on Merope. As punishment her father blinded Orion, who later traveled until he found the Greek goddess Artemis, who then fell in love with him. Her brother Apollo, angered by their love, tricked Artemis into killing Orion, who was then lifted up to the heavens by the goddess so that she could remember him always.

"Must all your stories involve love gone

awry?" Ewan asked. "Is there no such thing as someone actually marrying his love and living a happy life with her?"

She turned her head into his shoulder and smiled up at him. His stomach tightened.

"There is the story of Cupid and Psyche. They live together in happiness. Would you rather hear that one?"

"Aye, lass. Please."

As Ewan listened to the sweet cadence of her voice, he ran his hand idly down her arm to her hand. Her fingers were so delicate compared to his. So soft. He took her hand in his palm and ran the pad of his thumb over the careful curve of her well-manicured nails.

The urge to lift that hand to his mouth and suckle her fingers was so fierce that he wasn't sure how he managed to deny it. He tilted his head to look down at her while she talked. A light pink stained her cheeks as spoke in a gentle tone of love and trust.

How he wanted her.

Right now while she lay so peacefully in his arms.

What would it be like to have her sliding against him? To feel her warm and welcoming beneath him?

Instead, he laid his cheek against the top of her head and contented himself with just holding her like that. Letting her feminine softness soothe him.

By the time Nora had finished her tale, she realized Ewan was completely relaxed.

More to the point, he was completely asleep.

"Ewan?" she whispered, looking up at him.

He didn't stir.

Her bear lay with his lips slightly parted, her braid laced between his large fingers. She hadn't even realized he'd touched her hair.

But she had known every other move he'd made.

She had felt his tender caress as he held her hand in his and ran his fingers over her wrist and forearm.

And when he had leaned his cheek against her head, she had melted.

Rolling over, she lifted herself up on her arms to look down at him while he slumbered. A lock of black hair fell over his forehead. She brushed it back, then traced the slash of his eyebrow with her fingertip.

He was so delectably handsome. So strong and powerful even while he rested.

Why had he indulged her tonight? She had half expected him to chastise her and send her back to camp like some errant child.

Instead he had listened to her. Held her.

Encouraged her to tell him her stories.

What she wouldn't give for a husband to treat her thusly. She bit her lip as that thought played around in her mind.

Would Ewan be like this if she belonged to him?

He is unfitting for you.

Was he?

He played music for her and he did listen to her. He had even handed her his sword.

Surely such moments made up for his more unrefined ways.

It takes two to make a marriage. Her mother's words echoed in her head. Her mother had oft lectured her on wifely duties and what it took to make a marriage sound.

Marriage is a contract between man and woman. The wife is to care for the husband. To see to his needs, and he in turn is to protect and provide for her. But if the marriage is to be a happy one, then the two must respect each other. They must never belittle or discount the other's feelings. Take your father for instance. He would sooner cut out his own heart than make me cry. Your husband should always listen to you, just as you should always listen to him.

Nora studied him closely. Ewan didn't seem to be the kind of man to ever discount someone.

She traced the line of his lips, remembering what they had tasted like. The way they looked on the rare occasions when he smiled.

You'll have to marry someone. Why not —

"Don't even think it," she breathed.

True, she did have to have a husband, but Ewan MacAllister?

He lived in a cave!

184

Granted, it was a nice cave with glorious furnishings, but it was still a cave.

What kind of life could they have together?

Before she realized what she was doing, she was peeling back the corner of his shirt. She'd never before realized just how interesting a man's throat was. How inviting the skin of it could be.

She stroked his Adam's apple with her fingertips, feeling the roughness of his masculine skin and whiskers. He was all prickly and hard.

And his jaw . . .

Truly it was superb. Strong and well shaped. She'd never touched a man like this before.

Her parents would have vapors. Her father would have his sword after them both.

Ewan himself would most likely be terse from her exploration and study.

He didn't seem to like her touching him overmuch.

Tonight being the exception.

If you touch me, I'll kiss you, and if I kiss you . . .

Did she perchance drive him wild with desire? Could he feel the same urging for her that she felt for him?

Her mother had warned her much about men and their voracious, rutting ways. But instead of dishonoring her, Ewan had fallen asleep like a harmless pup.

Harmless pup, indeed! She laughed at the very thought.

There was certainly nothing harmless about a man as fierce as this one.

Nora laid her head back down on his chest and listened to his heart thumping under her ear. She'd only imagined lying with a man like this. It was something she had thought to share with her husband, never with a man she barely knew.

Ewan turned then, drawing her in closer to him. His arms tightened.

"Ewan?" she said. "You're crushing me."

His hold loosened a bit so that she could breathe, but he didn't release her. Instead he snuggled closer.

It wasn't so bad really.

It was actually quite nice.

Relaxing, Nora let the sound of his deep breaths lull her into sleep, too.

For the first time in years, Ewan dreamed of pleasantries. There was no Kieran to haunt his sleep. No sign of Isobail and her cruelty.

Only Nora was there with her catlike eyes and her barrage of questions.

He sighed in his sleep as he saw her out in a peaceful green meadow beckoning to him.

"Come, my lord, and be seated." She pulled him down by her side so that she could offer him cake and ale.

In his dream, Ewan closed his eyes to savor the taste of her fingers as she fed him the cake from her hand. 'Twas the sweetest thing he'd ever known.

He drank of the ale, then set the food and drink aside so that he could stare at the woman who made him desire again. She made him yearn for dreams he had forsaken long ago. Dreams he had purposefully thrown away.

He pulled her across him, then rolled over, pinning her beneath him.

"I want you, Nora," he breathed.

Her smile welcomed him.

Accepting her invitation, he lowered his mouth and tasted the sweetness of her lips. She laced her hands through his hair, raising chills over him as he teased her mouth with his tongue.

He groaned her name as he moved his mouth lower, down to the cream of her neck where he had been dying to taste her. She arched her back against him, thrusting her breasts against his chest.

Unable to stand the torment of her, he cupped her breast in his hand and teased the taut nipple with his palm . . .

Nora moaned as she was stirred from her dreams by the heat of someone kissing her. By the feel of someone touching her body in a way no one had ever dared before.

Startled, she opened her eyes to find Ewan holding her. His lips were hot and demanding on her neck while his left leg was buried between both of hers. His warm hand cupped her breast.

"Ewan," she said.

He pulled back groggily and blinked. "Nora?"

"Aye. Did you not know it was me?"

She expected him to withdraw, to at least pull his hand away from her breast.

He didn't.

"I knew it was you. I thought I was dreaming it." Before she realized what he was doing, he dipped his head to kiss her again.

Nora moaned at the fierce taste of him.

He tore away from her lips.

"Push me away, Nora," he said suddenly. "Tell me that I repulse you and that you don't want anything to do with a sullen, self-pitying drunkard."

She frowned at his words.

Who had said such to him?

"I don't find you repulsive, Ewan. Far from it."

He cupped her face in his large hand and stared at her. His eyes were dark and pain-filled.

"Tell me, Nora," he insisted. "Because if you don't, I'm going to make love to you out here in the woods like an animal."

His words shocked her as much for his

honesty as for the desperation she heard in his voice.

Her Aunt Eleanor had once told her that the most precious thing a woman possessed was her maidenhead. If a woman was lucky, she would get to choose whom she gave it to.

If not, 'twould be her father's choice.

Ryan's face drifted through her mind and she fought the urge to cringe. If they failed to make it to England, he would be her fate.

He would never make her feel the way Ewan did.

Her body was hot and shivery. Needful.

What if no man save Ewan ever made her feel this way again? If she turned him aside, she would go to her husband with her body intact.

Ryan cared not a whit about her virginity; 'twas only her coffers that concerned him.

But Ewan . . .

He needed her. She felt it deep inside.

She'd always wondered what it would be like to lie with a man. In her mind, she had always pictured a softspoken troubadour who won her heart.

But it was the quiet bear who called out to her.

Don't.

The word hovered in her mind. If she did this, it would change her forever. She would no longer be innocent. She might even conceive his child.

But something deep down inside told her that carrying this man's child would be far from a hardship.

In the end, it was her curiosity and desire that got the better of her. Her mother had always said it would lead her astray.

Tonight it had led her to Ewan MacAllister, and here she was where she wanted to be.

"Make love to me, Ewan."

Chapter 7

Ewan was dumbfounded by Nora's words. He had expected Nora to turn him away, not welcome him to her body.

She wasn't supposed to want him.

A decent man would pull away from her. But he wasn't decent.

He was feral and hard. The kind of man who took what he wanted without thoughts about tomorrow.

It was what had gotten him into trouble with Isobail. He had acted in the heat of passion and then paid dearly for it.

Decorum and he were strangers.

He'd never been that kind of man. He'd left manners and refinement to his brothers, while he had made his own way without those strict bindings that society and his mother would have placed on him.

Now he wished he did know the words to tell Nora how much this moment meant to him.

How much *she* meant to him.

He'd been so long without the comfort. So long without the warmth of a tender caress.

How could he walk away now? Especially since her sweet, precious taste was branded on his tongue. The silken heaven of her mouth was more than he could resist.

He was a mere mortal, not some saint.

Nay, he'd never been a saint.

Ewan traced the curve of her swollen lips with his fingertip before he parted her lips and kissed her deeply.

He closed his eyes and inhaled the sweetness of her breath as he let loose his tongue to dart against hers, to sweep up to the palate of her mouth until she moaned and writhed from it. Her supple body pressed against his while he loosened the stays of her chemise.

"You should push me away," he said, pulling back from her kiss to stare down into her gentle, welcoming eyes.

"Perhaps, but I oft do the opposite of what I should do."

"Aye, lass, you do. And that is one of your more endearing qualities."

"Are you mocking me?"

"Nay, love, I would never mock you."

Nora's heart fluttered as he offered her a real smile. It was unexpected and breathtaking.

His eyes fair glowed in the faint moonlight. His heat surrounded her as his arms cushioned her from the cold, damp ground. The heat and strength of him surrounded her.

And she wanted more.

She actually purred as he returned to her

lips to kiss her softly. She'd never been touched like this. Never thought a mere kiss could be such a wondrous experience.

And when his warm, callused hand closed around her breast, she jumped in nervous excitement. Pain and pleasure stabbed through her body as heat pooled itself between her legs.

What was this burning in her body? This strange ache that craved him?

She didn't understand these foreign sensations. They were confusing and consuming.

Electrifying. Tormenting. And they left her wanting more of him.

Ewan left her lips to kiss a trail down her throat to the breast he cupped. Nora swallowed at the sight of his dark head at her breast, at the feel of his tongue teasing her taut nipple. His tongue was rough and hot, his lips soothing and tender.

She clasped his head to her, and let the locks of his hair tease her fingers.

He was so beautiful there, tasting her, teasing her. His beautiful face showed the pleasure he received just from touching her.

She sighed in contentment and let the incredible earthy sensations sweep her away until she was nothing but an extension of the man holding her.

Tonight she would be his.

Ewan had never tasted anything like her body. She was so warm, so inviting. More so because he knew she was sharing with him what she had shared with no one else.

He was her first.

Why she would choose him, he couldn't imagine. He was so unworthy of what she offered. So unworthy of her, period.

She was lightness and joy.

He was darkness and sorrow.

But he was glad that tonight, for this one moment and for whatever reason, she was with him.

Nora tugged at his shirt.

Eager to oblige her, he pulled it off, and his trewes followed soon after.

She gasped audibly as she ran her hands over his tense arms. He clenched his teeth as his head reeled from pleasure.

The things her touch did to him . . .

It was incredible. Invigorating. It made him feel virile and wild.

He was hard and aching. Most of all, he felt vulnerable to her.

But he couldn't pull back. Nay, he needed more of her. Needed to touch every inch of her body and to claim it as his own.

Nora felt a moment of panic as he removed her chemise from her. She was suddenly exposed to him.

It was scary and strangely erotic. She couldn't recall ever being naked in front of another person. No one knew what she looked like bare.

No one but Ewan.

Her heart pounding, she stared at the large size of him and tried to imagine what it would feel like to take that into her body. Surely it would cleave her in two.

"Will you hurt me?" she asked hesitantly.

He stroked her cheek with his fingers. "I will do my best not to."

She smiled up at him, trusting him completely even though she wasn't too sure he spoke honestly. How could *that* not hurt? It was huge.

He lay down on top of her and gathered her into his arms. Her thoughts scattered at the glorious feeling of his skin against hers. Of his heavy weight that felt good instead of oppressive.

Ewan took her hand into his and guided it back to him. "Don't be afraid of me, Nora," he whispered.

Nora ran her hand down his shaft as the tip of it probed her maidenhead.

"Tell me to stop and I will."

She smiled up at him, knowing most men would not offer her that. It made her even more tender toward him. "Don't stop."

He kissed her again, then drove himself deep inside her.

She tensed at the burning pain of him filling her.

Ewan whispered sweet encouragements in her ear while he used his tongue to toy with the tender flesh of her neck.

She panted against the pain and tried to relax as he coaxed her. She had never imagined a man would feel like this, but she was glad it was Ewan who was inside her.

Glad for the strength of his arms around her and the sound of his deep voice in her ear.

She wrapped her arms around his shoulders and buried her face against his muscled neck and inhaled the warm scent of him. It gave her courage and strength not to push him away.

She wanted this. She wanted to share her body with him and to have it be Ewan who filled her for the very first time.

Ewan ached with want as he forced himself not to thrust even deeper into her.

But it was hard.

He wanted her in a way unimaginable. She surrounded him with heat, and her breath against his neck sent a thousand chills over him.

She felt wonderful and he never wanted to let her go.

"Relax, love," he said gently. "I promise I won't move until you're ready for it."

He waited until her hold on him loosened. She looked up at him, her face trusting.

He smiled at her courage and at the sight of her lying underneath him, her body bare and joined to his.

It was the most incredible thing he'd ever seen. A wave of fierce possession tore through him then, especially when he looked down to see them joined.

"You feel so strange inside me," she said.

Ewan laughed at that. He'd never had a woman speak of such things. But then talking was what she did best, and he found her innate curiosity fascinating. She was completely uninhibited with her questions and comments.

"How do I feel?" he asked.

"Full and deep. I can feel you all the way to my core."

He sucked his breath in at her words and the image they created. He liked to hear her speak of such things. "Can you now?"

She nodded.

He pulled back, then thrust his hips against hers.

They moaned in unison.

"Did that hurt?" he asked.

"Nay," she said breathlessly.

Ewan moved slowly against her, driving himself in as deep as he dared.

"Oh that feels so good." She sighed. "Is it supposed to be like this?"

"Are you ever out of questions?"

"Am I not supposed to talk?"

Ewan rolled over with them still joined. He sat her on top of him and watched her in the moonlight.

Her eyes widened even more. "Am I supposed to be up here like this?"

He actually laughed at that. "Do you like it?"

She bit her lip and nodded enthusiastically.

"Then we're supposed to do it."

Ewan showed her how to ride him slow and easy. He ran his hands down her thighs and watched the way the moonlight cut across her pale skin.

"May I ask another question?"

His mind was dazed from the feel of her naked body sliding against his, and it took a few seconds before he could respond. "By all means talk, my lady, if it gives you pleasure to do so. Tell me more about how I feel inside you."

"You are so hard and strong. I can even feel you throbbing here." She pointed to her lower abdomen.

The sight of her hand stroking her stomach almost shattered his control. He took her hand into his and led it away before he succumbed too early to the orgasm he longed for.

Nora wiggled her bottom against him. "What am I supposed to do?"

He lifted his hips up, driving himself deeper into her. "Whatever you want to do."

She ground herself against him in a way so sublime that he growled in satisfaction.

Nora felt so strangely free with him. She

ran her hands over the hard muscles of his chest and abdomen. It was so odd to see him lying there under her, between her spread thighs.

He held her hips in his hands and guided her movements. But what held her transfixed was the bliss on his face. His cheeks were flushed, his eyes dark and unfocused.

She moaned as he ran his hands up from her hips, to her breasts, where he toyed with their swollen nipples.

Had anyone ever told her she would sit on a man like this and enjoy it, she would have called him a liar, and yet here she sat with his thick hardness inside her.

"What do I feel like to you, Ewan?"

"Wet and soft."

"Have you been with many women?"

He stopped moving. "Nay, not many."

She smiled at that. It made this moment all the more special to her. "I'm glad. I want this to be special between us."

Ewan cupped her face in his hands. "Believe me, love, it is." He pulled her down and kissed her fiercely.

Nora trembled at the passion she tasted, at the way he teased her lips with his and twined his tongue around hers. His muscles bulged around her, making her tremble.

Ewan pulled back from the kiss, then rolled over with her and took control.

Nora arched her back as he moved faster.

Harder. It was as if he were racing for something.

What was this wondrous sensation of him sliding in and out of her body?

Every stroke brought more pleasure. Every kiss and touch reverberated through her.

"Make me yours, Ewan."

But in her heart, she knew he already had.

He claimed her lips again as he slammed himself into her even deeper than he'd been before.

She wrapped her legs around his hips and let his passion sweep her away.

He lowered his head down to her shoulder and growled as he released himself inside her.

She drew a ragged breath as he collapsed on top of her and held her tight.

"Thank you, Nora," he whispered in her ear as he panted fiercely. Then he kissed her lips again in a tender caress that sent chills through her.

He withdrew from her and rolled over onto his back and pulled her against his side.

She assumed he was through with her, so it surprised her when he spread her legs and touched the most private place of her body.

"What are you doing?" she asked.

"I want you to have your pleasure."

"I already had it."

He smiled wickedly at that. "Nay, my innocent dove, you didn't."

Nora swallowed as his long, lean fingers delved deep into her body. She tensed a bit as they burned the tender flesh of her nether lips.

"Don't dry out on me, Nora."

Confused as to what he meant, she frowned.

Ewan pulled her plaid to him and used it to wipe her between her legs. She blushed at his actions.

"What are you doing?"

His eyes were warm. "Trust me. I promise you'll like this."

He laid his body between her legs and spread her thighs wide.

Nora's face flamed as she realized he was staring at the center of her body.

He ran his long, tapered finger down her cleft. She shivered. Then he used his fingers to spread her open and dipped his head down.

Nora jerked as his mouth covered her. Every nerve ending in her body sizzled as she cried out in surprise. He stroked her with his tongue and lips.

She hissed and moaned as she cupped his head to her. No longer able to speak, all she could do was feel each and every luscious lick he gave her.

Who could have imagined? His breath was hot against her bared flesh, and when he slid a finger deep inside her and rotated it, she thought she would die.

She looked down to see him staring up at her while he tormented her with ecstasy.

He pulled back, but left his finger inside her. A strange sensation of intimacy overwhelmed her.

"Don't be embarrassed, dove," he whispered, then he returned to taunt her with his mouth.

With a mind of its own, her body writhed to his touch and kisses.

"Oh Ewan," she groaned.

And as he continued, she found herself unable to speak anymore. Unable to do anything other than feel him. Feel his tongue sliding around her, his finger swirling.

Her pleasure built to an unimaginable height, until she was sure that she would explode with the weight of it.

Then, in the span of one heartbeat, she did explode. Her body splintered apart, and she cried out.

Ewan didn't stop. He stayed there, licking and teasing until she'd come for him twice more.

When he seemed content to tease her more, she begged him for mercy. "Please, Ewan," she whimpered. "If I do that one more time, I fear I shall die of it."

He chuckled at her plea, then turned his face to suckle the tender flesh of her thigh.

Nora lay there, completely spent and weak. She breathed raggedly as Ewan gathered her into his arms and held her close.

"You weren't jesting," she said while her body slowly returned to normal. "I had no idea *that* existed."

He kissed her brow and cradled her head with his hands. "Neither did I," he whispered softly.

Nora smiled and snuggled into him, wanting to be as close as she could.

This was the single best night of her life, and she was so glad that she had shared this with him. If tomorrow forced her to marry Ryan, at least she had known one night of true passion. A night of lying in the arms of a man who wanted and respected her.

She would treasure it always.

Ewan listened to Nora as she fell back asleep. Guilt and regret overwhelmed him.

What he had done tonight was inexcusable. He had taken her virginity, something that was a husband's right, not his.

Her father and betrothed would be furious when they found out.

A fierce wave of rage swept through him at the thought of another man touching her as he had tonight.

At the thought of her encouraging another man with her words.

She was his!

You've no right to her.

Besides, what could you offer her?

Ewan covered them with her plaid and ran

his hands through her pale blond hair. He had nothing to offer her. All he knew was what he felt when he held her like this.

The way he felt every time she looked at him.

God help them both, for they were bound to pay for this night. But he would make sure he paid the lion's share of it. No one would ever hurt the lady for what she had given him.

He would make sure of it.

Catarina rose just after dawn.

Everyone was still abed, and she didn't notice that Nora wasn't in her pallet until she grabbed her bucket and headed for the stream for fresh water.

Whistling the lullaby her mother had taught her, she found Ewan and Nora lying entwined underneath a plaid. Though they were mostly covered, it was still apparent they were both naked.

And it didn't take a genius to figure out why the two of them were lying naked in the woods underneath a plaid.

She smiled, then tiptoed silently backward so as not to disturb them.

Against all Nora's protestations, the lady was enamored of the man.

Catarina felt a momentary stab of jealousy. How she wished she could find a man of her own to love.

Still, she wouldn't let that destroy the happiness she felt for Nora. Love was a beautiful thing, and everyone deserved to find her perfect mate.

She believed in love at first sight. More than that, Cat believed in predestiny. There was someone out there for everyone; one day she would find a love of her own.

But that would wait.

Right now Ewan and Nora needed her help.

"Oh, not that look."

She turned to see Viktor sitting up in his pallet, looking at her.

"What look is that?" she asked.

"You've got mischief on your mind, *cherie*. Just please tell me it doesn't involve me this time."

She laughed. "Nay, Viktor, you are safe."

He let out a relieved breath. "Thanks be for that small favor. So who is the fish about to be snared by your hook?"

" 'Tis no worry of yours."

Viktor groaned. "You're planning on putting the two of them together, aren't you?"

"And if I were?"

"I think Ewan would rather we have poisoned him than drugged him."

"Viktor! He loves the lady."

"Cat," he said, his voice gruff. "I know you've got your mother in you. She let her heart lead her astray, and what did it get her? Other than you, all she's gotten for her wayward love is a broken heart. To this day she waits for your father's notice. Is that what you'd have for the two of them?"

"My father had no choice of whom he married, but he loved my mother, you know that. Had he been anyone else, he would have married her."

"And Nora is promised to another. Did you know that? She is as bound to him as your father was —"

"Nay. Ewan won't allow her to marry another. I know it."

He shook his head. "Don't play with their lives, Cat. I beg you. I'm doing this only because I was told to, but you know I never agreed with it. Leave them in peace."

Cat understood his warning. He was right. In spite of her parents' love, they had been forced to live their lives apart. But it wasn't her starry eyes that had put Ewan and Nora together. It was their own actions.

And if she could do anything to help them, she would.

Nora came awake to find herself still lying atop of Ewan. Heat exploded across her face as she remembered what they had done in the late night hours.

Now in the light of day, she saw their naked bodies.

As she pulled back, Ewan jerked awake as if expecting to battle.

He relaxed as soon as he saw her. The tender smile he gave her went a long way in alleviating her embarrassment.

"Morning, sweeting."

"Good morning."

"Are you sore?" he asked.

The heat returned to her face. "Nay, are you?"

He laughed at that. Heavens, how she loved the sound of that deep rumble.

"Nay, love. Not a bit."

He sat up and the plaid slipped back, exposing his body to her. Nora couldn't stop her gaze from dropping down to see him hard again.

"Does it do that a lot?"

He looked down at himself, then met her gaze with a wicked grin. "Only when I look at you."

His kiss was both light and demanding.

At least until they heard the gypsies moving about and talking.

Ewan pulled back. "We'd best dress before they come looking for us."

Nora nodded.

As she reached for her chemise, she realized her thighs were smeared in blood.

Ewan turned at her dismayed gasp. He picked her up from the ground and carried her to the stream and helped her bathe. He was so incredibly tender.

She saw the frown on his face as he removed all traces of what they'd done.

"Are you sorry for what we did?" she asked.

Ewan looked up, his gaze a cross between shock and guilt. "I'm not sorry for what we did. How could I be? I'm only afraid of what might happen to you if someone else learns of this."

"I won't tell anyone. I promise I won't ask anything more of you."

Ewan froze.

Her words stunned him. He'd never known a woman so kind. He'd had countless friends forced to marry a wench because she quickly sought out her father with the tale of what they'd done.

Instead Nora offered him immunity.

She was truly a unique lass.

One he wished he could spend a lifetime learning.

He hesitated at the thought.

Dare he chance it?

Dare he not?

He stood before her, unsure of what to do. Unsure of what he should do.

But in the end, he had one truth that resonated inside him.

Nora deserved better than him.

After he bathed her, they dressed while he considered what he should do with her.

They made their way back to the gypsies, who were up and cooking.

"Where have you two been?" Viktor asked.

For the first time, Nora was at a loss for words as she blushed and looked up at him with fear in her eyes.

"We got up early and went for a walk," Ewan said.

If the gypsies didn't believe it, no one said anything. They merely kept on with their various tasks, ignoring them.

Catarina approached them with two platters of sausage and hard bread. "I figured the two of you would be a bit hungry this morning."

She cocked her head as she looked at Nora. "Though you be looking a bit tired, my lady. Did you not sleep well?"

"Very well, thank you," Nora said quickly, taking her platter and moving away from Catarina's inquisitive stare.

"And you, my lord?"

Ewan forced himself not to glance over to Nora. "Quite well, thank you."

They didn't speak while they ate, cleaned their platters, and then packed the wagon.

Nora found herself riding on the wagon at Ewan's insistence.

"You don't need to be riding a horse today, my lady," he said under his breath to her. "It will only make you more sore."

Then he had kissed her cheek quickly and

set her up beside Viktor.

Nora was warmed by his thoughtfulness, and so she spent the day chatting with Viktor as they rode north to meet the man who had paid the gypsies to abduct Ewan.

Ewan rode off to the side of the wagon and watched Nora, his heart aching for what he couldn't have.

"Tell me," Lysander said as he reined his horse to ride by Ewan's side. "How did you manage to tolerate her chatter without stuffing a gag into her mouth?"

"I don't mind her chatter."

Lysander snorted at that. "Surely you jest. How can it not make your ears ring? I'm surprised poor Viktor hasn't snapped at her."

Ewan shrugged.

He kicked his horse forward so that he could speak with her. "Nora?"

She turned to face him. The breeze tugged at strands of her pale hair that had come free of her brat. Her cheeks were bright red and her lips moist.

How he ached to taste them again. To drink the delectable sweetness of her mouth until he was drunk from it.

"Aye?" she asked.

Ewan felt sucker-punched as he looked up at her. "Would you care to ride with me for a bit?"

He saw the relieved look on Viktor's face

as the man passed him a grateful nod.

"Would that be proper?" she asked.

"Aye, it would, my lady," Viktor hastened to assure her. He stopped the wagon.

Ewan helped her from the wagon to his saddle. He pulled her across his lap so that she sat sideways before him.

Nora gave him a suspicious look as she adjusted her skirt. "Are you doing this because you wanted me to ride with you or to save poor Viktor's hearing?"

"Both."

She smiled. "So you're not concerned about your own hearing then?"

"Better I lose my hearing than Viktor wrings your neck."

She laughed at that. "Then I shall have to torture him more if it means I get to sit in your lap. I rather like it here."

So did he. More than he should.

Nora felt good in his arms and even better spread out in his lap.

Already he could imagine her as she'd been last night. Hot and welcoming to his touch.

"How much farther do you think we'll travel before we break to sup?" she asked.

"Are you hungry?"

"Nay, not at all. But I grow weary of riding. How do you stand to be in the saddle for so long? Don't you wish to be free to walk?"

Before he could answer, she went off on

her own. "I think if we could travel by foot it would be better. The horse would like it better, too, I imagine. It must be hard on your horse for both of us to ride astride him."

"You scarce weigh enough to bother him."

"Aye, but you weigh at least twice the amount of a normal man, I would think."

Ewan grimaced at her reminder.

"Did that bother you? I'm sorry, Ewan. I should think you'd be proud of the fact that you're so large. My cousin Sean often laments that he is shorter than most men. Indeed, he's a full head shorter than I am. Why would your size bother you?"

Catarina answered for him as she rode her horse beside them. "I imagine 'tis as big a curse to be too tall as it is to be too short. I am sure Lord Ewan lives in a world where nothing fits. Chairs and beds are ever too small."

"Aye," he agreed, "I'm forever banging my head, arms or legs into things that are designed for men half my size. I even had to have my horse specially bred to be larger, too, else my knees would be dragging the ground."

"I like your height," Nora confided. "There is nothing about your size that I would change."

Ewan stared at her, amazed.

"Catarina?" Nora called out. "Do you

think we will stop where there might be fresh berries to pick?"

Ewan rode in silence as the women talked to each other. He couldn't fathom why Nora's tireless conversation no longer bothered him.

"Would you?"

He realized Nora was speaking to him. "I'm sorry, I didn't hear you. What were you asking?"

Nora laughed and looked completely unconcerned for the fact that his thoughts had trailed off from her conversation. "Catarina wanted to know if you'd pick berries with me. Will you?"

"I . . ." He frowned at the question. "Pick berries?"

"Nora will need protection," Catarina said. "Else she might get lost or perhaps be mauled by some bear or other wild thing in the woods."

Ewan frowned at her words and at the odd note in her voice as she spoke of bears mauling Nora.

He hadn't picked a berry since he was a boy. But the thought of being alone with Nora . . .

Well, he'd most definitely like to maul her himself.

"I would be happy to."

Catarina nodded. "There you go then, Nora. We'll have fresh berries for dinner."

The women talked until they stopped to eat. It was a little after noon. Ewan and the other men tended the horses while the ladies made a light meal of cold meat and cheese.

But it wasn't food Ewan hungered for. It was the dainty woman who sat with her back straight and whose manners were as perfect as a queen's.

Whose laughter rang out while she talked to the men and Catarina.

As soon as they finished eating, Catarina handed Nora a small basket. "You fetch your berries while I clean up."

The men started to protest, but the vicious scowl Catarina directed toward them stopped them instantly.

"Take your time," Viktor said.

"We won't be overly long," Nora assured them.

That's what she thought.

If Ewan had his way, they would be gone for a while, at least.

They walked deep into the woods, until he could no longer hear the others and the gypsies could no longer hear them.

Ewan watched her stoop for the berries. His gaze was fastened on her bottom as she bent over.

He hardened instantly as he imagined lifting her skirt and burying himself deep inside her again.

"Have you ever made your own tarts?"

Nora asked, then stopped herself. "Nay, I guess not. You being a man and all. You probably never even picked berries, did you?"

"I did."

She straightened to look at him. "Truly?"

"Aye. My mother used to take me and my brothers into the woods to pick berries for her pies and jams." He smiled wistfully at the memory. "But we usually ate so many of them that she would shoo us away shortly after we begun."

"Who ate most of them?" Nora asked as she led him through the foliage in search of her fare. "You or one of your brothers?"

"Kieran. He was always hungry."

"And you weren't?"

"Nay, not really."

Nora started to climb over a fallen log.

Ewan picked her up easily and swung her over it.

"Thank you."

He inclined his head and jumped over it with little effort.

Nora watched him in the dappled sunlight. His black hair was curling becomingly around his shoulders. He was such a handsome man.

Before she could think better of it, she took his hand in hers. She half expected him to let go. He didn't. Instead he squeezed her hand in his and offered her that hesitant smile that was such a part of him. It was one where the corners of his mouth turned up ever so slightly, and if one wasn't paying attention, one might not realize it was a smile at all.

But she knew it.

Just as she was beginning to know the man who gifted her with it.

Then he led her hand to his mouth and placed a tender kiss on her knuckles.

Nora shivered as she recognized the fire in his crystal blue eyes.

"I've been wanting to kiss you for hours," he said, his voice deep and hoarse.

Nora smiled as she cupped his face in her hands. She stood up on her tiptoes and kissed him. Her brat fell from her head, down to her shoulders as he pulled her up to reach his mouth.

Her head swam at his taste.

She felt him reach around her and lift her skirt up.

Ewan knew he shouldn't be doing this. One of the gypsies could stumble across them at any moment.

But he couldn't pull back from her.

She was irresistible to him.

Nora gasped as he set her up on top of a tree branch and leaned her back against the tree trunk. Before she could ask him what he intended, he shoved her skirt back and spread her legs.

She trembled at the sight of him staring at the center of her body. His eyes were dark and hooded as he slid his fingers down her cleft and gently into her.

Then he dipped his head and took her gently into his mouth.

She bit back a cry of pleasure as she reached up to hold on to the branch above her.

Ewan was like a wild animal as he tasted her, and his caresses made her breathless and weak.

He pulled back, his eyes blazing as he loosened his trewes, baring his swollen shaft to her eager sight. He kissed her lips a moment before he slid himself deep inside her.

This time Nora did groan out loud.

"Oh Ewan," she choked.

His lips seared her as he thrust against her. Her body spiraled out of control, and when she came it was so intense that she couldn't keep herself from crying out.

With three deep, sharp thrusts, Ewan joined her.

Nora held him close as he breathed raggedly in her ear.

"What have you done to me, lass?" he asked roughly. "God help me, I can't seem to keep myself away from you."

She laid her hand against his flushed, stubbled cheek. His eyes were dark and stormy. " 'Tis a madness that seems to envelop us both. For I feel the same of you. I know I shouldn't. You are everything I find distasteful in a man."

He looked offended by that. "Thank you, my lady."

"Well, you are, and yet there is nothing about you that I find distasteful at all. Why is that?"

"I don't know. I should have taken you straight to my brother."

"I'm glad you didn't."

He kissed her. Then kissed her again and again until she was breathless and weak.

Nora sighed at the sensation of him around her while he was still inside her.

With a groan, he pulled back and left her with an aching void.

"We'd best not be too long or someone will come searching for us."

He helped her right her clothes and covered her hair again with her brat, then led her back in the direction from which they had come.

As they walked, a low-hanging branch caught her brat and pulled it free of her hair.

Nora hissed at the pain. The bowed branch snapped back, tearing the brat from her head and dress, and launching it up to a higher branch.

"Oh bother!" she said, her voice rife with aggravation as she tried to jump up to reach it.

"Here." Ewan moved her aside and tried to reach it. When he realized he couldn't, he moved to leave.

"Nay," she said. "We can't leave it in the tree."

"Why not?"

" 'Tis my favorite and was a present from my mother."

He growled at her words.

"Please, Ewan?"

His face softened. He handed her the basket and headed for the tree.

Nora watched in fascinated awe as he easily climbed the branches. He effortlessly worked his way out onto the branch where her brat was snarled.

The tree groaned in protest. Nora stepped back as a bad feeling consumed her.

Mayhap she shouldn't have sent him up there after all.

No sooner did he capture the wayward brat than the branch broke and sent him straight to the ground.

Her heart stopped at the sight of him falling.

"Ewan!" she gasped, rushing toward him.

He lay on the ground unmoving.

Chapter 8

"Ewan, please tell me that you dinna get hurt." Frantically, Nora searched his body, looking for injuries.

Ewan couldn't draw his breath for a full minute. The fall hadn't hurt anything much more than his dignity and had knocked the wind from him.

But he had to admit he liked the feeling of her hands running over his body. Liked seeing the concern on her face.

"I got your brat," he said around his aching ribs and back, handing it to her.

"Oh, forget the silly brat. You've been hurt."

Silly brat?

Now the brat was silly?

Ewan frowned at her. He wasn't really hurt, but he didn't want her to know that. She was running her hands up and down his body as if searching for injuries, and even though he should be sated after their tryst, he wasn't.

He could take her again, right now.

And that surprised him most of all.

"Should I go get Lysander or Pagan?" she asked.

"Nay," he quickly assured her. Those two would laugh and know in an instant he wasn't hurt. "I think I can manage with your help."

"What should I do?"

Ewan stifled a wolfish grin. He should feel guilty for taking advantage of her this way, but he didn't. He enjoyed her concern and care.

"Ow!" he said as she touched his thigh.

"Are you hurt there?"

"Aye."

She ran her hand around his leg to his inner thigh. Ewan clenched his teeth as a fiery need stabbed his groin while she rubbed his leg in an effort to alleviate his ache.

Little did she know, she was only adding to it.

"What about your back?" she asked. "Are you hurt there?"

"Perhaps. It throbs so that I canna tell."

She helped him to sit up.

Ewan closed his eyes as she explored his back with her hands. But in truth, he'd rather she do so with her mouth.

His groin jerked at the thought.

When she started to move away, he groaned as if in pain. "My right shoulder."

Nora massaged the joint. "Here?

"Aye."

Her hands dipped lower, and lower. Och, but the lass felt good.

Too good. Her hands were the most blessed pain reliever he'd ever known. For this amount of her undivided attention, he'd gladly fall out of another tree.

She helped him to his feet.

Ewan made sure he didn't put too much weight on her as he limped along beside her.

He'd never had anyone care for him like this. His brothers would have laughed, then kicked him up and told him not to cry like a lass. His mother had at times tried to pamper him, but with three other sons, she'd been ever occupied by their needs, and so he'd gone forgotten while she rushed to tend Braden, Kieran or Lochlan.

He had to admit he liked the way Nora cared for him. Liked the idea of having her complete and undivided attention.

Most of all he liked where his hand rested.

"Ewan? Could you please lower your hand a bit?"

He reluctantly moved it from her breast, and did exactly as she said and placed it just below her bosom so that he could still feel the curve of her.

Aye, a man could get used to this. But in truth, he'd rather still be cupping the soft mound. Feeling the hard nipple of her tease his palm.

Nora had nice breasts. Not too large and not too small.

A perfect handful.

And that thought made him even harder. He looked back at the trees and whimpered in need.

"Did I hurt you?" she asked.

"Nay, love," he said gruffly, wishing they didn't travel with the gypsies after all.

They approached the others.

"What has happened?" Catarina asked as soon as she saw them.

"Ewan fell from a tree while retrieving my brat," Nora explained. "I think he's injured his leg and his back."

Ewan saw the suspicious looks from the men and a knowing, taunting grin from Pagan.

"Fell from a tree, eh?" Pagan asked in a whispered tone just for Ewan.

Ewan gave him a wicked glare. When he spoke, he made sure to keep his words low enough so that Nora couldn't overhear them. "Och now, you're just jealous you don't have a beautiful lass to dote upon you."

Pagan surprised him with a laugh. "True enough. For a taste of those lips, I'd gladly throw myself down a mountainside."

Ewan watched him suspiciously, but Pagan merely walked off and left them.

"Did you now?" Viktor asked Ewan once Pagan had departed. He slid his gaze to Nora. "And just how far did he fall?"

"Quite a ways," Nora hastened to assure him.

Lysander snorted. "Too bad he didn't land on his head."

Bavel shoved at him.

Disregarding them, Nora helped Ewan into the back of the wagon. "You rest here, and I'll be right back with something for you to drink."

As Nora left him, Catarina approached her and whispered so that Ewan wouldn't overhear her.

"I don't think he's as injured as he appears, my lady. I think he's playing upon your sympathies so that he can stay close to you."

Nora flashed an evil smile. "And well I know it. 'Twould take much more than such a slight fall to hurt him, but I rather like having him close."

She winked at Catarina, who laughed.

She didn't think Ewan would have allowed her such freedom with his body if he wasn't "injured." And he seemed to enjoy her caresses too much for her to stop them.

If he wanted to be babied a bit, then she would certainly oblige him.

As she returned to the wagon, she caught sight of him with her brat. He had it pressed to his lower face as if inhaling it.

Seeing her, he quickly put it aside and straightened up.

Nora stared at him there. His long legs were stretched out in front of him, and he looked a bit guilty. Those piercingly blue eyes of his made her tremble.

He was so fierce and powerful, and at the same time there was something playful about him. But what warmed her most was the knowledge that he wasn't playful with the others.

Only she was allowed to glimpse the more tender side of him.

She liked that a great deal.

Nora climbed in to sit down beside him and handed him the wineskin.

He took a drink, then glanced at her in surprise. "You brought me ale?"

"I thought it would help with the pain."

Viktor looked in on them. "How you doing, lad?"

Ewan looked at her uncomfortably.

"He'll be fine," Nora answered. "He just needs a bit of a rest. Would it be all right if we rode back here for a while?"

Viktor nodded. "We'll be on our way then."

Nora listened as the others returned to their horses and Viktor tied both Ewan's horse and hers to the back of the wagon. After several minutes, they were on their way.

Again he had a guilty look about him that told her he wasn't as injured as he would have her believe.

So be it. She was more than content to ride back there alone with him.

"Who do you think this man is who paid them to abduct you?" Nora asked after a short span of silence. "Have you many enemies?"

"Nay. My only enemy was Robby MacDouglas, but since the feud ended between our clans, he's forgiven me and we've been friendly enough."

" 'Tis peculiar, isn't it? I wonder if it could be some woman who caught fancy to you and paid someone to bring you to her."

Ewan scowled at her. "What a strange thing for you to think."

"Nay, not really. You're rather fetching when you're not making that face."

"I'm not making a face."

She touched his forehead and smoothed his features. "You scowl overmuch."

"And you talk overmuch."

She smiled a smile that warmed him. "Aye, 'tis what makes Ryan so angry at me. He says I am ever a whirlwind of nonsense."

Ewan touched her cheek with his fingertips. Then he leaned forward and kissed her lightly. "I rather like your nonsense."

Nora sighed as she cupped his head to hers. She could drink from his lips for eternity.

Ewan nibbled on her lips for quite some time, stroking and teasing them.

It was the first time ever she had sat with a man like this and let him have free rein with her lips and body. She enjoyed it immensely.

Finally he pulled back, and Nora settled down by his side, safe in the shelter of his arms while the wagon rocked beneath them. Neither of them had slept much the night before.

So she let the soothing sound of his heart lull her to blissful slumber.

Ewan toyed with her hair as her gentle breath fell against his neck. How he loved the way this woman felt in his arms. She was so soft against his hardness.

He tried to remember Isobail. He couldn't even recall her face, only the pain she had left in her wake.

It was Kieran he remembered. He had tried to tell him that Isobail didn't love him.

Kieran had attacked him viciously, calling him a liar.

"Damn you, Ewan. You know nothing of what you speak. She was meant for me and no other. She has said it to me a thousand times."

"Listen to me, damn *you*. She told me herself that she has no feelings for you."

"Liar!" Kieran had backhanded him for those words.

Ewan had reached to attack, and Lochlan and Braden had come between them, forcing them apart.

"Why are you upsetting him, Ewan?"

Lochlan had demanded as he shook him forcefully.

"She loves me." The words had leaped out of his mouth before he could stop them.

All three of his brothers had laughed. The sound had echoed painfully in his heart.

How dare they scorn him for it. Was it so impossible to believe a woman could desire him?

"You?" Kieran had shaken his head as he continued to laugh. "Now I know you jest."

Ewan had never wanted to hurt his brothers before, but he wanted to then. He was tired of being pushed aside by all of them. Discounted. Mocked. "Why is that so hard for you to believe?"

It had been Kieran's final words to him that had set everything into motion.

"Look at yourself, Ewan. You're gangly and sullen. What few women you've had, I had to pay them to take you, and all you did then was talk to them instead of make use of their *charms*. The day will never come when a woman would have you over me. What could *you* ever offer a woman?"

"I know the answer to this one," Braden had chimed in. "A lifetime of brooding silence and evil glares."

Then Braden had clapped Kieran on the back and the two of them had left the hall, all the while laughing at him.

Ewan had stood frozen, unable to breathe

from the cruelty of their words.

"I know not what to do with that lad, Aisleen. He will never be what his brothers are . . ."

"They didn't mean that as it sounded," Lochlan had said after Kieran and Braden had left. "I'm sure Isobail is fond of you. In your own way, you are —"

"Silence, Lochlan," he'd snarled. "Bother me no more with your so-called comfort. I'm tired of all of you recounting my faults to me. I'm not as handsome as Braden, or as charming as Kieran, and I lack your intelligence. Believe me, I know well my shortcomings. Every last one of them."

Those comparisons had been branded into his heart from the hour of his birth.

Though he loved his brothers, he was well aware of where he fell in everyone's esteem.

Even Sin had mocked him when he offered to help him and Braden rescue Lochlan from the clan.

There was nothing he could do that his brothers couldn't do better.

Only Nora had never compared him to them.

Of course, she had yet to meet his brothers . . .

Would she care for him if they were around? Or would she be like Isobail and abandon him the first chance she got?

He didn't know for sure. But in the back of his mind was the thought that if she did, it would be the blow that destroyed him. He could take anything except her ridicule.

Viktor stopped the wagon on the outskirts of a small town. Catarina reined her horse to a stop as Lysander, Pagan and Bavel dismounted.

Catarina joined Lysander as he pulled open the door to the wagon, and they found Ewan and Nora sound asleep in the back.

Nora was lying against his chest, and he had one brawny arm slung protectively over her.

"Ahhh," Catarina said, happy to see them so entwined.

"Am I supposed to allow them to lie like that?" Lysander asked. "I'm thinking I might get a sword to my middle for it should her father ever learn of this."

"I'll take one to your backside if you don't leave them be," Cat said. "I think they make a beautiful couple."

"I knew she was too quiet," Viktor said. "I should have known she'd be fast asleep."

"Well, rouse them," Bavel added. "I'm hungry enough to eat my boots."

"I'm awake," Ewan said gruffly. "Who could sleep with the four of you yapping like a herd of puppies?"

Ewan gently shook Nora awake.

She blinked open her eyes, then smiled at him.

In spite of his best intentions, he smiled back.

"Where are we?" she asked as she realized the wagon was no longer moving.

"I'm not sure," Viktor said. "We've come up to a small village. I thought we might buy ourselves a nice supper and mayhap find a comfortable bed for the night."

Nora stifled a yawn as she scooted out of the wagon.

Ewan came out behind her and forgot that he was supposed to be injured. The minute he took a step, Nora clucked her tongue teasingly at him.

"For shame, my lord, feigning injuries and playing on my poor good nature. And to think I was worried over you."

Ewan scratched his chin and sheepishly averted his gaze.

Pagan laughed at them as he walked past.

Nora playfully patted Ewan's arm, then stood up on her tiptoes to give him a sisterly kiss on his cheek. "Not that you asked it, but I forgive you."

They took a few minutes to freshen their appearances. Ewan took Nora's hand and led them into the town.

He paused long enough to ask if there was a pub, and they were directed to the largest cottage in the village.

The gypsies were eerily quiet as they walked along behind them.

The pub's door was open and several men were seated at tables, drinking from goblets.

"Can I help you good people?" an older woman asked as she came forward to greet them. She had dark auburn hair that was liberally laced with gray and a large, full figure.

Ewan inclined his head. "We'd like some food and beds for the night if you have them."

The woman led them to a table near the hearth.

"They're not very friendly here, are they?" Nora asked as she sat down by the wall.

" 'Tis a small village, my lady, and most are rather suspicious of strangers. They fear we'll either steal their children or curse them to a pox." Catarina winked at her.

Nora frowned at that. "Well, I can't imagine why."

"Neither can I," Ewan said. "Especially since they drugged and then abducted us."

Nora elbowed him.

Viktor's cheeks darkened.

Catarina and Nora laughed.

"But admit it," Catarina said. "Your being abducted is the best thing to happen to you."

Ewan looked at Nora. There might be some truth to that. But he didn't want to admit it, especially not out loud.

After they were served their food, the door opened again.

Ewan saw a man a couple of years older

than he enter. He knew there was something familiar about him, but it wasn't until the man drifted past the table that he realized what.

'Twas Isobail's older brother.

His heart stopped. He hadn't seen Graham MacKaid since the day before Kieran had stolen Isobail away from her father's house.

The man looked older than his years. His face was bearded and haggard. His brown hair hung lankly around his shoulders, and he was thin and gangly.

It was obvious the MacKaids had fallen on hard times.

"Graham," the maid said in greeting. "Been a while since you passed this way. Are you heading home?"

"Aye, though I don't know why I bother. If I had any sense at all, I'd be heading myself for France and forgetting that I ever saw Scotland." He paused as if realizing he'd said too much, then added hastily, "You have a room for the night?"

"Sorry, love, I just rented my last one out a few minutes ago."

He cursed and turned to his right, which faced him toward where they were eating.

The man didn't move as his eyes narrowed and recognition hit him as well.

Ewan's hand tightened on his goblet as he saw rage descend on Graham's face.

"You," he snarled. "Fi, I would have expected better of you than to let filth into your establishment."

The woman stiffened and cast a suspicious eye toward them.

Ewan rose to his feet. He'd never been the kind of man to let an insult pass unanswered and he wasn't about to start now. "You'd best be calming yourself, Graham MacKaid. I'm in no mood for you."

Graham cast a disdainful look over Nora. "Which of your brothers did you steal *her* from, hmmm? Everyone knows Ewan MacAllister can't ever have a woman unless he takes her from someone else."

He heard Nora's sharp intake of breath.

Ewan roared in anger as he came around the table to attack.

Nora was dumbfounded as she watched the two men fight.

"You bastard!" Graham snarled as they punched at each other. "You ruined my life."

Ewan said nothing as he caught the man a blow that sent him straight to the floor.

Ewan picked him up by his shirt and shoved him toward the door. "Leave, Graham. Otherwise I might kill you."

Graham laughed, displaying a set of bloody teeth. "Why don't you then? What's my life to you? I might as well be dead since your family ruined mine."

"What did we do to you? 'Twas your sister

who killed my brother."

Graham spat blood onto the floor and snarled at Ewan. "Isobail would never have left home had it not been for you and your brother. You're the one who killed Kieran. Don't try and blame an innocent lass for your deeds. She was a good lass until you ruined her."

Ewan bent down and caught the man about his waist. He ran at the wall, pinning Graham to it.

Nora was on her feet and across the room before she even realized she'd moved.

"Ewan!" she snapped at him. "Put him down."

"Nay, not until I kill him."

Lysander and Pagan appeared at her side to help her separate them. Nora forced Ewan back while Pagan and Lysander escorted the other man toward the door.

"Calm down," she said as she met his blazing eyes.

Graham turned at the door and called out one last parting word. "You never answered my question, MacAllister. Who did you steal her from?"

Ewan took a step, but Nora stopped him. "What are you doing?"

She saw the pain on his face, the torment. She reached up to touch the cut on his lip, but he dodged her hand.

"Don't touch me."

He turned about and left her there to stare after him.

Nora followed after him.

He was already to the wagon.

"Ewan MacAllister," she said sharply, "stop right where you are."

"Go away, Nora. I'm in no mood for you."

"Why? Because of what that fool said?"

He clenched his teeth and looked away.

She reached up and cupped his face in her hands, then forced him to look at her. "You didn't steal me from anyone."

"Think you Ryan will feel that way? You don't belong to me, Nora. I have no right to you."

"You're right. I don't belong to you. I belong to no man on this earth. I am my own person and not the property of my father, Ryan or anyone else. Whom I give myself to is my concern, not theirs."

He tried to pull away, but she held him.

"Look at me."

He did.

"You're a good man, Ewan. One with a good heart. If Isobail couldn't see that, then she was an even bigger fool than her brother. But I see you. I know you."

His eyes were filled with agony as he stared at her. He took her hand into his and pressed it against his lips.

Ewan inhaled the sweet scent of her. He wanted this woman with every piece of his heart. But at the end of the day, he knew Graham was right.

He had stolen her from another.

For all he knew Ryan would be like Robby MacDouglas, pining away for her. Willing to risk life and limb to regain her.

And who would blame him?

Nora was wonderful.

He didn't deserve someone like her. He deserved nothing at all.

"Go back inside, Nora. Please."

To his relief, she nodded and obeyed.

Ewan stood back, trying to draw a deep breath to alleviate the pain in his chest.

He had to let her go, and yet all he wanted was to hold on to her.

Why couldn't he ever find a woman for himself? One who wasn't promised to someone else?

Pagan joined him. "Your friend has decided with a little help from yours truly to leave the village immediately. Are you all right?"

"Thank you. Aye, I'm fine."

Pagan glanced in the direction Nora had vanished. "She's a good woman. You're very lucky to have someone like that who's willing to appreciate you for what you are."

Ewan nodded in agreement. "That she is."

"Are you to marry her?"

He shook his head. "She's not meant for me."

Pagan scoffed at him. "Then who is she

meant for, Ewan? I can't imagine any other man showing her the patience you do. I for one would go mad if I had to tolerate her tongue for any length of time."

Ewan snarled at him.

Pagan grinned at his reaction. "There's what I expected from you. You'll tolerate no one to insult her. Sounds like love to me."

Ewan grimaced at his words. "You know nothing of it."

"True enough. I know naught of Cupid's arrow and have no wish to be educated. But if I were ever to be stricken by his machinations, I don't think I could just let go of the one who held my interest and see her in another's arms. I only know how to fight for what I want."

"And have you ever had to?"

He turned darkly serious, his eyes glacial, and in that moment Ewan was glad he wasn't facing the man in battle. There was something very deadly and sinister about Pagan. "Every day of my life."

Ewan's mind flashed to the sight of Isobail rushing toward her lover. The two of them had embraced and kissed.

Dumbfounded, he had watched them until his anger spurred him to attack.

Night after night, he had lain awake wishing he had beaten the knight that day. That he had continued to fight until the man killed him.

But he'd been too heartbroken to breathe.

Thank you, Ewan, Isobail had said coldly, her eyes icy as she regarded his beaten and bloody form. *Without you, I'd still be locked in the Highlands with no hope of ever seeing Gilbert again.*

Her lover had thanked him then, never knowing what Isobail had promised Ewan if he would help her, and the two of them had laughed as Gilbert's men escorted him out.

In the end, he had consoled himself with the knowledge that a woman so faithless and cruel, who could use her body to lure both him and Kieran, would never be true to the knight. Gilbert would come to learn her as they had.

God have mercy on him then.

Ewan sighed.

Life was ever confusing to him. Nora wasn't faithless. He knew that. She'd never used her body to get her way.

But she had given herself to him.

How he wished he had one of his brothers there to talk to.

Nay, he wished he had Kieran there to talk to.

His gut twisted as he remembered the last time they had been together.

"She doesn't love you!"

"She loves me, Kieran. Accept it."

They had fought like lions, trying to shred each other until Braden had come between them and pried them apart.

"You are brothers!" Braden had snapped. "Would you let a woman come between you?"

Ewan had wiped the blood from his face and glared angrily at Kieran. "You've never loved any woman more than a few weeks. You can have any woman you want. But Isobail loves me. Can't you leave us in peace?"

"How could you ask that after what you've done? She was to be my bride, and you went behind my back to have her. You're not a man, Ewan, you're a sniveling coward."

They had fought more until Lochlan had removed Kieran from the room.

That night, Isobail had come to him and told him that she was leaving.

"If you love me, Ewan, come with me and we can be together forever. We can never stay here in Scotland with your family. They will never forgive us for what we've done. The only chance for happiness we have is in England. Come with me."

Like a fool, he had gone.

It was a mistake he would pay for for the rest of eternity.

Nora sat in the pub with a heavy heart. What would it take to lift Ewan's spirit?

She looked over to Catarina, who had returned from outside with a change of clothes for the night.

"Cat?"

Catarina paused and looked at her.

"Do you know much about men?"

Catarina smiled. "Aye, my lady. I know a great deal about them."

"How do you entice them?"

"All men or just Ewan?"

Nora blushed. "Just Ewan."

Catarina smiled, then crooked her finger for Nora to follow after her. "Let me share with you the secret my mother gave to me. 'Tis guaranteed to win over any man, be he beggar or king. Trust me, Nora. You do as I say and you'll be able to command any man who suits your fancy. Lord Ewan will be powerless against you."

Chapter 9

Nora spent hours with Catarina as she taught her numerous exotic tricks to entice Ewan with exotic dances. How to roll and undulate her hips in a duplication of Catarina's wild movements.

She felt strangely erotic and womanly as she learned the dance, and she found it hard to believe Cat's mother had taught her all this.

All Nora's mother had ever done was teach her to be circumspect and proper. Her graceful, decorous mother would be possessed of vapors to know Nora was practicing such heathen antics.

But if they would gain her Ewan's notice . . .

"Will this really work?"

"Trust me," Catarina assured her. "Men are easily led astray by their desires. All you have to do is cater to them, and voilà, they are yours."

"Aye," she said as she thought of Isobail and the grief she had caused him. "It's why Ewan is in so much pain now. Perhaps I shouldn't do this," she said as Catarina dressed her in one of Catarina's low-cut gowns. "My mother always told me that it is evil to tease a man."

"It's only evil if you have no intention of keeping him."

Nora bit her lip. "What if I am unsure yet whether I want him?"

"Are you?"

She hesitated as she thought about the matter. "Aye . . . nay . . . maybe?"

Catarina shook her head. "My lady, what more could you want from a man? He is handsome and concerned for you. He looks at you as if his very life hinges on your happiness. I would give aught to have a man dote on me as he does you."

Nora bit her lip in indecision. "Aye, you are right. If I must marry, and I must, I can think of no one I would rather have than Ewan."

"Then why are you fretting?"

"What if he doesn't want me? He likes his quiet solitude, and I am most certainly not quiet."

Catarina tied a thin, gauzy blue veil around Nora's waist. "I wonder if he likes it so much or if he is just used to it."

Nora frowned. "What do you mean?"

"I just wonder if he chose it because he liked it or if it was forced upon him by others."

Catarina stepped away and swept a critical gaze over her.

"Perhaps," Nora concurred. "I said as much to him myself, but he never commented on if it was true or not."

Nora paused as Catarina moved to style her hair. "Why are you helping me, Cat? You should be scandalized by what we're doing, not participating in it."

Catarina smiled at that. "Life is short, Nora. Like my mother before me, I believe in seizing what you want while you're young enough to enjoy it. All we have to console us in old age is happy memories, and I want my fair share of them. Ewan needs you. I can see it in his eyes. You make him laugh when nothing else does. How can that be wrong?"

Nora sighed at the thought of his deep, rumbling laugh. "He has beautiful laughter, doesn't he?"

"Aye, and a smile to match it."

Nora's heart fluttered as she remembered Ewan's tentative smile. The way his face looked when it softened.

He was a gorgeous man.

"Oh Catarina, I hope you are right. I never anticipated liking him, especially not after the way I met him while he was drunk in his cave. I thought he was a great, nasty beast. But he's so much more than that."

Catarina laced ribbons in her hair. "What made you seek him out?"

"My maid suggested it. She said only a MacAllister would have the ability to get me to England. She said they would have the connections that would allow them to transport me to my aunt without my father's interference."

"You must have been scared."

"A little," she confessed. "It helped that my maid talked one of my father's men into going with us. He balked at first, then conceded. He said if I was bound to go, better he keep an eye on me than I be harmed. If anyone ever learned he'd known about my flight and I was hurt while escaping, they would hold him responsible."

"True, no doubt."

Nora stared at the floor as her mind replayed everything that had happened to her since she started her quest to flee Scotland.

The miracle she had found in Ewan. A man who listened to her.

A man who touched her heart and her soul.

Almost everyone else she'd ever known had merely humored her while ignoring her questions. She would start to speak, and a glazed look would quickly come over them.

Ewan never had that look.

He always appeared interested in her and what she had to say.

But would he ever allow her to stay with him? If what Sorcha said was true, he would spend the rest of his life alone, trying to make amends to his brother's ghost.

"Cat? Do you think it's possible to get Ewan to . . ." She trailed off, unable to say anything more.

The thought of losing him was just too painful.

"To what?"

"Nothing. 'Twas a bit of foolishness."

Catarina stood back and looked her over. "You're perfect. A complete vision."

She handed Nora a handheld looking glass.

Nora stared at herself. Her hair had been swept up and left to fall haphazardly around her face. Catarina had added kohl to her eyes and henna to her lips.

She looked strange and ethereal.

"Think you Ewan will like it?"

"There's only one way to find out."

Ewan lay in silence on the too small bed, missing the sound of Nora's voice. Strange that he should now find the quiet night oppressive when he had always taken solace in it.

The stillness rang in his ears and made his heart heavy as he imagined what Nora would be saying if she were there with him.

He held the lute in his hands and smiled at the memory of her practicing with it. She so loved this worthless piece of wood.

How he wished he could have bought her one worthy of her devotion.

A fine lute made of good rosewood and

polished to a fine sheen with gold frets and beautiful carvings.

Listless with his want of her, Ewan idly strummed it. He'd tried earlier to give it to her, but Catarina had shooed him away from their room, telling him they couldn't be disturbed.

Somewhat stung, he'd left and had missed her ever since.

How could that be? He'd lived the whole of his life without her, so why now did he find an hour without her hard to bear?

He toyed with the strings, his thoughts drifting, his body aching.

A knock sounded on his door.

"Come in."

He expected to see one of the men, but it was Nora who opened his door.

His heart stopped. She wore a shimmery pale gown that clung to her soft curves. The material was so light that when she walked, it slid up to reveal her bare feet and ankles.

Her pale blond hair looked sublime caught up on her head. It looked as if it were ready to tumble down around her shoulders at any moment.

He couldn't breathe as he stared at her, his mouth gaping. She looked like some fey creature come to capture him, and at the moment, he could think of nothing better than being ensnared by her.

"Play for me?" she asked.

Ewan managed to close his mouth and did as she asked.

To his dismay and delight, she began to dance to the music. And it wasn't just any dance. She rolled her hips and moved her arms like some Saracen courtesan.

She was all fluid grace as she spun about the room. The skirt of her dress flared out, showing her legs off to perfection. His heartbeat hinged on every move she made, every gesture.

His body erupted into fire as he watched her. He needed her in a way that made him burn from the inside out.

"Where did you learn to do that?" His voice sounded strange even to his own ears.

Her face falling, she paused. "Cat taught me. Do you not like it?"

He nodded as he struggled for breath. "Aye, lass. I like it. A lot."

She smiled at him and started dancing again. And as she danced, she started pulling off panels of the dress . . .

Ewan's throat went dry.

She lifted the hem of her skirt and crawled up on top of his bed to rest on her knees. Och, how she looked wild and wanton there. Like some manifestation of his dreams.

Not real, but a fey creation sent to torment him.

She pulled off another section of the dress and wrapped it around his neck, then used it to pull him close enough for her to kiss him.

Ewan moaned at the taste of her as every piece of him screamed out for the lady before him.

She was unlike anyone else on this earth.

He tossed the lute aside and gathered her forcefully into his arms.

Drunk with her sweet floral scent, he buried his head between the deep valley of her breasts so that he could taste the creamy skin.

She pulled at his shirt until he shrugged it off.

Nora hissed as she ran her hands over his shoulders and down his arms, where she flexed her hand over his muscles. "I love the way you look."

He felt the same way.

She placed her hands on his biceps. "Now move your arms."

He did, and she bit her lip as if in the throes of pure sexual bliss.

"I'm not doing anything, Nora."

"I know, but the way your muscles feel . . ." She purred at him.

He shook his head in wonderment of her.

She laced her hands through his hair and nibbled his lips. How he loved the way this woman kissed him. The way she looked at him as if he were the only man in the world to her.

She pushed him back on the bed and straddled his waist. "Tell me how to please you."

"You do that just by being with me."

She smiled. "Do I?"

He nodded.

Her smile widened as she rubbed herself against his swollen groin. He groaned at the feel of her there and imagined how much better she would soon feel as he removed his trewes.

"Is there nothing else I can do?"

"That is a good start, my love." He reached up and unlaced her dress until her breasts were free to his starving gaze.

Ewan held her close, his heart pounding.

How strange, the only place he'd ever felt at home was in her arms. She made him feel warm and welcomed.

No one else had ever offered him so much.

Marry her.

How he wished he could. But he didn't know who she was. Who her family was.

Does it matter?

Aye, it could. Politics was a large part of his family's life, and any decision he made would affect all of them. Even the simple act of running off with Isobail had caused a feud that had killed countless members of their clan.

That feud had taken the lives of almost all his sister-in-law's brothers. It had caused years of deaths and property waste. Total devastation.

He wasn't free to just pick a lass and marry her.

Everything he did could have a major impact on his clan and his brothers' lives.

And yet even though he knew that, he couldn't bring himself to get out of this bed and leave her. She was like some missing part of himself.

A vital part of himself.

Nora watched Ewan's face as he pulled back from their kiss to look down at her. His arms were braced on each side of her, and he stared at her as if trying to memorize her face.

There was a dark, deep sadness to him tonight. One that seemed more severe than the other times she had seen that look on his face.

"What is on your mind, my lord, that you look as if the Second Coming is upon you?"

"Tell me who you are, Nora. Who is your family?"

"Does it matter so much? Can I not be a peasant?"

"Are you?"

"If I said aye, would you toss me out?"

He ran his forefinger over the arch of her brow and studied her face as if he were trying to discern the truth.

"Nay," he breathed, "I would not."

"Then pretend I am peasant born. Let me be a gypsy like Catarina with no family ties to bind me."

"And when your father finds you?"

Her throat tightened at the thought of her father's fury over her absence.

I wish you to marry Ryan, Nora. He'll make you a fine husband . . .

Even now she flinched at the thought of what her future might hold.

Nay, she would run until she died.

She would never submit to Ryan. Not like this. She refused to share her body with him while it was Ewan she loved.

No one but Ewan would ever touch her like this. Only he could fill her . . .

She froze as she realized what she had just thought.

She loved Ewan MacAllister.

Nora loved everything about him. Even that harsh, furious frown that he wore so often.

She never wanted to leave him, and yet she dare not admit it to him.

He couldn't welcome the news. That much she was sure of.

"I have no wish to think on that, Ewan," she whispered. "Especially not while I'm with you. Let me love you, my lord. For tonight, stay with me and pretend that we have no families. Pretend there aren't any obligations or fear for either one of us. No past. No future. There is only now. Just me and you, and nothing else."

Ewan trembled at her words. He trembled

at the warmth of her soft woman's body contoured to the hardness of his own. Her stomach was feather-soft against his erection. Her hands were tender on his shoulders.

He stared into her ever-curious amber eyes and lost himself there. What would it be like to spend the rest of his life staring into those eyes?

To hold her like this when they were old?

At this moment, he could see her ripe with his child. See her warm and welcoming in his bed forever.

The thought both terrified and thrilled him.

How could he even think of such a thing as keeping her when he had his oath to Kieran?

The day of his return whispered through his memory, and he saw himself again on the shore of the loch where Kieran had drowned himself.

The winds had been fierce and cold, the water dark and choppy. He'd looked out across the waves, his heart sickened by the news that his brother was gone, his soul burdened by grief and self-hatred.

I will never again take any pleasure in my life. I swear it to you, Kieran. I shall make my home here by the loch so that I can look out every day at where you rest and remember what I did to you. I will spend the rest of eternity paying penance for my stupidity.

Nora reached up and cupped his face with her hands. Her touch brought him back to the present. Back to the only pleasure he had known since the day he had released Isobail into the arms of her lover.

"Have I lost you this night?" she asked quietly. "You look as if you're far away in your mind. Will you come back to me, or should I go?"

"Stay with me, Nora."

Stay with me forever . . .

How he wished for the courage to say that last bit aloud.

But he couldn't.

He didn't dare.

She opened her legs to him and wrapped them around his hips, then leaned up to kiss him blind with bliss.

Ewan let her taste roll over his senses. He inhaled the precious scent of her hair and breath as he lay flat against her.

Her touch reached deep inside him, setting him free of his past. Free of his guilt.

Nora ran her hands through Ewan's hair and down his whiskered cheeks. How she loved the manly feel of him lying atop her. She ran her feet down his legs, feeling the crisp hairs that dusted them, and reveled in the differences between their bodies.

And it was then she realized just how much she did love this man. How much she treasured his rare smiles.

Her unrefined bear was so much more than what she wanted. He was what she needed.

This man whose kisses set her afire. Whose strong touch made her weak.

He was her heart.

This man who could bellow louder than any she knew, who could melt steel with his grimaces. The same man who could climb a tree to retrieve her brat. Who could show her how to play her lute and who could make love to her with the tenderest of care.

How could she not love such a man?

Och now, and what use was her love of him?

She couldn't stay with him. Even if Ewan would accept her, her father would not. He was set on her marrying Ryan.

And then there was the matter of Ryan himself. Greedy little beggar that he was, he wouldn't graciously step aside. He would demand she marry him.

The beast!

It was hopeless, this love.

Nora wrapped her arms around Ewan's neck and held him tight as the pain wracked her body.

"Nora," he rasped. "You're strangling me."

She loosened her grip, then buried her face in his neck so that she could inhale the warm, manly scent of him. His hair fell across her face, and she took comfort in the rough whiskers that scraped her cheek. She didn't want to let him go.

You'll have to.

Nay, it wasn't fair. Not when all she wanted was to love him. Be with him.

Why couldn't it be?

Because you are promised to Ryan . . .

A man she despised. A man who could barely be in her presence without starting to criticize her.

You make enough noise for ten women. Had I been your father I would have broken you of that habit right quick.

She shivered at the thought.

Ewan moved to nibble her lips.

Pushing away all thoughts of Ryan, she sighed contentedly and forced herself to forget all that.

For now, she was where she wanted to be and with the man she wanted to be with.

She closed her eyes as he trailed kisses over her body, down to her breasts, where he teased and played. Arching her back, Nora melted under the onslaught of his tender care.

Ewan moaned aloud at the taste of her salty skin. If he lived forever, he would remember this night. Remember her dance and her taste. The way she felt beneath him.

The way her hands played in his hair.

It was heaven.

Growling deep in his throat, he left one

breast and made his way over to the other so that he could draw that taut peak into his mouth and let his tongue sample it.

He slid his hand down her body, through the moist tangle of curls until he could touch the part of her he craved. She gasped and moaned, then opened her legs even wider for his exploration.

"Tell me what you want me to do to you, Nora."

"I want you to kiss me."

"Where?"

She touched his lips with her fingers. "On my lips."

He obliged her until he could scarcely breathe for the fire inside him. "Where else would you have me kiss you?"

"Here," she said, turning her head so that she bared her neck to him.

Again he licked and teased her neck. He felt the chills spread over her body, felt her nipples harden even more against his chest.

She made little noises in the back of her throat as he nipped her skin with his teeth.

"Is there anyplace else you would have me?"

Her face pinkened, and she looked away sheepishly.

"Here now," he said, capturing her chin in his hand and turning her face until she looked up at him. " 'Tis not like my Nora to be timid. You've never shirked from talking before."

Her eyes softened.

Ewan turned serious as he leaned on his arms and met her gaze. "Never be afraid or embarrassed over telling me what you want, Nora. So I ask again. Where would you have me, my love?"

She bit her lip and slowly trailed her hand down her body. Ewan watched the path of it, his breath rattling in his chest. It was the most sensuous thing he'd ever seen.

She braced one leg up, spreading herself open to his hungry gaze, and touched herself between her legs.

Nora shivered at the hot look Ewan gave her. She still couldn't believe what she was doing, but there was no shame in her heart.

Only love for the man who was with her.

Ewan kissed his way down her body, slowly, languidly. The touch of his lips on her skin made her burn with fiery need. Who could have imagined a man's touch could be so pleasurable?

When he took her into his mouth, she cried out.

His hot tongue licked and teased, around and around, stroking and delving. The room spun out of control while she lay there, weak and panting from the ribbons of pleasure that shredded her.

She reached down and took his large, masculine hand into hers.

Ewan laced his fingers with hers and gave

a light squeeze. Nora smiled as her love washed over her. There was truly nothing more sublime than having him like this. Feeling him with her body, holding on to his strong hand.

She looked down to see their entwined hands. Her skin was so pale compared to his. Scars marred his knuckles and ·stood out against the darkness of his skin.

She sighed as his thumb stroked her palm in time to his tongue stroking her body.

"Oh Ewan," she breathed. She lifted his hand up to her lips so that she could kiss his scars.

But she didn't stop there. She opened her mouth and suckled his fingers one by one, tasting them. Nibbling them.

Ewan looked up, startled by her actions. No woman had ever kissed his hand, let alone given it so much consideration.

No woman had ever given his fingers such lush and warm attention.

But he had to admit that her tongue felt heavenly sliding over his skin, between his fingers.

He crawled up her body and then stared down at her, warm and open, beneath him.

The sight tore through him.

How he craved her. Needed her.

Her hands released his. Then she trailed them over his chest, his hips, ran them down until she could sheathe his hot, rigid shaft.

His body jerked in response.

Ewan moaned at the sensation of her hands sliding down his shaft, of her reaching down lower so that she could cup his sac.

"Tell me what you want, Ewan," she breathed.

You.

The word hung in his throat. He was unlike her; words were strangers to his tongue.

"I would rather show," he breathed.

Dipping his head down, he claimed her lips, then slid himself deep inside her body.

He growled at her warm, sweet wetness that surrounded him. At the feeling of her body welcoming his intrusion. He made love to her slowly, delighting in the sensation of her holding him. Knowing it couldn't last. Knowing that he'd have to let her go.

But letting her go would be the hardest thing he'd ever done.

Ewan kissed her lips as he thrust against her. They had only a few more days together. Then fate and circumstance would separate them.

Fight for her.

Did he dare?

Do you dare not?

He tried to imagine going back to his cave without her. Tried to imagine making it through one day without her smile.

He couldn't.

The pain of the thought was too much.

Nay, he would keep her with him no matter the consequences.

She was the only thing that was good in his life. The only thing that made him happy, and no one would take that away from him.

Not without a fight.

Nora saw the determined set of Ewan's jaw as he quickened his strokes.

"Are you all right?" she asked, wondering what caused the sudden change in him.

"Aye, love," he said, punctuating his words with his thrusts. "When I'm with you, I'm always all right."

She melted at that. Wrapping her arms around his shoulders, she held him close and reveled in his hot, naked skin sliding against hers.

She teased his jaw with her lips and tongue and trailed her hands over the smooth plane of his back to his hips. She splayed her hands over his delectable rear and closed her eyes as she urged him on.

Her body quivered and tightened until she could stand no more.

Moaning deep, she let her orgasm take her and held him close until the last tremor had shuddered through her.

He cupped her face with his hand and kissed her deep.

Then she felt it. He growled into her mouth as his own release took him.

He buried himself deep and froze.

"Oh lass," he breathed in her ear. "There is truly nothing better than the feel of you in my bed."

"There is nothing better than the feel of you in my body." Heat exploded across her face as she realized what she'd said.

But her embarrassment faded the instant she saw the warm, satisfied look on his face.

He gave her a light kiss, then withdrew. He rolled over onto his back and gathered her into his arms.

Nora draped herself over his chest and listened to his heart pounding under her cheek. The deep thud was so incredibly soothing. How she wished she could lie like this forever.

She traced circles around his chest and toyed idly with his nipples.

"You keep doing that, Nora," he said huskily, "and neither of us will sleep tonight."

It was a threat he proved well before the dawn came.

It was close to daybreak when Ewan finally faded off to sleep while dreaming of something he hadn't thought of in a long, long time.

He saw himself at home with Nora. Saw her with his children, and for the first time since Isobail had ridden off with her lover, he dared to hope for a dream that had left him.

Even in his sleep, he could feel Nora beside him, feel her warm breath on his skin. He took comfort in her and in the knowledge that he was going to make her his.

No one would ever come between them.

Nora woke up first to the late morning light streaming across the room. She yawned and looked to see Ewan still fast asleep.

He was completely bare.

Her face flamed, but she couldn't take her eyes off his long, lean limbs bulging with hard muscles. His dark, tawny skin looked luscious against the white linens, and it made her mouth water for a sample.

Not that she should crave him after the night they had. For that matter, she shouldn't be able to move.

Ewan had shown her ways for a man to take a woman that she wouldn't have thought possible. But never once had he hurt her.

Nay, her bear was ever tender.

And as she stared at his naked body, she remembered all too well licking those hard pectorals. Feeling his raw strength surrounding her as she held him in her arms.

Glorious, that was the only way to describe him.

She slid out of bed and quickly dressed in the gown she'd borrowed from Catarina, trying her best not to wake him. No doubt he would be exhausted for the whole of the day.

Smiling, she bit her lip impishly at the thought.

Once she was dressed, she headed toward the room she was supposed to share with Catarina. She would need her own clothes before she went below to break her fast.

As she left Ewan's room, she met the inn's owner in the hallway. He glared at her as she excused herself and headed back to where Catarina had slept.

Catarina was already awake, and by the smile on her face, Nora knew she didn't have to tell her where she'd been.

"My lady . . . did you have a good evening?"

"Shh," Nora breathed. "I will have to spend the rest of my life doing penance for this."

"Then make an honest man of him."

Nora laughed at her words. "If it were only that simple." She sighed wistfully as she gathered her things.

What would it be like to spend the rest of her life with Ewan as they had been these last few days?

Would they ever have laughter and happiness? Or would he return to his sullen ways?

She had to admit, the thought of having him as husband was a glorious one indeed, and she fully intended to make an honest man of him as Cat had suggested.

Catarina excused herself to give her privacy.

Nora washed herself and dressed, then gathered their things and went below.

Viktor took her satchel from her hands and went to take it to the wagon. Nora thanked him, then headed over to where Catarina sat with a loaf of bread.

When Catarina pushed the bread toward her, the pub owner's voice cut across the room like thunder. "We don't serve no whores here with decent people. If she wants to eat, she can eat outside with the dogs."

Nora had never been so horrified or insulted in the whole of life.

Several patrons turned to stare at her curiously.

Her throat tightened in embarrassed agony that was only aggravated by the stares directed at her.

The thin, balding owner grabbed her arm and pushed her toward the door. He'd barely taken a step when a tall shadow fell over them.

Nora looked up to see Ewan's eyes blazing at the man.

He twisted the owner's hand away from her and shoved the man back. "You touch her again, and so help me I'll rip your arm off and beat you with it."

The owner gulped in fear, but his wife took up his tirade. "We're allowed to serve who we choose. And we'll not —"

"You insult my wife again, woman, and I'll

see you flogged for it."

Nora didn't know who was more stunned by Ewan's words. Herself, the pub owners or the gypsies.

"I . . . I beg pardon, my lord," the owner quickly apologized. "I saw her head to the room with the other lady and assumed you to be unwed. So when I saw her leave your room this morning I thought she . . ."

"We were fighting when we arrived."

"My lady, forgive me, please." The man turned to his wife. "Aida, quick, fetch the lady and lord steak and eggs."

His wife hastened to do his bidding as the owner led them back to the table where Catarina was still waiting.

Catarina quickly excused herself and forced Bavel, Pagan and Lysander to get up and leave with her.

"But they're bringing steak," Lysander groused.

Catarina glared at him. "You won't be able to eat it if I bash you in the head until you pass out. Now move."

He got up reluctantly.

Once they were alone, Nora took Ewan's hand and held it tight. "Thank you."

Ewan inclined his head to her. "I'm sorry I couldn't think of a better lie, and I'm truly sorry they treated you that way because of me."

He saw the shame that she tried to hide.

"Nora, I . . ." Ewan stopped himself before he made an even bigger ass of himself. He had almost proposed to her.

That was the last thing he could do. He didn't even know what clan she belonged to.

There were protocols that needed to be followed if he was to have her.

He would have to get her to trust him with that information and then he would have to ask her father.

If the man said nay . . .

Well, they'd be heading to England after all.

"Aye?" she asked.

"Nothing."

They ate in silence. After they were finished, Ewan paid for the food and lodging, then led her outside to where the gypsies waited.

In no time, they were on their way again.

Nora spent the rest of the day trying to get Ewan to open up, but he had closed himself off from her again.

No matter what she tried, he ignored her.

Finally she gave up and rode silently on her horse as they made their way to the rendezvous point where the man was supposed to meet the gypsies and pay them.

They reached the village of Drixel late in the afternoon. The tiny town was bustling with activity as people rushed in and about the small cottages and shops.

Viktor directed them over to the stable that was set up on the edge of the village. A large blacksmith was at work outside at his forge underneath an awning. The stout man paused at his work to watch them.

"Can I help you, good people?" he asked.

"We're meeting someone here," Viktor said.

The blacksmith nodded and returned to pounding out his horseshoes.

Viktor indicated the back of the stable. "We were supposed to meet him in the last stall."

Ewan nodded as he considered the best way to go about this confrontation.

The last thing he wanted was for Nora or the gypsies to be harmed.

He looked around the crowd. "Do you see anyone who looks like the man who hired you?"

Viktor shook his head.

"Fine then." Ewan ordered Lysander to keep the ladies back while he, Pagan and Viktor went to meet the man who would pay them.

"What if he sees you?" Catarina asked. "It might make him scared to know that you're here. No offense, Ewan, but you're a large man, and I'm sure he'd be frightened to know you've come for retaliation."

She had a point with that.

"I'll have Viktor tie my hands then. We can pretend he brought me here for the man's scrutiny."

"But we were going to be paid to ride you around, then let you go," Bavel said. "If he sees you here, he might run."

" 'Tis a chance we'll have to take. I'm a little too large to hide anywhere. It's not as if he'd have any trouble figuring out who I am."

"Point well taken," Viktor said.

Viktor told Lysander to fetch a piece of rope.

Once Lysander returned, Ewan allowed Viktor to loosely tie his hands behind his back so that he could escape if need be.

"I think this is a bad idea," Nora said. "I dinna cherish the thought of you going in there like this."

Ewan winked at her. "I'm a big lad, lass. I can handle my own."

Nora and Catarina exchanged unamused looks as they were left behind.

"Men," Nora muttered under her breath. "They think they're invincible and that *we* are fragile."

Catarina nodded, then turned to look at their "guard." "Lysander," she said. "I am thirsty. Think you, you could fetch my tankard from the wagon so that I could get a drink of water from yon well?"

Lysander agreed, but no sooner had he climbed into the wagon than Catarina locked him inside.

"Cat!" he snapped angrily, rattling the door

so fiercely that Nora half expected him to wrench it from the hinges. "Release me. I hate it when you do this."

Cat smiled impishly at her and wiped her hands in triumph. "Ready to find out about this man?"

"Absolutely."

United in mischief, the two of them made their way to the stable to find Viktor, Bavel, Pagan and Ewan in there all alone, looking sour.

"Maybe we're early?" Viktor said hopefully as he and Bavel walked around the last stall.

"Maybe we were duped," Bavel added. "Maybe he had no intention of ever paying us."

Ewan's reasoning made the most sense. "Or maybe he saw us arrive and is hiding."

Viktor nodded. "That is most likely it. Bavel stay here, and let us look about and see if we can find him."

Ewan loosened the ropes on his hands and handed them to Bavel.

Catarina stood up as the men passed by.

Ewan's face darkened dangerously as he saw the two of them there alone.

"Where's Lysander?" he growled.

Catarina didn't even flinch at his tone or fierce demeanor. "Back of the wagon. You men are ever easy to trap when a woman knows how."

Ewan didn't appear to appreciate her

words. "What is it with you locking people inside your wagon, Catarina? I think someone should set fire to it."

Catarina gasped. "Don't even say such a thing. That wagon belonged to my grandfather and his father before him."

"Aye," Bavel said. " 'Twould be bad luck to lose it now. Their ghosts would haunt us forever."

Ewan apologized, and then the men left her and Nora alone. Verbally at least.

They did, however, accompany the women to let out poor Lysander, who chastised the women greatly.

"Next time, Cat," Lysander growled, "I swear, father or no, I'm taking a hand to your backside for that."

Catarina made a rude noise at him.

Ewan ignored their sniping and deposited the women and Lysander in a small pub before he went back to help Viktor, Pagan and Bavel search for the unknown man.

The little room was crowded with people coming and going. There were four serving wenches and a heavy-set man who kept ordering the women about.

They went to sit at a table in the rear corner that had just been cleared.

A buxom blond woman paused as they neared the table. She had the old dishes from another table balanced carefully on a large serving tray. "No offense, my lord and ladies, but if you're needing food, one of you'll need to follow me to order it. We're dreadfully busy and equally short-handed. But you shouldn't have to wait too long for your meals."

Lysander followed after the woman to order their food, and while they waited for his return, Catarina left Nora so that she could attend to her personal needs.

Nora sat alone at the table. She watched two men break out into a fight and saw the owner toss both of them out the door. The luscious, rich smell of baking bread and roasting meat filled the air.

It was enough to make her stomach rumble.

Lysander held up his hand to her to signal that he would be right back.

Nora waited patiently while the room's conversations buzzed loudly in her ears.

Until one sentence rang out more loudly than the others . . .

"What are you doing here?"

Her heart stopped at the voice behind her. It was a voice she knew all too well. One that made her blood run cold and her heart pound in trepidation.

Nay, it couldn't be . . .

Turning around, she saw Ryan MacAren standing between her and the faded wood wall. His dark brown eyes were furious. His light brown hair was swept back from his face, and he looked none too pleased with her.

"What are *you* doing here?" she asked him angrily.

He didn't answer her, either. "I swear, woman, you never do as you're told. You should have been on your way home by now, *not here*."

She frowned at his angry, commanding tone. "What the devil are you talking about?"

"Get up." He took her roughly by her arm and hauled her to her feet.

"Let go of me!" she snapped, trying to pull free.

He refused to.

Nora grimaced as he pulled her roughly through the crowd. She slapped at Ryan's hand, but still he refused to loosen his grip.

"What has possessed you, Ryan? Have you gone mad?"

"Silence, Nora. I'm in no mood for your talk, and there's no telling what I might do to you if you don't hold your tongue. One day you're going to learn to keep your mouth closed and to listen."

Suddenly Ewan was there, in the middle of their path to the door, his eyes dark and deadly. "Release her."

Ryan pulled his sword out so fast that she gasped. He angled it at Ewan's throat. "This is between me and her, MacAllister. Don't make me kill you."

In total silence, every eye in the pub fixed on the two men, and the people gathered there wondered what was going on.

Ewan looked from the tip of the sword to her. She saw his steely, cold look of determination, and it made her blood run cold.

This was a man who really could kill someone. It was the face of the man who had started this trip with her.

And she had forgotten just how dangerous a man Ewan could be.

"Come along!" Ryan ordered her.

Ewan moved so fast that she couldn't even follow his actions. One second Ryan had him pinned with the sword point, and in the next Ewan had knocked the blade aside with his forearm and seized Ryan by his throat.

Ewan picked him up from the floor by the collar of his shirt and let him dangle from his fist.

Ryan fought Ewan's hold, but it was useless. Ewan was so much larger that he held him in his fist like an angry dog with a puppy.

"Who are you?" Ewan growled.

Now that she was calmer and relieved that Ewan was there, Nora saw Viktor, Pagan and Bavel standing behind Ewan. Pagan watched with his usual silent composure while Viktor's eyes narrowed.

"He's the one who said he'd pay me," Viktor said.

"Why?" Ewan asked Ryan. "And what do you want with my woman?"

"Your woman?" Ryan repeated in disbelief, his face bright red from Ewan's hold. "She's not your woman, MacAllister. She's mine. I'm Ryan MacAren and she's promised to me."

Nora saw the color and anger fade instantly from Ewan's face. His eyes looked suddenly dazed as if someone had struck him a staggering blow.

His hurt gaze went from Ryan to her.

"Your betrothed?" he asked her for confirmation.

Nora couldn't answer him. The words lodged themselves in her throat.

"Aye," Ryan choked out. "Now let me go."

Ewan was dumbstruck enough to do as he asked. He lowered the much smaller man to the floor, then faced him with a scowl. "You paid to have me abducted? Why?"

Ryan jerked angrily at his clothes, straightening them. "Because I didn't want you around my Nora. I heard she was running to you, and I wanted to make sure you weren't there to help her. Everyone in Scotland knows that if you want a woman to flee the country, send her to Ewan MacAllister, especially if she's promised to another."

Ewan slugged him for that.

Ryan fell to the floor, where he lay whining like a child. "You hit me!"

"You're lucky I didn't kill you for that."

Ryan wiped the blood from his nose, then looked to Nora. "She's mine, MacAllister. I won't let you have her."

"I don't belong to you, Ryan," Nora snapped. "I will never marry you."

Ewan felt sick at the words.

The man loved her so much that he would pay someone to abduct him to keep him away from her. He might not like the man's actions or logic, but he certainly couldn't fault the fool for his motivation.

Ryan loved her so much that he was willing to dare the MacAllister wrath to have her.

Just as Robby MacDouglas had loved Isobail.

Just as Kieran . . .

Nora saw Ewan's face and knew what he thought. She could see his anguish. If he thought Ryan loved her, he would never let her stay with him.

He would be lost to her forever.

"Ryan," Nora said desperately, "tell Ewan the truth. Tell him that you can't stand me. Tell him what you really think of me."

Ryan was aghast as he came to his feet again. He looked at her as if she were a rare treasure.

If she didn't know better, even she would think he spoke honestly.

But unlike Ewan, she knew the heart of

this treacherous adder.

"How can you say that, Nora?" Ryan asked, feigning hurt as he clutched his heart. "Our parents have planned for our marriage since we were children. I love you. I have always loved you. I want no other bride."

Ewan winced as if he'd been struck.

His eyes were bleak as he met her gaze. "You lied to me, Nora."

Panic welled up inside her. She had to make Ewan see the truth. She couldn't let him think that she had lied to him when she hadn't.

Damn Ryan and his lies.

"Nay, I did not." She turned on Ryan with a glower. "Tell him the truth, Ryan, or I'll beat you myself."

"It is the truth," Ryan said sincerely. "I *need* you for my bride. May the Lord Almighty strike me dead if I lie."

Ewan took a deep breath as he tried to stave off the bitter agony he felt. Something inside him had shriveled with Ryan's words.

So Ryan did love her.

Damn you, Fate, for replaying this.

It was just as before.

Only this time Ewan would make sure the woman went where she belonged. Nora would go home with Ryan, and he would go back to . . .

Unable to finish the thought, Ewan turned around and left the pub. The soundless crowd parted, letting him pass.

Bavel, Lysander, Pagan and Viktor exchanged awkward looks before they followed after him.

Nora started to go after Ewan as well, but her anger with Ryan was too great.

First she had a score to settle.

The crowd surrounding them slowly began to resume their own business and speculate on hers.

"Why did you do that?" she demanded.

"Because I *have* to marry you."

"Why? You don't love me. You can't even stand me. All you've ever done is berate and mock every part of my person."

Ryan looked away sheepishly as if the truth were almost too hard for him to face. "Because I need your dowry. If I don't have it, I will die in less than two months."

Her shock at his words overrode her anger. That was the last thing she expected, but then given his odd behavior, she shouldn't be surprised by anything he said or did at this point. "Why?"

Ryan sighed wearily and moved away from the crowd that was still mostly focused on them.

He lowered his voice so that only she could hear his words. "Remember last spring when I went to the continent?"

"Aye."

"I went trying to find myself another bride.

My mother was pressing me to ask your father for your hand. She told me that it was past time I settle down and take you for my wife. I was horrified by the very idea of spending my life tied to you. I thought if I could go to the tourney circuit and build a solid reputation and fortune for myself, I would have my pick of brides."

Nora shook her head at him. "Oh Ryan. *I* can best you at swordsmanship."

His eyes blazed at her. "I'm not *that* incompetent, Nora. I'm just not excellent. Believe me, I need no reminders from you of just how painfully average I am."

She almost felt sorry for him.

Almost.

But after what he'd done to Ewan, she wasn't anywhere near ready to forgive him for his actions.

"What happened?" she asked.

He rubbed his face with his hand and looked weary and tired. Aged, in fact. "Every time I lost, I signed vouchers for the value of my horse and armor. I kept thinking that if I could just win one tournament, I would have enough to pay everyone back."

He let out a long-suffering breath. His eyes appeared haunted and were tinged by humiliation. Now she did feel sorry for him and his foolish quest.

"But I lost time and again," he continued. "When the season came to an end, everyone started demanding I make good on my vouchers. I didn't know what to do so I borrowed enough money from Stryder of Blackmoor so that I could come home, marry you, and repay what I owe."

Nora couldn't believe what she was hearing. "Stryder of Blackmoor? Are you mad? They say he is the devil incarnate."

"Aye, but I had no choice. Oddly enough, he alone hasn't pursued me for the money I owe him. But everyone else has hounded me to ground. I have to marry you, Nora. There's no other way."

Nora pressed her hand to her temple to fight the ache that was starting there as she thought of everything Ryan had put her through.

The fright she'd had reaching Ewan. The worry and fretting. Now he was completely unrepentant for his actions.

She could strangle him!

"I can't believe this," she said. "Debt is the only reason you asked for my hand?"

"Well, I do care for you in a pesky little sister sort of way. And you're not bad-looking when you're silent. Unfortunately that is almost never, but —"

"Ryan! I knew you were vile, but this . . . How could you borrow money and then rely on me as your banker?"

He sighed again. "I know what I did was wrong. The only way I was able to continue on the tourney circuit was by telling everyone that I was betrothed to King Henry's niece."

He gave her a pleading, sheepish stare. "So you see, I do need you, Nora. I really, truly will die without you because if I fail to repay some of the men I owe, they will kill me as an example to others."

"You don't need me, Ryan," she said testily. "What you need is a banker."

"King Henry's niece, eh? Och now, this just got better."

Nora turned at a voice that sounded oddly familiar to her. It took a minute to recognize Isobail's brother Graham from the day before.

But this time, he wasn't alone.

There were two other men with him.

"What are you doing here?" she asked them.

Graham gave her an evil sneer that was cold enough to set her teeth to chattering. "We're setting things right."

"I beg your pardon?" she asked.

Before she could move, Graham pulled out a dagger. "Come quietly, lass, and we won't hurt you. Fight us, and you'll be much worse for the dare."

Chapter 10

Ewan stood in the stable, brushing his horse as his mind whirled with the day's revelations. He didn't know why he was out here, except that he couldn't think of anything else to do with himself and the horse needed a good brushing.

Maybe.

Not.

Basically, he needed something to focus on other than the burning pain inside his heart.

Ryan loved Nora.

But then, so did he.

He loved her more than anything. There was nothing he wouldn't do for her. Nothing he wouldn't give her.

Except his hand in marriage.

His stomach twisted even more as he felt hopelessness deep inside his heart.

Why was it ever his plight to love women he couldn't have? What were the chances of Nora's father siding with him and breaking Nora's betrothal with Ryan while Ryan loved her? Especially given the fact that their families knew each other. That Nora and Ryan had grown up together.

It was impossible.

Her father would never allow her to marry a man with so few prospects. He wasn't Lochlan who was laird or Sin or Braden who were titled lords.

He was a simple landowner with a slightly better than modest income.

One who lived in a cave.

You could take her.

Aye, he could, but to what purpose? Another feud for his clan. More death. More sorrow.

How could they have a happy marriage based on that?

There were so many lives at stake here. Things much more important than his own happiness, which seemed paltry when compared to what could happen again.

Ewan cursed as pain assailed him anew.

He should have stayed in the mountains. He should never have helped her.

Now that he had . . .

Ewan couldn't get her out of his mind. He needed her more than he had ever needed anyone or anything. The mere thought of living without her was enough to send him to his knees.

How could he go back to what he'd been before her winsome smile had set him free?

"Ewan?"

He looked over his shoulder to see Catarina approaching. The lass was toying with the tip of her long braid. She looked hesitant as she drew near.

"What is it?" he growled. "Can't you see I'd rather be alone?"

She ignored his surly tone and stood by his horse's head. She patted the horse on the nose as she watched him. "Nora didn't lie to you."

He felt his nostrils flare as more pain wrenched his gut. "What do you know of it?"

"I know enough to say that she would much rather have you for husband than Ryan."

He tightened his grip on the brush, refusing to let her see how much her words bothered him. "And I would say that you are not Nora and know nothing of her mind or mine."

"I know what I see," she said softly. She reached out and stopped his hand from brushing the horse. "You two belong together."

Ewan stared at her hand on his. Her skin was pale, like Nora's, her nails every bit as well manicured.

But that hand didn't make him tremble.

It didn't cause his body to burn, his manhood to stiffen.

Only Nora did that.

And she was the one woman he couldn't have.

Alone he could fight for her. Was willing to fight for her. But if Ryan refused to let her go, it would be like Robby MacDouglas all over again.

Another feud.

More unwarranted deaths . . .

"She belongs to Ryan," he said insistently, shrugging her hand away. "You heard what he said. He wanted her so much that he dared my wrath to hire you to keep her away from me."

Ewan paused as he thought about that. "Wait . . . how did he know to hire *you?* How could he have found out about Nora's plans, and then having learned of them, why did Ryan go to you and not her father to stop her from fleeing?"

Catarina looked rather sheepish.

She stepped back, her brow fretful.

A bad feeling came over Ewan as he watched her sudden nervousness. Just what was going on here?

"Cat? What are you not telling me?"

She visibly cringed. "Promise you won't be angry at us?"

"Nay," he said sternly. "I never make a promise I can't keep, and by the looks of you, lass, I be thinking I'm going to be good and angry at this explanation."

She took another step back.

Ewan grabbed her wrist to keep her from fleeing. "You'd best be telling me, Cat."

She squirmed uncomfortably under his scrutiny, and when she finally spoke, it came out in a flurry. "Her father wanted Nora to marry a MacAllister. He's been trying to arrange a marriage for a while now between your families, and since Braden and Sin are both recently married, he got a bit worried that some woman would grab *your* interest and he would lose out on uniting your two families."

Ewan scowled at her words. It didn't make sense that Nora's father would want him for a son-in-law. "Why would he wish to marry her to a younger son?"

Catarina cleared her throat. "Because the MacAllister clan will ever come first to Lochlan. Alex wanted a younger son who could take over his clan's leadership and yet be able to pull MacAllister strength if needs be."

Ewan went cold at the name.

"Alex?" he repeated slowly in disbelief.

There was only one Alex who had ever broached the subject of marriage with one of his brothers.

"Are you saying Alexander Canmore is her father?"

Catarina nodded.

Ewan cursed. Loudly.

This was truly unbelievable. Aye, her father would have his head.

Both of them.

"Her father is the cousin to the king of Scotland?" he roared.

Catarina offered him a forced smile. "Surprise."

Ewan felt sick to his stomach as the full weight of what he'd done with Nora came crashing down on him.

He was a dead man should her father ever learn what they'd done.

"She said she was Eleanor's niece."

"She is. Her mother is sister to Eleanor. She married Alex years ago when he was in Paris."

Ewan cursed again as he remembered Alexander had married a French lady. It had never dawned on him that she would be sister to one of the most powerful women in all of Christendom.

Anymore than he would have *ever* believed Nora to be Alexander's daughter. No wonder she had failed to tell him her clan's status or her father's name. No man in his right mind would dare lead her out of the country and risk her father's wrath.

Alexander Canmore was known for his furious wrath and quick retaliation.

Sweet holy Mary, he'd slept with the niece and cousin of two kings!

Lochlan would kill him for this, and God only knew what her father would do to him . . .

How could this have happened?

Well, he knew *how* it had happened, but why?

Aye, he was a fool. One destined for an ugly castration.

With a blunted instrument.

As his mind played through the horror of his situation, Ewan realized Catarina seemed to know a lot about this whole affair, and he wondered what other information she was withholding.

"You knew Ryan was the one who hired you to abduct me?"

This time she didn't even try to hide from him. "Aye, I knew it. Viktor and Bavel didn't. They had never seen Ryan before, but I had."

"When?"

"A few times at Alex's castle."

Ewan scowled. "You seem rather familiar with Alexander Canmore."

"He and my mother are friends. They were very close in their youths."

Something in her tone made him wonder if she might be one of Alexander's illegitimate children. But that was none of his business.

He had more pressing worries at hand.

"So why did you bring me here to meet Ryan, then, if you knew what he wanted?"

"To be honest, I didn't think Ryan would have the audacity to be here when we arrived with you, and her father wanted me to keep the two of you together for as long as possible. When I told him Ryan had tried to hire Viktor to kidnap you, he thought it would be a good way to give you two more time together. He was certain you would grow to love Nora if you were around her long enough."

Ewan let out a long, deep breath.

Suddenly everything made sense.

Well, not *everything*, but many things were a lot clearer.

Her guard abandoning her at his cave.

Some of the odder comments the gypsies had made over the last few days.

But one thing still didn't make sense.

"Why would he entrust her to me?" Ewan asked. "How did he know I wouldn't hurt her?"

Catarina looked as if he'd just asked her the dumbest question on earth. "Because you're a MacAllister and your family honor is the law all of you live by. He knew you would never let her come to harm."

Ewan snorted at that. "The man is still a fool. I would never have taken such a chance with *my* daughter's life, and I find it hard to believe that he would be so careless with hers."

"Well to be honest, that's why he sent us. We were to keep you together and to keep watch on you to make sure you didn't hurt her."

"But why send gypsies?"

She smiled at that. "We're not all gypsies. Lysander is one of Alex's men and Pagan is a good friend of his. That's why the two of them refused to fight you with a sword after Nora disarmed Lysander. Had you engaged either of them, you would have known immediately they were knights trained for battle and not peasants."

"And you?"

"My mother is a peasant and I fall under Alex for my protection. Viktor is my uncle and Bavel my cousin."

Ewan shook his head. "I canna believe I was duped so easily."

"Don't blame Nora —"

"Believe me," he said, interrupting her, "I don't. 'Tis her father I want to murder. How could he play with people's lives like this?"

"Ewan?" Nora's voice rang out.

Ewan looked past Catarina to see Nora standing at the opening of the stable.

Nora seemed nervous and uncertain as she looked at them together. "Could you please come out here for a moment?"

He frowned at her words. "Nora, there's nothing —"

"Please, Ewan," she stressed the words. "I *truly* need you to come outside alone. Now."

His frown turned into a scowl at her insistent tone. She sounded more like a mother trying to rein in an ill-bred child than a woman who should be contrite for her father's behavior.

Angry, he headed for her.

It wasn't until he neared the entrance that he saw she wasn't alone.

Graham MacKaid was with her, and he had a dagger held to her throat. His two brothers flanked him.

"Make a move and she's dead."

Ewan froze. He wanted to turn around to see if Catarina was still in the stable, but didn't dare, lest he get her into trouble as well. With any luck, she would be able to sneak out and get one of the others to help with this.

"You wouldn't dare harm her," Ewan said slowly, stepping forward with his arms held up nonthreateningly so that Graham wouldn't get nervous and hurt Nora out of fear.

"Wouldn't dare kill the king's cousin?" Graham said his next words loudly as if wanting everyone to hear them. "Ewan MacAllister will kill whomever he pleases."

Ewan took another step forward, intending to end this once and for all.

"One more step," Graham snarled, "and she's headless."

Ewan stopped instantly.

He met Nora's fear-filled eyes and tried to offer her comfort. He had no intention of letting her be hurt by Graham or anyone else.

Whatever it took, he would see her safe.

"What do you want?" Ewan asked.

Graham smiled snidely. "You to stand there while my brothers take you."

Ewan heard Catarina in the stable, and his

heart lurched in fear of Graham and his brothers finding her there. They wouldn't hesitate to kill Catarina.

He didn't know what Cat had planned, but she always had something planned. He only hoped she executed it carefully.

Ewan stood in silence as Graham's two brothers tied his hands behind his back.

"Excuse me," a villager said, drawing near them hesitantly. "Is there a problem here?"

"King's business," Graham snapped. "Isn't it, my lady?"

By her pale face, Ewan knew Nora longed to tell the truth, but didn't dare. The truth would get both of them killed and probably the good Samaritan too.

"Aye. There's no problem."

The old villager looked less than convinced but went on his way.

The taller of Graham's brothers was still a full head shorter than Ewan. He had dark brown hair and mean brown eyes. He grabbed Ewan by the hair and forced him onto a horse.

Ewan kept waiting for Catarina or one of the others to come and distract them.

They didn't.

So in the end, the MacKaids mounted their horses and he had to watch helplessly as Nora was placed in front of Graham.

He saw the pallor on her face. The fear and concern.

"It'll be all right, Nora," Ewan assured her.

The doubt in her eyes tore through him.

"Aye, Princess Nora. It'll be just fine." Graham laughed evilly and kicked his horse forward.

"Why are you taking us?" Ewan asked.

Graham's younger brother, Rufus, was the one who answered him. Shorter than Nora, Rufus might have been passably handsome had he ever taken a bath and if he could get the distasteful smirk to leave his lips.

Ewan had met the man only once, years ago when Rufus had stopped with Isobail and their father to visit with his father at the MacAllister castle.

"For the sake of justice," Rufus snarled. "You ruined our family and so we ruin yours."

Graham laughed again. "And here I thought the best revenge would be in just taking the woman you wanted and making her my own. Little did I know who she was. Just imagine how her father will react when he learns that she was killed by Ewan Mac-Allister. He won't rest until he's destroyed every single member of the MacAllister clan. There won't be a single member left standing."

Ewan was aghast at their plan.

Surely they weren't serious.

"Are you mad?"

"Not at all," Rufus said. "We lost everything when you ran off with Isobail. Robby MacDouglas demanded her dowry and then when our father failed to give it to him, he killed Father and banished us."

"Aye," Graham said, his lips twisted cruelly as he rode. "We've been struggling just to live only to find that none of our family will even admit they know us. 'Tis time for the MacKaids to be regaled again while the MacAllisters get what they deserve . . . humiliation."

Ewan clenched his teeth to keep from telling them who was really to blame for what happened. Reminding them of the fact that their sister was a faithless, lying whore wouldn't accomplish anything.

They blamed his family, not Isobail.

And he doubted if they would ever listen to reason where she was concerned.

"If it's vengeance you want, then kill me and let Nora go."

"Oh nay," Graham said. His eyes glowed with cruel mischief. "See, here's where we regain our position. Who better to fall into the king's good graces than the man who tried to save his cousin and who killed her murderer."

Nay! the word screamed through Ewan's mind.

Ewan was appalled at the man's plan.

He should have known Graham MacKaid was insane. He should have killed the man in the pub when he had the chance.

Why had he ever allowed Graham to leave the pub without killing him?

Damn!

Nora's heart pounded as she listened to the men brag to one another what they intended to do to her and Ewan. She was terrified of their insidious plan.

Guilt, horror, and anger warred within her. Over and over she saw Ryan in her mind.

As soon as she saw Graham, she'd known something was wrong, so she'd tried to run.

Rufus had caught her.

And Ryan, God have mercy on his soul, had finally found a moment of bravery. Seeing her threatened, he had reached for his sword.

But it hadn't even cleared the scabbard before Graham ran him through with his dagger.

Ryan had staggered back, holding his stomach as blood poured from his body.

Nora had tried to help him, only to find Graham in her way.

"Do as I say, or I'll give you worse than that."

Ryan had reached out to her with one bloodied hand, then he'd fallen to the ground, dead.

Nora sobbed at the memory.

Ryan was dead because of her, and now Ewan was taken. If she didn't come up with some way to free him, he, too, would die.

And so would she.

Nay. Nay, she would never submit to these brigands. She was Eleanor's niece. She was her father's daughter. Ruffian Alexander Canmore might be, but no man had ever defeated him in battle or practice.

She would get them out of this.

And heaven have mercy on the MacKaids when she did.

They rode for hours until they came to an abandoned keep that appeared to have been burned down. The skeleton of the building remained, but it looked far from safe. Weeds and vines covered the fallen and charred stones.

It was an evil place. An aura of death and decay clung to it.

Nora had never tasted real fear before, but she tasted it now. The place looked like a crypt. A place that had no purpose except to house dead remains.

The MacKaids dismounted, then carefully pulled Ewan from his horse.

Ewan glared at the men. Though he didn't know how at the moment, he was determined to get them out of this.

And once he had Nora safe, all three of the brothers would pay for this. He would make sure of it.

Graham kept his dagger at Nora's throat the entire time.

"One move," he warned.

It was a threat Ewan heeded.

They led him into the crumbling great hall and roughly forced him to kneel by the hearth. The only thing that made him obey was the knife at Nora's neck.

Ewan didn't take his eyes off it or her while Sean and Rufus tied him to an iron ring that was buried deep into the stones by the hearth.

Only then did the dagger come away from her neck. Ewan took a deep breath in relief.

Now the real fun could begin . . .

Graham smiled evilly at him. " 'Tis a pity I can't kill you now. But I have to make sure you stay alive until her ransom comes to us. Tell me, how would you kill her? Would you choke her? Cut her throat?"

Ewan eyed him with all the hatred he felt for the man. "You harm her, and so help me, I'll defy death itself to rip your heart out."

Sean sucked his breath in sharply. "I can almost believe the rumors that say you've sold your soul to the devil when you look like that."

Ewan turned his black stare toward the man. "You can more than believe it, Mac-Kaid. Harm her and I'll introduce you to the devil myself."

"Leave them be, Sean, Graham," Rufus snapped. "Let us write the note to her father and see about putting this into motion. The sooner we get the message off, the closer we'll be to having us a home again."

Graham shoved Nora toward Ewan and sheathed his dagger.

Nora fell to her knees by his side. The sight of her there, trembling, made him want their blood all the more.

"Don't fret, Nora," he hastened to assure her. "I won't let them hurt you."

"They killed Ryan," she said, her voice shaking as she cuddled up to his side like a child needing comfort.

Ewan winced at the news and wished his arms free so that he could hold her and soothe her worry and fear. "What happened?"

"After you left, I was talking to him when they came in. Ryan tried to keep them from taking me, and Graham stabbed him dead for it."

Tears were shining brightly in her eyes, but to her credit, she held them back. "Oh Ewan, what have I done? I only wanted to go to Eleanor's. I never meant for anyone to be harmed. The saints know I never really wanted Ryan dead. I just didn't want to marry him, but I never truly meant for evil to befall him. He didn't deserve to die like that. Not over me. Whatever will I tell his parents? His poor mother lives for him. She'll never recover from this."

He nuzzled her head with his cheek, offering her what solace he could while bound to the wall. "Shh, love. None of this is your fault."

"Aye, it is. All of this is my fault. I never meant for Ryan to die. He was an annoying pest, but still . . ."

"He loved you."

"Nay," she said, holding on to his waist as she buried her head against his chest, "not really. We were childhood enemies in that our parents were always putting us together. We never got along."

Ewan glanced to Graham and Sean, who were arguing over what the letter to her father should say and over how much money they should ask for.

He had to find some way to get them out of this.

He wrenched at the ring that held him to the wall. It wiggled only enough to make him think that maybe he could work it free. Provided the MacKaids didn't turn around and see what he was up to.

Nora saw him twisting at his ropes. She pulled back from him. "You'll hurt yourself."

"I'll heal."

She shook her head, then glanced around the overgrown floor where weeds and rocks were scattered. She looked back at the Mac-Kaids, who were still arguing, and motioned for Ewan to be silent.

He watched her go to a small pile of

stones. After a few minutes, she returned with one.

But before she could hand it to him, Sean saw her.

"Give me that," he snapped, rushing over to them and pulling it from her hand.

"What is it?" Graham asked as he joined them.

"The little tart was trying to help him escape."

Rufus came forward with a snarl. "I say we tie her up with him while we write the note."

"Aye," Graham agreed. He pulled his belt off and handed it to Sean. "Then after we finish with the note, what say we have a bit of fun with her?"

Ewan went cold. "Don't even think it."

Graham smiled evilly. "Why not? She's going to die as soon as we get the money. The only one who'll ever know we tasted her is you, MacAllister. And you won't be able to tell anyone after we cut your throat."

His smile widened as he eyed Ewan with malice. "That bothers you, doesn't it? The thought of us using her? Aye. You used our sister and cast her off. The least we could do is return the favor."

"Your sister left him."

Ewan flinched at Nora's words.

Graham drew back to hit her.

Ewan slung his leg out, knocking Graham

away from her. "You touch her, and by all the powers of hell, I'll see you pay for it."

Graham walked over to Ewan. He raked a cold glare over his body, then kicked him hard in the ribs.

"Ewan!" Nora screamed.

Sean held her back.

Ewan grunted at the pain as he tried to shrug it off.

Graham would pay for that. When he got free, he was going to make sure this was the last mistake Graham ever made.

"You're worthless, MacAllister," Graham sneered. "There's nothing you can do to me now."

Ewan laughed at that, and the sound of it made all three MacKaids back away.

"You've no idea what I'm capable of, Graham MacKaid, because if you were, you'd be on your knees praying right now for the Lord to send His angels to protect you from me. I will see you dead." He looked to each of them. "All of you."

Sean actually crossed himself at those fiercely uttered words.

Graham spat on the ground and shoved Nora toward Rufus. "Secure the wench and let us finish our business."

Ewan pulled at the ropes that held him. Somehow he was going to find a way to escape this. God help the MacKaids when he did. They were all going to learn firsthand why no one crossed a MacAllister.

Only death awaited such fools.

Once Rufus had Nora tied up with Graham's belt, he sat her roughly next to Ewan, then returned to his brothers to help write their note.

Nora licked her lips, but held herself together with a strength of will that amazed him. She was truly spectacular given what she'd been through this day. Brave.

Even so, he could tell just how shaken she was from all this, and he ached to soothe her nerves. But he doubted if anything short of their escape could do that.

"It's hopeless, isn't it?" she asked.

"Nothing's ever hopeless," he said with conviction. He would get her out of this no matter what it took.

She sighed and shifted her bound hands in her lap. "I don't know, Ewan. I'm thinking this is as hopeless as it gets."

"Look at me, Nora."

She did.

"If this is as hopeless as it gets, you and I are in good standing. I promise you. This, in the grand scheme of life, isn't so bad."

She shook her head at him. "You're a strange man, Ewan MacAllister. But I love you anyway."

His heart caught at her words. "What?"

"I love you," she repeated. Then she leaned forward and laid her head on his chest and snuggled up to him. "I'm so sorry I got you into this."

Happiness, disbelief and anger tore through him.

How could a woman like her have a single care for him?

And yet he knew she spoke the truth. She wasn't Isobail to spread her lies and walk away. Nora would never be so cruel.

She loved him.

And he loved her even more now than he had before.

"I will not let them hurt you, Nora. Do you understand?"

Nora offered him a small smile that she didn't really feel. She appreciated what he was trying to do, but she didn't hold out any false hopes.

How she loved her big bear. She could almost believe him when he said that. "Aye."

Ewan nuzzled his face against hers. She could hear his intake of breath as if he were inhaling her. He pulled back ever so slightly and kissed her cheek.

She watched in awe as he moved away from her. He stood up slowly, turned to face the wall, and braced one leg against the old stones next to where the ring was embedded.

He took the ropes into his hands and used his leg to pull against the iron ring.

Every muscle in his body tightened as he tried to pull it free.

Nora was aghast at his actions as much for the fact that he might succeed as for the fact that what he was doing had to be excruciating for him.

"Hey!" Rufus shouted as he looked up to see Ewan on his feet.

Ewan didn't stop.

The wall shook as Ewan panted and strained even more.

Nora pushed herself to her feet and moved away from the wall before her strong bear pulled it down on top of her.

She'd never seen anything like it.

An instant before the brothers reached him, Ewan pulled the ring free.

He turned on them with a vicious snarl.

Nora wanted to help him fight as the brothers attacked Ewan, but as long as she was there tied up, she was a liability to him and she knew it. If one of the brothers caught her, they would again threaten her life to control Ewan.

So she did the only thing she could.

She ran for the horses as the MacKaids ran for Ewan.

Her gamble worked. They were so intent on subduing Ewan that she was on Ewan's horse before Graham realized she'd left the area.

Nora wasn't used to riding bareback, but it didn't matter. It was up to her to see them safely away from this, and she wouldn't fail Ewan.

After pulling herself up on the horse's back, she clamped her legs tight around the horse's ribs and ran Ewan's horse straight at the men.

The brothers scrambled away.

With a grunt, Ewan swung himself up behind her.

He brought his bound arms down over her head, placed them around her, and took the reins, then turned the horse about.

He ran it toward the other horses, scattering their mounts before he headed them into the dense forest.

She could hear the brothers cursing angrily as she and Ewan rode away from them while they tried to recapture their own horses.

Nora wanted to turn around and see if they were behind them, but couldn't. Ewan's hold on her was far too tight.

So instead she focused on remaining as still as possible so that Ewan could maneuver them.

Her entire body was tense and ready as they sped through the forest. His spirited horse flew through the trees easily, but she was terrified the MacKaid brothers would catch them.

After a time, Ewan reined to a stop and turned to look behind them.

"Did we escape?" she asked, her voice high-pitched from fear and trepidation.

"I think so." He hugged her close to him.

"You were brilliant, Nora."

She laughed triumphantly. "The horse was the easy part. You did the hardest part, what with pulling the ring from the wall. Are you all right?"

"A bit sore, but damned glad you kept your wits about you." He kissed her quickly and soundly on the lips.

She smiled at his praise. "Were you expecting me to lose my wits, my lord?"

"Nay. I know you better than that."

She was warmed by his words and wanted desperately to kiss him for it. And that she would as soon as they stopped.

She would kiss the poor man blind for everything.

Ewan led them through the woods, farther away from the MacKaids.

"Shouldn't we head back toward town?" she asked.

He shook his head. "They'll be expecting us to do that. No doubt it's where they pulled back, too, and they're waiting for us. I say we go farther north, then west before we head back toward Lochlan's."

It amazed her how much she trusted him.

How much she loved him.

He slowed the horse so that he could untie the belt from her hands and free her. Nora tried to return the favor, but his ropes were so tight that she couldn't.

She gingerly touched the red welts on his

wrists, some of which had already started bleeding. "It must hurt dreadfully."

"I'll live until we find some way to cut it off."

"Do you not have the dagger in your boot?"

"Nay, I loaned it to Lysander earlier this morning and forget to get it back."

She sighed. " 'Tis a pity," but even as she spoke those words, she frowned.

Ewan looked somewhat pale and he was perspiring quite a bit as if he'd been running for a while.

Attributing it to his exertion at the wall and their close escape, she leaned back against him and let him lead them to safety.

They didn't stop until nightfall.

Ewan removed his arms from around her and helped her down as best he could.

It wasn't until he slid from the back of the horse that she saw the bright red stain on his clothes. It looked like blood. A *lot* of blood.

Nora's heart stopped at the sight. Surely he wasn't injured. If he were, he would have mentioned it.

Wouldn't he?

And yet there was a pinched paleness to his handsome features. He was still per-spiring, and she noticed the uneasy way he moved. There was no sign of the lethal grace she was used to seeing from her giant.

"What's that?" she asked, pointing to the stain.

"Nothing." He pulled the horse to a cleared area and secured it so that it could graze.

Nora frowned at his actions, and when she looked down to see that the side and the back of her own dress was also coated in red, her heart pounded even more.

"You're hurt?" She rushed to him.

He wiped the sweat from his face with his arm and shook his head as if to clear it. "Graham stabbed me while we were fighting. The blade glanced off my rib."

She blinked in disbelief of his blasé tone. How could he be so nonchalant about a stab wound?

"Ewan MacAllister, sit!"

He arched a brow at her as if he couldn't believe her commanding tone.

"I can't believe you," she muttered. "You play helpless when you have a minor fall out of a tree, but let you have a serious wound and you get all noble on me. 'Oh, it doesn't hurt. I'll be all right.' How dare you! Now you sit down and let me take a look at you."

He growled at her, then did as she said. "I'm not an infant, Nora, and I've no need to be coddled like one. I've suffered much worse wounds than this and I'm still here."

She didn't even deign to respond to that, because if she did, his ears would be ringing with her insults until the world ended.

Nora took a deep breath and fought the

urge to loose her tongue on him.

How could he do this?

The wound had to be excruciating.

She forced him to lie down so that she could lift his shirt up to see the injury. She felt the color drain from her cheeks as she saw it.

Graham had laid open a long gash. The evil-looking wound was still oozing blood.

"Oh, Ewan," she breathed. "I can't believe you didn't bleed to death. Why didn't you tell me you were hurt?"

He reached up with his bound hands to touch her cheek with his fingers. The intensity of his crystal blue gaze made her hot and shivery all at once.

"We couldn't stop, Nora. Had I told you I was wounded, you would have made me stop so that you could tend it, and I didn't want to see you retaken."

Her love for him tripled with those words. For her, he had suffered this for untold leagues without a single comment or complaint.

She took his hands into hers and kissed his fingers. "Thank you. Now lie still and let me see to you."

He nodded and pulled his hands away.

Ewan steadied his breathing as he lay there, staring at the woman who had come to mean so much to him.

For her, he would walk through the very fires of hell.

She laid her hand against his cheek and chastised him with her worried gaze. "You've a fever started."

"I know." He could feel it. He was already shivery, but then he was often shivery whenever Nora touched him.

She tore her chemise and used it to make a bandage. "Hold this while I fetch some water."

He did as she bade him.

She rushed over to the stream near the horse and after a few minutes, returned with another part of her chemise that she had torn off.

She pressed the cool fabric to his wound.

Ewan breathed deeply as the cold water stung and the material scraped against the ragged edges of his injury. Aye, but it hurt. He wanted nothing more than to curl up and sleep for a bit, but he didn't dare.

The MacKaids might be headed back to the village or they might be trailing them still.

It was a gamble he didn't mention to Nora. He wanted her to have the illusion they were safe. The truth would only worry her unnecessarily when there was nothing she could really do.

He did need a little time to rest before they went any farther.

"I wish I had something to stitch this with," she mumbled. "But we'll have to make do with just bandaging it."

"Bandaging it with what?"

She lifted her skirt high, gifting him with a luscious view of her legs, and ripped more of her chemise. A large portion of it.

"You keep doing that, lass, and you'll be naked by the time we get back to the others." He smiled wolfishly at the thought. "Not that I'd mind that, of course, but I'm thinking you might be embarrassed."

She rolled her eyes at him. "Just like a man. You're lying there half dead and all you can think of is me taking off my clothes."

"Half dead, not *all* dead."

She shook her head at him as she bandaged his ribs. "You're incorrigible."

"Nay, my lady, I am *en*-courage-able."

Her cheeks pinkened. "That's not a word, my lord."

Ewan had to admit he loved teasing this woman. "Sure it is. It's a perfectly good word."

She leaned over him and kissed him lightly on the lips.

Ewan closed his eyes and inhaled the scent of her as he savored the softness of her mouth on his.

Aye, the lady was the world to him.

He drew a ragged breath as she pulled back from him. "You rest here while I —"

"Nay!" he roared, sitting up in spite of the pain that lacerated him. "It's not safe."

She gave him a peeved glare. "I have needs to tend to, Ewan, and if you don't let me do so privately, I'll not be kind to you in the future. I'll only be right through yon trees and I won't be gone long."

Ewan looked at the trees where she indicated, trying to see if there was anything lurking there to grab her. He didn't want to let her out of his sight, but he could understand her need for privacy. "Very well. But you talk the entire time so that I know you're safe."

She laughed at that. "I think this may very well be the only time in my life anyone has ever *invited* me to talk."

He kissed her gently. "I cherish your tongue, my lady," he said, then he tasted said tongue with his own. He moaned at the feel of her.

"Aye," he said, pulling back. "I find myself quite taken with it."

She gave him a delighted grin. "So you've changed your mind about having it cut out?"

He laughed at her reminder of what he'd said to her the day they met. "Aye, lass. I've become quite attached to it. Now be off before it gets any darker."

She bit her lip, then did as he said. As she left him, she began chattering about her favorite ballad.

"You know," she said, her voice drifting back from the forest. "I miss my lute. 'Tis a pity I didn't have it when Graham showed up. I could have used it to bash him."

Ewan smiled at her as she continued on.

Heaven above, how he loved to hear her prattle.

"By the way, Ewan, I am very sorry for all this."

Ewan considered everything that had happened to them since he had awakened to find her standing over his bed.

"Don't be," he said loudly as he sat back down to rest. "All in all, it's been rather interesting, hasn't it? Besides, you said you were always up for an adventure."

"True," she said from the other side of the trees. "But I never meant for this to happen."

"I'm sure your father didn't, either."

"My father?"

"Aye, Catarina told me that he paid them to put us together."

Total silence rang for several heartbeats.

"Nora?" he asked worriedly. "Are you still there?"

She ignored his question. "Just what do you mean, my father paid them?"

Ewan explained it to her between his attempts to loosen the ropes on his hands with his teeth.

"So my father *wanted* me to marry you?" she asked as she rejoined him.

He looked up to see her less-than-pleased

visage. "Apparently so."

She appeared flabbergasted as she stood there with her hands on her hips. "Oh, I am a fool."

"Why do you say that?"

"I should have known something was up. My father telling me that I had no choice but to marry Ryan, then my maid telling me that the only hope I had would be to get to England. 'You'll be needing an escort, my lady,' Agnes had said. 'And I'm thinking there be no better man than Ewan MacAllister. He'll see you to England fast enough and you won't have to worry about him. All the MacAllisters are good men . . .' "

She paused in her tirade to curl her lips. "Oh, they are evil. I should have known when Agnes brought the guard as escort. Why didn't I see it?"

"Because you were scared."

Nora sighed disgustedly. She felt ten kinds of foolishness. How could she have let her father manipulate her so? The man was the devil, no doubt about it and when she got home again, she fully intended to let him know exactly what she thought of his machinations.

While she silently condemned her father, she heard Ewan's stomach rumble. "We need to eat, don't we?"

He let out a tired breath. "I'm afraid I'm not quite up to catching anything other than a cold in my current condition, and even if I could, we dare not start a fire while I'm outnumbered, wounded, weaponless, and bound."

She patted him on the arm. "I can gather greens and make a salad for us. It won't be the best, but it'll keep our strength up."

Against her protests, Ewan got up to go with her.

He refused to let her out of his sight while he followed her. Even though it perturbed her, there was a small part of her that reveled in his care.

He might not have said it, but she rather fancied that he did love her. Surely there was no other reason for him to be so concerned for her welfare?

After she gathered the greens, she went to the small stream for fresh water to wash them.

Ewan knelt down on the bank and bent over with a grunt to drink. Because of the way his hands were tied, he couldn't do anything more than suck the water from his fingertips.

"Here," Nora said, setting the greens aside. "Let me help." She cupped her hands and helped him drink.

He smiled gratefully, then dipped his head down to kiss her lips.

Nora sighed at the tenderness of his lips on hers. After everything that had happened, she found his kiss strangely fortifying.

"Do you think they can find us tonight?" Nora asked after he had drunk his fill of both her lips and the water.

Ewan lay back while she used her lap as a place to break and blend the leaves together.

"Nay," he said. " 'Tis too dense in the woods and too dark now. They'll have to stop for the night. We should be safe until morning."

Nora nodded as she fed him her greens. While he chewed his, she ate some herself.

"It must be frustrating not to be able to get loose," she said after she swallowed her mouthful.

"I have to say 'tis not one of my more favorite situations."

Nora took his hands into hers and was awed by the strength of the man before her. She'd never met anyone like him. "You were incredible back there. I can't believe you pulled that ring from the wall."

"There are times when being a bear is a benefit."

"Aye, there are . . ."

Tears gathered in her eyes as she thought about what had happened that day. "Poor Ryan. I can't believe he's dead. Had he been larger . . ."

"Shh," Ewan whispered. "It's not your fault he fought them."

"Had I not been there —"

"He's the one who . . ." Ewan trailed off as he almost echoed the words she had said to him earlier about Kieran's choice to kill himself.

She was no more responsible for what Ryan had done than he was for Kieran.

Kieran had been the fool who had walked into the loch.

And for what?

For a worthless whore who had destroyed every man she'd ever known, including her own family?

Isobail had never cared for anyone other than herself, and Kieran had been a fool to throw his life away over the likes of her.

Ewan had lived these last years in seclusion with guilt eating away at him. Blaming himself for the decision Kieran had made. He hadn't forced his brother into the loch.

Kieran's stupidity had done that. In the end, his brother hadn't given a care to anyone other than himself. In his grief, he had destroyed not only his life, but Ewan's as well.

And all because Ewan had allowed it. He had let his own grief, guilt, and pain blind him.

Kieran should have been stronger.

Had Isobail meant so much to him, he should have gone after them and taken her back.

Kieran should have fought for what he wanted.

Ewan would have.

He would never allow someone to just take his Nora from him . . .

He blinked as he realized the significance of that thought.

His Nora.

When had he started thinking of her that way?

And yet he did.

When he thought Ryan had come back for her . . . It had damned near killed him. Now that he had her with him again he didn't want to let her go.

She was the world to him.

She was everything . . .

Dear saints, he *loved* her.

He truly, truly loved her.

Nora hadn't realized a tear had fallen down her cheek until Ewan wiped her face with the backs of his fingers.

"Don't cry, love."

He pulled her gently toward him and held her close to his chest so that she could take comfort in the sound of his heart pounding under her cheek.

Nora returned his embrace and was just grateful she hadn't lost him, too.

Graham MacKaid was a madman who would have gladly killed them both.

But they were safe now. She had Ewan with her, and they were both in one piece.

She hugged him even more tightly, so glad

for that one basic fact.

Ewan cupped her face in his bound hands and kissed her.

She tasted him with more than just her mouth. She tasted him with her soul.

"Make love to me, Nora," he whispered. "I need to be inside you right now."

She should be shocked by his words, but she wasn't. In truth, she wanted the same thing. "You're hurt."

"I'm not *that* hurt."

"But you're tied."

He grinned wickedly at her. His hot look made her blush profusely. He lifted his hands over her head and lowered them so that she was in the circle of his arms. He leaned back, drawing her with him.

Careful not to hurt him or touch his side, Nora couldn't help laughing at what they must look like, entwined like this. But when he kissed her, her mirth died under a wave of profound desire.

He nibbled her lips, then pulled back. "I'll need you to take my trewes off."

Nora had never contemplated such a thing. She should be mortified by the mere suggestion, and yet a part of her thrilled at the idea.

Ewan lifted his arms, giving her freedom again.

Taking courage from the needful look on his face, she did as he asked and loosened his trewes, then pulled them free of his long legs.

He was already fully erect.

Her heart pounded at the sight of him lying exposed and somewhat helpless. It was strangely erotic.

One corner of her mouth quirked up.

"Should I be concerned by that look?" Ewan asked.

Nora bit her lip. "I'm not sure. I was just thinking that I have you all to myself."

"Aye, love, that you do."

"You're virtually helpless . . ."

"I'm always helpless where you're concerned."

She smiled at that. Nora didn't know where her boldness came from, but as she watched him, curiosity took hold of her. She wanted to explore his body.

Running her hands up his bare legs, she saw his shaft jerk in response.

"May I touch you?" she asked.

"Aye," he said, his voice deep and husky. "You can touch me anywhere you want to, and I won't mind."

Tentatively she moved her hand over to his rigid shaft. He groaned the instant she brushed her fingers over it.

His breathing ragged, he moved his hand to cover hers and show her how to stroke him.

Nora was thrilled by the pleasure on his

face, by his deep, masculine moans. He was so hard and yet soft to the touch. She'd never before really examined a man's part; now she took her time exploring it.

She ran her fingers over the tip, letting his wetness coat her skin. Then she went down the length of him to the base and gently cupped his sac.

He arched his back, growling at her.

Ewan watched her innocent exploration of his body. He'd never known anything more splendid than her hands on him. He wished he had his hands free long enough to return her caresses.

"Does this feel good?" she asked as she ran her finger over the tip of him again.

"Aye."

"Why is the tip leaking?"

He groaned. The woman was completely unabashed with her questions. "It's just something it does when I'm aroused."

"Can I taste you like you tasted me?"

Ewan groaned again at the very thought. "Aye."

He watched as she lowered her head tentatively to his shaft. And when she took him into her mouth, he thought he would die of the ecstasy of it.

He growled as he forced himself to lie still while she discovered him. The last thing he wanted to do was scare her or cause her to pull back.

But the feel of her tongue stroking him while her mouth wrapped him in moist heat was almost more pleasure than he could bear.

No woman had ever done this to him before. It was something a man didn't ask a lady to do for him, and yet she had done it on her own.

Aye, he loved her boldness. Her curiosity.

Most of all he loved her.

He ran his bound hands through her hair and reveled in the feel of her. She sucked and teased him to the heights of pleasure, until he was nearly bursting.

Then suddenly she pulled away and stared up at him. "I want you inside me, Ewan."

"Straddle my waist."

She did as he asked.

Arching his back, Ewan guided her hips to his.

Without undressing, Nora slid herself slowly onto him.

They moaned in unison.

Ewan took her hand into his and led it to his lips so that he could nibble her fingertips as she gently rode him.

It was so strangely evocative for her to make love to him while his hands were tied and she was still fully dressed. Her bare thighs burned against his hips as she writhed above him.

He was at her mercy, and she was in control of their pleasure.

He would never have imagined the thrill this gave him.

Nora watched him watch her as she ground herself against him. "You feel so good inside me," she breathed. "I think I can feel you all the way to my womb."

Ewan moaned at her words and at the thought of his seed taking root there. He had long ago given up the hope of a wife and children.

But as he watched her, he wanted those things now. He wanted to see her belly grow with his child. Wanted to hold her in his arms as she suckled his baby.

He could imagine no better paradise.

She came calling his name.

Ewan thrust himself against her, then growled as his own release came swiftly and carried him away to a place that only Nora had ever shown him.

She collapsed on top of him, carefully avoiding his wound. "What is it about you that makes me crave you so?" she asked innocently.

"I know not, my lady, I only pray that whatever it is, you never grow immune to it."

She smiled at that and slid herself off him.

They cleaned themselves and then Nora helped redress him.

He settled down near the horse on the damp ground. Nora lay down beside him and cuddled close.

She went to sleep while mumbling to him about the stars.

Ewan watched her as she slept on him, but his own sleep didn't come. He didn't dare let it.

So he lay for hours, listening to the night, grateful that the MacKaids hadn't found them.

At least not yet.

Every time he dared to doze, he immediately came awake with a jerk.

As dawn approached, he heard the sound of footsteps approaching.

Chapter 11

"Nora," Ewan breathed, shaking her awake.

She woke up slowly. "Aye?"

"Someone's coming."

She jerked up instantly. "Where?"

Ewan indicated the direction with a tilt of his head. He pushed himself to his feet, then hid her behind a shrub.

He grabbed a limb from the ground and waited in the early dawn light for whoever it was to show himself. It was a poor weapon, and his hands were bound in such a way that he held it awkwardly. Even so, he planned to make good use of it.

The footsteps drew closer.

Closer . . .

He lifted the branch.

It sounded as if someone stumbled, and then a curse rang out. "Oh bloody hell, that hurt!"

Laughing at the words, Ewan breathed a sigh of relief as he heard Viktor's irate voice.

"Shh, Viktor, you'd wake the dead," Cat said, but Ewan still couldn't see either one of them for the thick foliage that surrounded him.

"Catarina?" Ewan called.

The gypsies broke through the forest into the small clearing in front of him.

Catarina smiled triumphantly. "See. I told you he would head north. Only a fool would head back to the village knowing someone was after them. And Ewan is anything but a fool."

Ewan tossed the limb aside as Nora came out of her hiding spot.

Catarina rushed to Nora and gave her a hug while Viktor stood back, his face showing the relief Ewan felt.

"What are you two doing here?" Nora asked. "Not that we're not thrilled to see you. But how did you find us?"

"The finding was easy. The MacKaids left a large trail to follow," Catarina said. "We found them not long after the two of you had escaped them. They were plotting a way to retake you once they reached the village. Since we were coming from the village and hadn't seen you, I knew you had to be going north to avoid them.

"I then had Lysander and Bavel backtrack so that they could pretend to be you to lead the MacKaids away from your trail while Viktor and I continued to search for you."

"Pretend to be us?" Nora asked.

Catarina laughed. "We shall have to make it up to Bavel that he's wearing a gown and your brat."

Viktor agreed. "I'm sure the MacKaids

won't get close enough to realize they're not you, and even if they do, Pagan is trailing behind them to catch any of them in case they do become smart and think to divide. Once they reach the village again, Lysander will bribe the villagers to verify that they were you and had passed through. Knowing Lysander as I do, I'm sure he can accomplish this rather well."

Ewan held his tied hands out to Viktor, "May I borrow a dagger?"

Viktor pulled the dagger from his waist and sliced through the ropes.

Ewan winced as his wrists stung even more from their release. Still, it was good to be free again.

Nora gasped as she looked at his wrists. They were bloodied and chafed with large bruises all around. "Oh, Ewan. First your side and now this. I honestly can't imagine how you can stand the pain of it."

She looked to Catarina. "Cat, have you anything we can put on his wrists? And I'll be needing a needle and thread to stitch his side."

"Are you hurt?" Viktor asked.

"Graham stabbed him," Nora said before Ewan had a chance. "And it hasn't been properly tended."

Catarina motioned for them to follow her. "Come, I should have something in the wagon."

They walked through the woods until they reached the wagon that had been left behind once the woods became too dense for it to pass easily.

Ewan paused as he caught sight of the short, lean man sitting on the back of the wagon in the open doorway.

His blood ran cold.

It was Ryan.

He sat at the back with a snide smirk on his face as his legs dangled down.

Personally, Ewan would have rather seen Graham or one of his brothers waiting for them.

"Ryan!" Nora gasped, rushing toward him.

She pulled Ryan into a fierce hug and squeezed him tight.

The sight of it cut through Ewan.

"I thought you were dead!" she said excitedly before she kissed him happily on the cheek. "Oh, thank the Lord for His mercy."

Ewan felt as though someone had dealt him a staggering blow. He hadn't wanted the man dead, but . . .

"Careful," Ryan snapped, pushing her back. "They damned near did kill me, and I fear my stomach shall never be the same again."

Nora disregarded him and his surly warning. "I'm just so happy *I* didn't kill you."

"As am I," Ryan concurred. "Though to be honest, I feel as though I've died and been sent to hell where the devil torments me with constant pain."

Catarina stepped past Ryan and fetched a pot of salve out of the wagon. She brought it over to Ewan.

Angry and hurt, he spread the salve over his bleeding and torn wrists, which throbbed and ached unmercifully.

Nora seemed to have forgotten all about him while she chatted with Ryan about *his* injuries.

And why shouldn't she?

Ryan was her betrothed.

Ryan would be her husband.

By the way she was acting, it was what she wanted. Nothing like near death to make a woman realize where her affections truly lay . . .

Nora paused in her fussing over Ryan. She looked back to see Ewan with Catarina.

There was a pinched look to Ewan's features. A pain in his eyes that hadn't been there before.

She left Ryan to check on him. "Are you all right?"

"Fine."

She looked down at his raw wrists that were now covered in white salve. "Do they hurt overmuch?"

He shook his head, then handed the cream back to Cat.

Nora reached for Catarina's sewing basket.

"Here, you go lie down and I'll —"

"I think it best that we get moving," Ewan said, interrupting her, his tone deep and clipped. "Viktor, hand me your sword. I'll take the seat on the wagon since I know this area best."

Viktor nodded and unstrapped his sword from his hips, then handed it over.

"Ewan," Nora said, her voice thick with warning. "You are wounded."

His tone was curt and cold. "I'll live."

Whatever was wrong with him?

She glanced back to where Ryan was glaring at Ewan.

Surely Ewan didn't think . . .

Nay. Ewan had to have more sense than that. He couldn't be jealous over Ryan the Toad. Surely he realized the only reason she'd gone to Ryan was that she was relieved he hadn't died because of her.

Nora started for the front of the wagon.

"You need to be in the back, Nora," Ewan said sharply. "We'll move quicker that way."

"How so?"

"Just get in the back." His gruff tone offended her. She hadn't seen him like this since the first day they'd been together.

Where was her gentle bear?

Her feelings hurt, she did as he said.

Fine. If he wanted to go off and sulk, so be it. They'd have to stop soon and eat. By then he should be more level-headed and she would check and clean his wound then.

If he wanted to be a baby until then, so be it.

Viktor went to ride with Ewan while she, Catarina and Ryan rode in the back.

As soon as they were settled inside, Ewan clicked at the team of horses and got them into motion.

"How did you find Ryan?" Nora asked Catarina as they took comfortable positions on the wagon's floor.

"He came out of the tavern wounded and was babbling for someone to help him get to you."

Nora could imagine what a spectacle Ryan must have been. The man hated to make a scene more than anything and yet he had made one for her. It was probably the kindest thing Ryan had ever done for anyone. She might not like him, but that went a long way in assuaging some of the nastier things he had done to her over the years.

"Thank you, Ryan."

He inclined his head to her. "I'm just sorry I wasn't more adept at protecting you to begin with. Believe me."

"But at least you tried."

Ryan was silent while Nora talked to Catarina about what they should do to avoid the MacKaids and every other topic.

Ryan lay back in the wagon, moaning every time he took a breath about how much pain he was in and how neither of them understood the grueling misery that was his stomach.

Nora didn't comment. Instead, her thoughts were on the man who was driving the wagon. The one whose side was unstitched and whose wrists were still raw.

The man who said nothing at all about his pain.

Inside or out.

They rode for hours without stopping to break their fast. It was almost midday before Ewan finally reined the horses.

He helped Nora down, then left Catarina for Viktor.

Nora tried to speak to him, but Ewan refused.

Without a word or backward glance, he returned to the horses to care for them.

Angry at his behavior, Nora went to him. "Why are you being so cold toward me?"

"I'm not being cold toward you."

"Nay? Then why do I get a shiver every time you meet my gaze? Or should I say *when* you meet my gaze, which all of a sudden isn't often."

He glanced past her shoulder to where Ryan watched them with an arched, curious brow. "Ryan is wounded. You need to see to him."

Understanding floored her. "You're jealous?"

"I'm not jealous, Nora. Believe me."

"Then what are you?"

"I'm angry."

Ewan clenched his teeth, unable to believe he'd allowed that to escape.

"What have you to be angry over?"

Fate. Destiny.

Everything that kept him from being able to claim her for his own.

Everything that made Ryan more appealing to her than he was.

"Just leave me alone."

She reached to touch him.

Ewan wanted that touch so badly that for a moment, he couldn't move.

He waited for it. Desperate. Needful.

But he had no right to that, either.

He moved away from her.

"Ewan, please speak to me. Don't push me away."

Though it ruptured his heart, Ewan ignored her plea. He had to.

If he didn't . . .

He brushed past Ryan roughly, and went to tend private matters in the forest.

Nora watched Ewan leave and felt a profound urge to follow after him and beat him with a branch until he shaped up and talked to her.

"He loves you."

She blinked at Ryan's voice. "What did you say?"

"He loves you, doesn't he?"

"What makes you think that?"

Ryan sighed. "The expression on his face when he looks at you and the hatred in his eyes when he walked past me just now. I half expected him to strike me."

Nora gazed at the forest where Ewan had vanished. How she wished she could see inside his heart for a minute to find out how he felt about anything. "I know not what he feels. I only know he is a stubborn, aggravating man."

"A stubborn, aggravating man that you're in love with as well."

She frowned at Ryan.

"Don't bother lying, Nora," he said gently. "I've known you every day of your life. There's something about you that brightens whenever he's near you."

She scoffed at the very idea. "There is not."

"Aye, but there is. You fair glow with it." A muscle worked in Ryan's jaw. "You never glow around me unless it's your face turning red because you're angry at me."

"Then will you forget our betrothal?"

Ryan's face hardened, and when he met her gaze, the steely, determined look made her heart ache.

"I can't, Nora. I'm in debt too deeply. Some of these men will kill me if I don't pay what I owe. I'm sorry."

She looked away as her heart broke a little more. "So am I, Ryan. So am I."

It took them three days to make it to Lochlan's keep. Ewan didn't speak to her at all, even though Nora did everything she could to engage him in conversation.

He wouldn't even look at her.

He acted as if she didn't exist at all, and every time he refused to address her or even look at her, her heart ached more. What would it take to make the man be reasonable again?

"Nay," Catarina had said when she had told the gypsy of her feelings. "He acts as if the sight of you is more than he can bear. He knows Ryan has a claim on you, and it's tearing him apart."

Nora prayed that wasn't true.

But in the event it was, she set about making Ryan's life miserable. She chattered endlessly every time he came near her. She played her lute until he begged and threatened her to stop. She did everything she could think of to unnerve him.

And more times than not, she would send Ryan off in a hurry within minutes of his drawing close to her.

"Release me from the betrothal," Nora had asked him repeatedly.

His only answer was the ever steadfast "I can't."

And so it went until she was ready to scream.

Now as they neared the end of the journey, she watched Ewan atop the wagon while she rode on a horse beside him. He kept his eyes focused straight ahead, and yet she had a sneaking suspicion that he knew exactly where she was and what she was doing.

"I suppose you'll be glad to be rid of me," she said to him as he tried to ignore her. "You'll be able to go back to your cave now."

He didn't respond.

"I'll be glad to have a bed again," Ryan whined from where he rode behind her. "I fear my stomach has been damaged eternally. This pace the last few days has nigh killed me."

'Twas a pity Lochlan lived so close.

Nora! She chastised herself.

How uncharitable!

It was, but at the same time, she couldn't bring herself to feel more kindly toward the man who was about to ruin her only chance at happiness.

She'd lost one man to another woman.

Now she was going to lose Ewan because of his honor.

Och, men and their honor. They were quite beastly about it when they wanted to be. Oh for the day when they would let love rule them and not their stupid code of nobility.

She sighed wistfully as she watched him.

Please, God, please help him to see that I need him as much as he needs me.

They rode silently through the gates of Lochlan's castle, only to be pulled into full-scale pandemonium.

Her parents, Lysander, Pagan, Bavel and Ewan's entire family were all gathered in the bailey, and not a one of them looked any too pleased.

Nora wanted to turn her horse about and ride straight to England alone.

Only the fact that they closed the gate behind her kept her from it.

She could tell by the tenseness of Ewan's body that he had much the same inclination, but true to his character, he headed straight for the maelstrom.

On the steps outside the castle's door was a short, dark-haired woman who looked so much like Ewan that Nora was certain it was his mother. Two black-haired men flanked her, and by their heights and proximity to the woman, she assumed them to be two of Ewan's brothers.

One was dark and deadly, his stare sinister. Judging by rumor, she would assume him to be Sin MacAllister, who had married the lairdess of the MacNeely clan. A beautiful redheaded lady stood beside him. Her noble stance confirmed her station. No doubt she was Caledonia of the Clan MacNeely — a distant cousin to Nora whom she had never met.

The other dark-haired man was so handsome that to look at him was to ache. He was truly perfection, and the woman to his side was surrounded by children. Her red hair wasn't as vibrant as Caledonia's, and her features leaned toward plainness.

But when she nudged Braden and he looked to her, the love on his face said that he thought her to be the most beautiful woman on earth.

It made her own heart ache. Not long ago Ewan had held such a look when he glanced at her.

Catarina gave a low whistle. "Who is that man standing next to Alex?"

Nora looked to her father and saw the man Catarina had noticed. He was tall, blond and extremely handsome.

Frighteningly so.

"That be my brother Lochlan," Ewan answered for her. "Sin is to the right of my mother, who is on the steps, and Braden to the left. Braden's wife, Maggie, is the lass surrounded by children, and Caledonia, Sin's wife, is by his side."

Nora was pleased that she had pegged them correctly.

"You have brothers most handsome, Ewan," Catarina said, her voice filled with awe.

"So they tell me."

Nora realized that for the first time in days, Ewan was watching her.

He drove the wagon to the steps, then stopped and locked the wooden brake.

As soon as she reined her horse in, her father and mother came rushing to her side. Even though she was frightened by what might happen, she was glad to see her parents again.

"Are you all right?" her father asked as he helped her from her horse. His handsome brow was crimped with worry as he ran his gaze over her as if seeking an injury.

Nora soaked in the sight of her father. He was only slightly taller than she, with a stout build. His thick beard was the same golden blond as his hair and his brown eyes managed to look both relieved and angry.

"I am fine, Father. Truly."

He pulled her from the saddle, gathered her into his arms and held her closely. Nora was speechless. It was so unlike her father to ever be emotional. He'd always acted as if she were a fragile flower who would be crushed by his touch.

And crushed by his touch was definitely how she felt at present.

Her mother's pale blue eyes were filled with tears as her lips trembled. "Welcome home, precious," she said, removing Nora's father from her and grabbing her into a hug of her own.

Then, to her further astonishment, her father turned toward Ryan, who had dismounted and ambled over to them.

He glared at him, and for a minute she thought him angry. Then his face softened. "And you, lad, I was completely wrong about you."

To her utter stupefaction, he embraced Ryan like a long-lost son and pounded him on the back.

Ryan choked and sputtered as if unable to withstand her father's strength.

Still her father pounded on him. "Lysander told me how you were almost mortally wounded for my Nora. Thank you."

Nora looked at Ewan, whose face was unreadable. At least to anyone other than her. She saw the tightness around his lips. The emptiness of his eyes.

Without a word, he climbed down from the wagon and headed for the donjon.

His mother spoke to him, but he ignored her and kept walking.

His brothers fell in behind him, and none spoke while she was barraged with questions from her parents, and Lysander, Pagan and Bavel greeted Catarina and Viktor.

Ewan needed a drink. A large one.

But in his heart, he knew it would take more than an ocean of ale to drown the pain he felt.

"What happened, Ewan?" Lochlan asked from behind him.

"Nothing." He stopped at the cabinet outside the pantry and pulled out a pitcher of ale, along with a goblet.

He cursed as he saw every member of his family behind him. His mother's face was worried and pinched while his brothers all looked ready to fight him.

His sisters-in-law excused themselves and made for the stairs.

Grateful for their kindness, Ewan poured himself a drink.

"Nothing?" Braden repeated. "Alexander Canmore has been here for two days now wanting to know what you've done with his daughter. He's been threatening war and dismemberment at every turn should she not appear unscathed, and yet you say nothing happened."

Ewan downed the goblet of ale, poured more, then turned and glared at Braden before he downed the second cup. "I don't want to hear it from a man who tricked his daughter and then forced her to run to me. If Alexander was so worried for her welfare, he should have kept her home where she belonged."

"What are you saying?" Lochlan asked, his face skeptical.

Ewan gestured angrily with his goblet toward the door. "It's true. You can ask the gypsy lass, Catarina, yourself. Canmore wanted to align his family with ours and sought to trick her and me."

Ewan laughed bitterly at that. "But the trick it seems is on him since he promised her to Ryan, who won't release her from the betrothal. So you see, it was all a buggering waste of time."

"Ewan!" his mother snapped. "You watch your mouth."

He clenched his teeth and bit back the nasty retort he longed to utter. Angry though he was, he wouldn't hurt his mother by his nastiness.

Ewan started to pour more ale, but Lochlan stopped him by covering the goblet with his hand.

Lochlan gave a hard stare at Sin, Braden and their mother. "Could you leave us alone?"

They withdrew reluctantly.

Lochlan took the goblet from him.

Ewan growled, but as usual his brother ignored him and pushed his hand away when he sought to reclaim the goblet.

"I need you sober a bit longer to explain this to me. Her father is outside ready to tear this clan apart and to bring the kings of both Scotland and England down on our heads unless you do right by his daughter. Now tell me why it is she has been traveling alone with you."

Ewan glared at his older brother. He didn't need this lecture and he hated being toyed with. Alexander's plan had been ill laid, and now all he wanted was time alone to forget his part in the whole debacle. "I told you everything."

"You've told me nothing."

"Ewan?"

Ewan closed his eyes and clenched his teeth at the sound of his name on Nora's lips. It tore through him.

He couldn't face her now. Not here in this hall where he had once fought Kieran over possession of Isobail.

He picked up the pitcher of ale and headed toward the stairs. "I want to be alone."

He had barely taken a step before Nora rushed forward and planted herself firmly in his path.

He felt his jaw twitch at her actions. "Move, Nora."

She stood there unflinching with her hands on her hips. "Or what?"

"I'll move you out of my way."

She lifted her chin defiantly as she obviously braced herself to face him. "You wouldn't dare."

Tired, angry, heartbroken and filled with physical and mental agony, he was in no mood for her challenges.

Setting the ale aside, he faced her. He

knew his mother, brothers and her parents were watching them, but he was past the point of caring.

Damn all of them.

And damn anyone who got between him and those stairs . . .

Nora gasped as Ewan actually tossed her over his shoulder and headed away from the stairs.

"What are you doing?" her father demanded.

"I'm removing the obstacle from my path." Ewan sat her down in Lochlan's padded chair by the hearth.

Nora sat stunned for a moment, unable to believe he had done this.

Granted, he had set her down easily, but still.

How dare he!

"You're bleeding again," Nora gasped as he moved away from her, and headed back toward his ale.

"Aye, I know, and all I want is to lie down and drink."

She stiffened. "You can't drink while lying down."

He cast her a feral glare over his shoulder, grabbed the pitcher and headed for the stairs.

This time it was Lochlan who blocked his way.

Ewan sighed disgustedly. "Will I have to

move you one by one?"

"Why are you bleeding?"

"Graham stabbed him," Nora explained as she rejoined them by the stairs. "Ewan has refused to let anyone tend the wound for days."

"I don't need your coddling," Ewan snarled.

He shoved Lochlan aside roughly.

Lochlan caught his arm and pulled him away from the stairs.

Ewan swung at him, but the pain from his arm was such that he staggered back from it.

The next thing he knew, Lochlan had his hand on his forehead. "You're burning with fever."

Ewan struggled to breathe. He just wanted to lie down and forget the past week with Nora.

He wanted the pain inside him to stop.

All he felt was agony. Bitter and aching, it tore through him.

Nora was lost to him.

Honestly, he just wanted to die.

Knocking Lochlan's hand away, he took a step and felt the room spin out from under him.

Nora gasped as Ewan sank to the floor. The pitcher skittered across the cobblestones as he knelt down, and his mother rushed toward him.

He collapsed a moment later.

Nora joined them at his side, only to find him completely unconscious.

"Ewan!" Lochlan shouted, trying to shake his brother awake.

Ewan didn't respond at all.

Nora pushed Ewan's shirt up to see the wound in his side. It was red and swollen with infection.

"You stubborn man," she snarled at him. "You couldn't stand to let me help you, and now look what you've done. I swear, Ewan MacAllister, if you don't die from your stupidity I shall kill you for it."

"Out of the way, woman," Sin MacAllister said rudely, pushing her aside.

He and Lochlan carried Ewan upstairs.

Without thought, Nora followed after them while her parents stayed below.

Sin and Lochlan took Ewan into a room at the top of the stairs and laid him gently on the bed.

Their mother came forward, her brow worried. "Why wasn't the wound stitched?"

Nora's throat tightened at her innocent question. "I had nothing to stitch it with the first night and after that, he wouldn't allow me to even see it, let alone tend it."

Sin cut Ewan's shirt off while Lochlan turned toward her. "You need to be leaving now, lass. It's not proper for you to be here when we disrobe him."

"But . . ." Nora caught herself before she

told them that she had seen him bare. No doubt Ewan was in enough trouble; she wouldn't make it any worse on him. "I shall wait outside."

She found herself quickly ousted.

Both her parents were waiting in the hallway.

"How does he?" her father asked.

Nora chewed her fingernail in fearful worry. "I know not. He's not spoken of the wound since it happened."

"He didn't act wounded when he arrived," her mother said.

"Aye," Nora agreed. "He handles his pain well."

Her heart heavy, she looked up at her father. "How could you do this to us, Father? How could you have manipulated me into running to him?"

He opened his mouth, snapped it shut, then sighed. "You're a lovely lass, Nora. I wanted a good match for you and thought that if I could get the two of you together, Ewan would see what a fine wife you'd make."

"And Ryan?"

"I thought that once you ran off with another man, Ryan would recant his offer. I had no idea how much he really loved you."

She duplicated Ewan's feral growl at that. If she heard those words one more time she was going to seriously hurt someone.

"Ryan doesn't love me!"

"Not true," her mother said. "While you spoke to your father outside he told me how much he feared for you and that the whole reason he paid the gypsies to abduct Ewan was so that he could return you home before he harmed you. He was worried about you, Nora."

Nora started to tell them what a liar Ryan was, but she bit the words back. At the end of the day, her parents looked on him as a son. She wouldn't destroy that for them or for Ryan.

Yet.

But if she were forced to this, she would decry him from the tallest tree.

"I don't want to marry Ryan."

Her mother glanced to the door. "Would you rather have Ewan?"

Tears gathered in her eyes as she nodded. "More than anything."

Her father smiled. "Then I shall see what needs be done."

"If he'll have me, you mean."

Her father looked offended by that. "And why wouldn't he?"

Nora bit her lip as she thought about Ryan below. Ewan would never agree to marriage with her as long as he believed Ryan loved her.

She knew that.

The question was, could she ever make Ryan tell the truth?

Chapter 12

Nora spent days sitting by Ewan's bed. He lay in delirium, his body ravaged by fever. They bathed him repeatedly, trying to bring the fever down, but it was of little use.

It seemed he would never come back to them. And every day that passed without his eyes opening, Nora despaired more.

He had to wake up. She couldn't bear the thought of losing him over this.

His brothers took turns helping her and his mother watch over him, but as the days went by she began to fear he would never awaken again.

Her nervousness made her chatter more to him. Coaxing him to eat and drink. Begging him to wake up and look at her.

Bellow at her even.

She would give anything to hear one of his bearish growls.

Only when they were alone did she dare speak to him of her love. Tell him how much she needed him to come back to her.

"He whispers your name."

She looked up from her sewing to see Lochlan watching her from his seat by the window as she sat by Ewan's side.

Lochlan had relieved Sin barely five minutes ago, and she had been grateful. There was something very sinister and dark about Sin MacAllister. If not for his endearing love of his wife and small baby, she would have been terrified of him. But since her arrival she had seen enough of his tenderness with them to know he wasn't as fierce as he appeared.

Braden she liked a great deal. He was ever charming a smile or laugh from her while they watched over Ewan. And he had told her numerous stories of youthful pranks he had pulled on Ewan.

But when it came to Lochlan . . .

There was something very stern and sad about this particular MacAllister, and he made her terribly uncomfortable.

The only time she saw a break in his seriousness was when Catarina nettled him. Which was a habit the gypsy had taken to right away.

Lochlan was a young man to wield such power and authority, and she wondered if he ever found the burden oppressive.

"I know," she said in response to his words.

"Can you tell me why?"

"Most likely because he wants to wake up and tell me to spare his ears while he heals."

Lochlan's face softened a degree. "He can be a bit overbearing."

"Not really. He is rather charming, point of fact."

Lochlan arched a brow at her declaration. "You think so?"

"Aye. He's very gentle and sweet."

Lochlan choked. "Ewan? Sweet? The devil you say. The man is surly at best."

"He is not surly . . . often. He's just sensitive."

His handsome face was aghast at her words. "My lady, I fear you are the one who is delirious if you believe that. There's nothing sensitive about him."

Her anger was fired by his words.

How dare he say such a thing!

"You don't know your brother very well, do you, my lord?" She reached out and touched Ewan's hot hands. Hands that had made her want to weep with pleasure.

Hands she would sell her soul to be able to hold on to for the rest of eternity.

"You love him." Lochlan's deep voice rang out in the stillness of the room.

It was a statement of fact.

Nora didn't bother to lie. "Aye, I do."

"Does he know it?"

"I've never hidden the fact."

She felt the weight of Lochlan's gaze. It was heavy. Frightening.

Discerning. "Does he love you?"

She sighed weakly. "I think so. But with Ewan, one never knows really where one stands."

Lochlan leaned forward in his chair. "Nora, look at me."

She did.

Lochlan's stern gaze didn't falter or waver. It was intense and oppressive.

"Did he . . . did you . . ." He looked greatly uncomfortable, and she knew what he was asking.

Her face flamed, and she looked away without answering.

Lochlan cursed. "Your father will have his head for it."

"My father will never know, and if you say a word, Lochlan MacAllister, I will deny it."

Lochlan actually smiled at her. "You would protect my brother?"

"Always."

The smile crept up his face, all the way to his eyes, turning them a gentle, friendly blue instead of their normal iciness. "Ewan is a lucky man to have found you."

She frowned at his unexpected comment.

Lochlan excused himself and left her alone with Ewan.

Nora stared at his pale features. His sweat-dampened hair was plastered to his skin.

Setting her sewing aside, she moved to fetch a cloth to bathe his brow.

"I wish you would wake up, Ewan," she

said as she always did when she tended him alone. "I miss seeing your crystal blue eyes, hearing your fierce growl when you get aggravated at me. Mostly I just miss you."

His eyes fluttered opened, shocking her.

Nora gasped at the sight.

For a second she feared he was still gripped by his fever-induced madness, but his gaze was clear and sensible.

He frowned, then tried to sit up.

"Nay!" she said, forcing him back. "You shouldn't be moving."

His frown grew sterner. He glanced around the room, then looked under the sheet. His face perplexed, he looked at her. "Why are you here in my brother's home while I lay naked in his bed?"

She laughed at him, giddy with relief that he was awake and still his surly self.

Before she could respond, the door opened to admit his mother and brother Sin.

The instant they realized he was awake and alert, the two of them rushed forward.

"So he lives," Sin said, his voice relieved, his dark eyes bright.

Aisleen took Ewan's hand and pressed it to her lips. "Praise be to God. I had feared I would lose another son."

Nora wanted to stay, but as Braden, Maggie and Caledonia burst into the room with their children, she realized she didn't belong there.

Though she might wish it otherwise, she wasn't Ewan's family. They were.

Turning around, she made her way quietly toward the stairs.

Once she was on the ground floor, she saw Lochlan, who was just leaving the great hall, and headed for the stairs behind her.

Worry creased his brow. "Did something happen? You haven't left Ewan's side since he took ill."

"He's awake."

His face delighted, Lochlan bolted for the stairs.

Nora smiled in his wake, then moved to where her mother sat in the great hall by the hearth.

"How does he?" her mother asked.

"I think he shall live after all. He seems quite well. Where is Father?"

"He's outside with Ryan."

Nora felt strange. She wasn't quite sure what to do with herself now that Ewan was awake again. She'd been so focused on his getting better that she hadn't really contemplated what his recovery would herald for her.

Now she did.

Would he keep her or force her to marry Ryan?

Her heart shriveled.

Knowing him as she did, there was very little doubt what he would choose.

And God have mercy on them both when he did.

"Where did Nora go?" Ewan asked, looking around the crowd gathered at his bed.

"She was below a moment ago," Lochlan said.

Ewan started to get up to find her, but Sin stopped him. "You've been ill for almost a fortnight, little brother. The last thing you need is to get up and walk."

"I . . ." He paused as he remembered everything that had happened.

Ryan — the bastard who would not die.

Ewan sat back as reality came crashing down upon him.

"Nora was a blessing to us these days past," his mother said. "She watched over you like an angel. Ever vigilant and kind."

Ewan turned his head toward her to see her thankful smile. "What do you mean?"

"She hasn't left your side," Maggie said.

Ewan thought back to the way Nora had cared for him after he'd been wounded.

The way she'd run off to Ryan . . .

"Would you like for me to go fetch her?" Braden asked.

Ewan shook his head. "I would rather you fetch me something to eat and then leave me in peace."

"He must be feeling better," Sin said. "Already he wants his solitude."

His family gave their good wishes and love, then left him alone with Lochlan.

Ewan looked at his brother, then meaningfully at the door. "Why are you still here?"

"I want to make sure you don't do anything foolish."

"Such as?"

"Withdraw back into yourself while there's a beautiful woman downstairs who loves you."

Ewan snorted at that while inside he could actually feel his heart shriveling from the mere thought of losing her. "What do you know of it?"

"Nothing, truly. I've never been blessed with a woman's love. But if I were, I'd make certain that I kept it."

Ewan snorted. It was much easier for a man to give advice than to take it.

The giving of it cost Lochlan nothing, but should Ewan yield to it, the results could be disastrous.

"Aye, but at what cost?"

"What do you mean?"

"She is promised to another, Lochlan. A man who loves her and who has said repeatedly that he will not let her go. His clan will feud with ours if I take her from him. I already caused one feud and killed my brother over such a thing. Think you I want to kill another man?"

"Ewan —"

"Leave me!" he roared.

Lochlan tensed, then turned about and left.

Alone, Ewan let his thoughts drift over the last few days with Nora. Over the happiness that she had brought into his dismal world.

His gaze fell to the embroidery that lay on his bed. Picking it up, he frowned. It was the image of a troubadour playing the lute with a lady.

His fingers shook as he traced the picture.

How could he let her go?

"I beg your pardon, Lochlan MacAllister, you are not my lord and master!"

Nora watched as Catarina started for the door, and Lochlan caught her arm in his hand. "Would you listen to me?"

Catarina childishly covered her ears with her hands and hummed. Loudly.

Lochlan appeared ready to throttle her.

"What are they fighting over now?" she asked her mother.

Her mother shrugged. "They have done nothing but argue since they met. Poor Catarina can't stand him."

As Catarina stormed outside with Lochlan trailing after her, Nora's father and Ryan came in.

Ryan appeared completely recovered from his wound.

"Is Ewan better?" Ryan asked.

Nora nodded. She still didn't want to speak to the ogre.

"Nora," her father said. "Ryan and I have come to an understanding. If Ewan makes an offer for your hand, Ryan will stand aside."

Unexpected joy filled her.

Until she thought better of it.

"And if Ewan doesn't?" she asked.

Ryan wagged his brows at her. "You're mine, Nora. To have and to hold until death we do part."

As Ryan spoke those words, she saw Ewan coming into the hall. He paused and looked at them darkly.

If she lived out eternity, Nora would never forget the look on his face as he heard Ryan's declaration.

She wanted to curse at his timing.

"Ewan?" she asked. "What are you doing up?"

He didn't speak. He just turned about and started back for the stairs.

Nora rushed to his side.

Ewan handed her the embroidery cloth she'd left in his room. "I thought you might have need of it," he said simply, his voice and eyes empty.

"Let me help you back to bed."

He curled his lips at her. "I don't need any help. Go back to your betrothed."

"Ewan," she said insistently, "Ryan has

agreed to release me if you want me."

He glanced back at Ryan.

"It's true," Ryan said as he joined them. "I will not stand between the two of you."

Ewan wanted to laugh at those haunting words.

Fate was indeed mocking him.

Instead, he heard the sound of his mother's shocked gasp as she came into the room and heard words that were almost identical to the ones Kieran had once said in this very same hall.

Take her, Ewan, if she'll have the likes of you. I willna stand between the two of you. But know that if you leave with her, I will never again call you brother.

He wondered if Ryan was as sincere as Kieran had been when Kieran had spoken those words to him.

Or would Ryan ride home, gather his men, and then start the feud he'd promised?

In his mind's eye, Ewan saw the death and destruction that had reigned over the Mac-Allister lands as they fought with the Mac-Douglases.

Wincing from the pain of the memory of then and the reality of now, he turned away from the face of the only woman he would ever really love.

"She belongs with you, Ryan. I have no need of a wife."

Nora felt as if Ewan had slapped her.

Nothing had ever hurt her more than his cold announcement.

"I was wrong about you, Ewan Mac-Allister," she said, her voice breaking on his name. "You are heartless and mean."

With a dignity she didn't feel, she lifted her chin and returned to her parents. "I wish to leave."

"Now?" her father asked.

"Aye. I'll go with you or on my own, but I willna stay in this place another instant."

Ewan couldn't breathe as he heard her words.

She was leaving him.

You told her to go.

Aye, he had. It was kinder this way.

Why then did he feel as if his stomach and heart were being shredded?

Fight for her, damn you, fight!

But he didn't have it in him. He couldn't let his clan be torn apart.

Nora's parents said a quick and embarrassed goodbye to his mother while Nora stalked from the hall without even glancing back at him.

So be it.

He was better off without her.

And yet the thought of returning to his home alone made his blood run cold.

Ewan made his way up the stairs and to his bed. He had barely lain down before his brothers stormed into his room and surrounded his bed.

The three of them appeared angry and ready to battle.

"May I be the one who beats him?" Braden asked.

Ewan frowned at them. "Beats me for what?"

"Stupidity," Sin hissed.

Lochlan thumped Ewan on the arm. Hard.

Ewan grimaced and rubbed the sore spot his brother had caused. "Do that again and I shall rip your hand off."

Lochlan glared furiously at him. "Try it and I'll have your worthless hide for a rug before my hearth. Now tell me how you can be so foolish as to let her leave?"

Ewan ground his teeth as rage filled him. "What are you, daft? You do remember what happened the last time I took a woman from her betrothed, do you not?"

Lochlan pierced him with a feral glare. "Ryan is not Robby MacDouglas, nor is he Kieran."

Ewan said nothing.

"He's closed us out again," Braden said disgustedly. "He'll not hear a word we say."

"Then may I kill him?" Sin asked.

"Nay," Lochlan said, "I want the privilege."

Braden scoffed. "You're just angry that she took Catarina with her when she left."

Lochlan shoved at Braden. "Leave off that

line of taunting. I never want to hear that woman's name pronounced in my presence again."

"Out!"

All four men jumped at the sound of Aisleen MacAllister's commanding tone. "Leave your brother be, lads. He needs no more pestering from the likes of you."

Reluctantly they withdrew. But the combined looks on their faces warned him loudly that they would be back to pester him more.

"Thank you," Ewan said as silence once again claimed the room.

Then, to his utter shock, his mother came to the bed and smacked him hard across the side of his right hip.

"What was that for?" he asked, unable to believe she had done such a thing.

"I wish you were small enough that I could give you the spanking you deserve."

"Mother, I'm injured."

"Aye, and in the head to boot."

He was aghast at her. She'd never spoken to him in such a manner. "What has possessed you?"

"Anger mostly. I want to know why you let such a fine lass go off with that good-for-nothing. He'll only make her miserable, and well you know it. I canna believe you would do such a thing. Saints preserve me, but I thought I had raised you up better than this, and now I find out just how wrong I was."

She crossed herself and started praying for his lost and wayward soul.

Ewan gaped at her, unable to believe her and her actions. "*You* of all people would have me come between them?"

She broke off mid-prayer to glower at him for a full minute.

Then his mother sighed wearily and sat down on his bed. She sat there for several heartbeats, not moving or speaking.

He couldn't tell if she was really gathering her thoughts, or getting ready to hit him again.

When she spoke, he leaned away from her just in case her madness should again possess her.

"Ewan," she said as if the weight of the world were upon her, "I have tried all your life to bring happiness to you, and it saddens me that I have failed you so miserably."

"Mother —"

"Nay," she said, holding her hand up as she interrupted him. "Let me say my piece."

A faraway look came over her, as if she were remembering his childhood.

Ewan gave an involuntary shudder. If she remembered too much of his errant childhood, he really would be in trouble.

"Unlike your father and your brothers, I know why you are withdrawn. I've always known. Do you think I don't remember the way you looked when at age four you were too large for me to pick up and carry? You used to stare at me holding Braden, and I could see the hurt in your eyes."

He opened his mouth to deny it, but she silenced him by placing her hand over his lips.

"I would sit for hours and weep, wishing that I had been born larger so that I could take you into my arms and carry you about as you wanted. But it was too late. From that day forward, you pushed me and anyone else who would draw you in away from you. It broke my heart that you decided you had no use for me and my hugs."

"That's not true," he insisted, even though in his heart he knew it was. He'd always been wounded that his brothers seemed to get everything else while he was left on his own.

That was why Kieran had meant so much to him. Their father had taken up with Lochlan to the exclusion of the rest of them. Braden was favored by their mother, and Kieran had always doted on him.

Braden had forever picked at and harassed Ewan, while Lochlan lost patience with virtually everything he had ever said or done. Kieran alone had taken time to befriend him.

"Aye, it is true," his mother said. "Any time I have ever reached out to embrace you, you have tensed up and immediately moved away."

She stared intently at him. "You don't tense when Nora touches you, Ewan. When the two of you were in the hall below and you were fighting, I saw the way you looked at her. The need you had in your eyes when she reached for you."

Ewan stared at the wall as her words sank in and the pain of the past and present ran rampant through him.

"I know you were never happy when you lived here with us. Your father was ever cruel while you tried so hard to please him. He judged you harshly, and I won't make excuses for him. But he did love you, Ewan. The last words he spoke on this earth were about you."

"Because he didn't think I could care for myself."

"Nay, that was not what he said."

Ewan looked at her.

"He knew there at the end that he'd been too demanding on all of you. He'd tried so hard to make Lochlan strong enough to be laird, to make Kieran shoulder the burden of family. Braden to stand up to the rest of you so that the lot of you didn't run over him. Your father wanted me to find Sin and make amends to him for what we'd both done to him and you . . ."

Ewan held his breath as he waited.

"He wished that he had never let you hear his cruel criticisms. He regretted the times he wounded you with his words. The times he told you you disappointed him. You didn't disappoint him, Ewan. He was always proud of you."

Tears filled his eyes as he remembered what his father had said to him when he had come home to find Kieran dead.

His father had viciously backhanded him. *You disgust me. You stole what didn't belong to you, and you killed your own brother by doing it. Never again will I welcome you into my sight. You deserve nothing but my scorn.*

Embittered and grief-stricken, Ewan had left the MacAllister castle that day and had refused to ever set foot in it again until after his father's death.

He would never have returned at all had Lochlan and Braden not come after him and told him that their mother needed to see him.

That she was dying of her grief and that if he didn't return home with them, they would lose her as well.

And so he had come home, ever reluctant, back into their family fold. A missing part that had never really fit.

His mother leaned forward and kissed him on his forehead. "*I* have never blamed you for Kieran's death, Ewan. Never once. It is you alone who carries that in your heart, and if I could, I would exorcise it from you. I would give up my very soul to bring you peace and happiness."

She brushed a lock of hair back from his forehead. "Nora is a good lass, and she cares for you a great deal. 'Twould be a pity to live in a cave when you could just as easily live in comfort with a woman who loves you. But 'tis your life for you to make."

She patted him gently on the arm and got up to leave. "Sleep well, my son. If you can."

Chapter 13

Two weeks later

Nora stood outside the kirk, her broken heart pounding in trepidation and pain. She still couldn't believe that everyone was forcing her to do this.

Her parents.

Ryan.

Most of all, she couldn't believe Ewan would do this to the two of them.

Damn him!

Her eyes widened at the involuntary curse. Nay. Not involuntary. She was furious with him. He deserved that and more for his callous actions.

How could he have tossed her aside so easily?

May a pox roast his hoary soul!

By now he was probably back at his cave, lying in a drunken stupor, oblivious to the fact that she had ever loved him.

That she would spend the rest of her life pining away for him.

And why should she? He didn't deserve her devotion. He definitely didn't deserve her love.

What he deserved was a swift kick to his backside. One that left him limping for eternity, and if she ever saw him again, she would definitely deliver it to him.

And in a few minutes, she would be bound to Ryan for eternity.

She felt ill with the thought.

Even more so at the idea of doing with Ryan what she had done with Ewan. Of Ryan touching her, loving her . . .

A tear fell down her face.

"Shh," Catarina said from beside her as they waited for her father to lead her up to the kirk. She didn't know why the gypsies had stayed with them for so long, but she was glad they had.

She needed Catarina's strength to see this day through.

Lysander had been sent back three days ago to Nora's father's southern estate, which rested on the border of England and Scotland.

Pagan had gone farther north, toward the Hebrides, saying there was a matter he needed to investigate. But he had promised to return in a few weeks and check on her.

And if Ryan didn't give her the respect she deserved, he had vowed to make a widow of her.

One could only hope Pagan was a man of his word.

Tomorrow Catarina, Viktor and Bavel would leave as well.

Then she would be all alone as Ryan's bride.

Her stomach sank even more.

Was there no one who could save her from this madness?

She looked up at the sky, praying for some tragedy to befall her. Mayhap she could break her leg on her way to the altar and delay the events . . .

Nora glanced about the smooth pathway hopefully, but there was no help there, either.

She was doomed.

Catarina patted her arm affectionately. "Ewan will come for you, Nora. I know it."

How she wished she shared her friend's conviction.

"Nay, Cat. He's abandoned me. I meant nothing to him when compared with his honor." She spat that hated word. "That is all that matters to him. I just hope it keeps him warm in his old age."

Catarina gave her a knowing smile. "No real man would ever willingly let the woman he loves be touched by another man. He will come for you. Trust me."

It was a nice thought, but Nora didn't believe it for a minute.

Her father came forward to lead her to Ryan.

Please, let me break a leg or fall down dead.

It was all she could do not to turn around and run, screaming, through the village.

But no matter how distasteful this was, she wouldn't embarrass her father or herself.

So she walked woodenly toward the crowd that was gathered there to see this living nightmare fulfilled.

Ryan waited with a grim look on his face.

Run, Nora, run.

Her father's tight grip on her arm was the only thing that prevented it.

"Don't embarrass me, lass," he whispered under his breath as if he knew her thoughts.

Nora kept her gaze forward, focused on the gathered crowd. Ryan's plump mother was weeping in happiness. His father looked rather aggravated. The two of them stood off to the side, waiting for the moment when she would become their daughter.

They still didn't know how much money their son owed.

Not even she could bear to tell them. That was for Ryan to do.

Ryan stood at the door with the priest, but he refused to meet her gaze. He glanced at anything other than her as if ashamed of what he'd done.

And well he should be.

They paused in front of the priest.

Nora locked her legs together, afraid she was going to faint before this could be done.

She trembled as her father passed her hand from his arm into Ryan's hands. It was all she could do not to curl her lip.

Her father publicly renounced his ties to her and moved away from them. He went to stand next to her mother, who watched with misery burning bright on her beautiful face.

Her feelings were mirrored in Nora's tight belly.

"I'm sorry about this, Nora," Ryan whispered to her. "But I promise I'll make you a good husband."

Nora's thoughts whirled at his words and at the memory they evoked.

My wife . . .

A momentary slice of happiness slashed through her as a glimmer of hope appeared.

Something that just might save her.

Could she have found her reprieve?

Oh please, let this work.

The priest began the ceremony to bind them . . .

"Do you, Eleanor ingen Alexander of Canmore, take Ryan —"

"Wait!" she said, her heart pounding in fear and excitement. "May I ask a question?"

"Nora," her father's voice boomed. "This isn't the time for your curiosity."

She flashed him an impatient scowl. "But 'tis an important question, Father. *Really* important."

Ryan rolled his eyes and gave a long, disgusted sigh. "Best let her have at the asking, or we'll have no peace from her tongue."

She glared at him and fought down a

sudden urge to kick his shin.

"Ask your question, lass," the priest said charitably.

Drawing a deep breath, she spoke. "Can a woman marry one man while being handfasted to another?"

There was an audible intake of breath at her question.

The priest frowned. "Why would you ask that?"

"Nora," her mother said, her tone suspicious, "what are you saying?"

Nora squirmed a bit as she hoped this worked to her benefit. Ewan might not want her, but at least this would save her from being tied to Ryan.

"Well . . ." she began slowly. "Ewan told everyone that he was my husband while we were traveling."

"Aye," Catarina said, a smile breaking across her face as she caught on to Nora's plan. "I heard his proclamation myself. He said it proudly before an entire gathering of people."

"Aye," Viktor concurred. He indicated him and Bavel. "We heard it as well. You may check with any person who was there. Ewan made no pretense of hiding it."

The roar of the shocked crowd became deafening.

Ryan's father decried it as trickery. His mother sobbed uncontrollably.

"And where is this Ewan now?" the priest asked, having to shout to be heard over the cacophony.

Nora felt heat rush to her cheeks.

How did she tell the man that she had no idea?

"He's in the back of the crowd, bleeding," came a deep, rumbling English voice.

Nora couldn't breathe as she recognized the voice.

It belonged to Sin MacAllister!

Shaking now, she searched the crowd to find him. There at the very rear of those gathered was one man who towered over all the others.

It was Ewan, and he was flanked by his three brothers.

She smiled so widely that she had a good idea she looked foolish.

She didn't care.

Ewan elbowed Sin in the stomach for his announcement, then moved forward through the crowd that now parted before him like the Red Sea before Moses.

Ewan moved slowly, carefully.

Deliberately.

Nora wept at his approach. His face was pale, and he had a fine sheen of perspiration on his brow.

It was obvious that he was in pain, but why?

Surely his injury had healed.

"What are you doing here?" she asked as he climbed the stairs to stand by her side.

His eyes danced with love as he took her hands into his and kissed each one in turn. "I've come to claim my wife, if she'll agree to have a fool for her husband."

Joy exploded through her. He had come!

Catarina had been right.

Ewan had come for her . . .

But why had he waited so long?

Why had he put her through such torment?

'Twas cruel what he'd done, and had he waited another few minutes, she might have found herself Lady MacAren.

That didn't sit well with her.

In fact, it made her want to torment the man who had tortured her.

"Why did you wait so long to come?" she asked.

He brushed his finger down her cheek, raising chills all over her body. "The infection from my wound returned and I couldn't."

"He shouldn't be here now," Lochlan said as he stood at the foot of the stairs. "He's still too weak to travel, but when he learned you were to marry Ryan, he refused to stay abed. No doubt you'll be paying for this bout of stupidity as well."

Ignoring his brother's words, Ewan tipped her chin up so that she had no choice but to look up at him and see the fire in his blue eyes that devoured her.

"Run away with me, Nora," he breathed. "I'll take you anyplace you want to go. England. France. Rome. Outremer. You name it, and I'll gladly take you there."

Tears fell down her cheeks at his loving words. It was more than she could have asked for. "Anyplace?"

"Aye."

"Then I wish to take you to bed . . ."

Shocked gasps filled the crowd.

"To heal!" she said irritably as she glared at them as a whole. She shook her head at them. "What good would he be if dies of his wounds? Then I still end up married to Ryan. What good would that be?"

"I should be offended by that," Ryan said as the crowd laughed. "But she's said much worse to me than that over the years."

He clapped Ewan on the back. " 'Tis just as well, I would have more than likely killed her within a year anyway, or run off with another. Peace be with the two of you, Ewan and Nora, and may the saints in their mercy bring early hearing loss to all the MacAllisters."

Nora gaped at Ryan's words.

"Nay," Ewan said. "I want no deafness in my life to deprive me of the beauty of her voice."

She smiled up at him, then threw herself into his arms.

Ewan staggered back, and only Lochlan's quick actions kept him from falling with her.

"I'm sorry, Ewan," she breathed. "I forgot."

"I don't mind." By the happy look of his face, she could tell he meant that.

"So, do I need to retire from this?" the priest asked.

Ewan shook his head. "Nay, Father. You've a wedding to be about. I want no one to ever question my right to this lady again."

"Ewan," Lochlan growled. "You'll pass out before it's through."

"Then toss some water on my face, prop me up and make sure I say 'I do' when I need to."

Nora squeezed his hand as the priest began the ceremony.

Ewan listened to the priest while he stared in grateful relief at the woman before him.

He'd been terrified that they wouldn't make it in time. His body throbbed and burned in protest, but he didn't care.

Nora was his.

There was no way he would ever let her leave him again.

No way he would ever allow anyone else to come between them.

Luckily, he made it through the ceremony and Mass, but Nora refused to partake of the feast that awaited them.

Instead she forced him up to her room and into her bed.

Ewan sighed as he lay on the softness of her feather tick mattress and she fluttered about the room.

The walls of her room were painted soft pastels that were soothing and cheerful. Just like the lady herself.

Someone knocked on the door.

"Nora?"

Ewan recognized Catarina's voice.

Nora went to answer it while he closed his eyes and inhaled the pillows underneath his head. Pillows that smelled of flowers and woman.

Nora's scent.

It burned through his body, making him instantly hard for his wife.

His wife . . .

Even now he couldn't believe it. How had he been so lucky as to have her stumble into his life?

She rejoined him on the bed.

"What did Cat want?" he asked.

She bit her lip, then held up the dress she'd worn the night at the inn. "She thought you might want me to dance for you tonight."

Ewan forced himself up on his elbows as he raked a hot, lustful stare over her body. "Aye, my love. I want you to dance for me tonight. But I'd rather you do it *naked*."

Nora squeaked at his suggestion. "Why, Ewan MacAllister, you are an evil one, aren't you?"

"To the bottom of my rotten and depraved soul, Nora. Now come here, wife, and let me make sure we consummate our union."

She lifted the hem of her gown and stepped up into the bed. Leaning over him, she straddled his swollen groin.

"Hmm," she said as she rubbed herself against his erection. "What have we here?"

Ewan cupped her face in his hands and pulled her to his lips for a scorching kiss.

He pulled back a moment later to answer her question. "What we have here, my lady, is a bear who wants to be tamed. Know you someone with a stout enough heart to lead him home and suffer his dismal ways?"

She kissed him lightly on the lips. "Aye, my lord, I do. But having been brought home, is it possible for the bear to stay happily away from his cave?"

He smiled at that and the winsome look on her face. "Aye, it is. I want only you in my life, Nora."

"Only me? What then should I do with our baby when it comes?"

Ewan couldn't breathe as her words permeated his head. "What do you mean?"

"Well, 'tis early yet, but I missed my flow. I think my bear may have a cub coming to follow in his father's footsteps."

Joy made him delirious. "When will you know for sure?"

"A few weeks."

He pulled her on top of him, then groaned as her body contracted with his wound.

But he didn't care.

His wife, nay, his heart, carried his child. This was the sweetest moment of his life. "I love you, Nora. With every fiber of my soul. I love you."

She smiled at that. "And I love you, too."

Chapter 14

It was long after dark when Lochlan, Braden and Sin sat with Nora's father alone in the great hall of Alexander's keep. The overhead candles had been doused and the hall was illuminated only by the fire in the large fireplace that was built along the right wall.

Its light played against the banners and weapons that decorated the whitewashed walls, dancing strange shapes all around them while they joked and sampled the food that had been left out before the servants had taken their leave of them.

The happy couple had retired hours ago, and no one had seen a single sight of Nora since.

Not that they expected to.

Indeed, Lochlan fully expected days would go by before either of them showed themselves again.

It was something that made his heart soar.

He was glad happiness had finally come to his brother. Ewan had needed it.

"I can't believe we got Ewan married off before Lochlan," Braden said as he picked at a platter of sliced fruit that was set before him. "We needs be careful, Sin. I think the

Second Coming might be upon us. I feel the sudden urge for confession."

Sin laughed. "Perhaps."

"Have you any more word about the MacKaids?" Alexander asked.

Lochlan shook his head. How he wished to find them. And he would. He wouldn't rest until they paid for what they had attempted to do to his family.

"None of my men have found a trace of them," he said to Alexander. "Have yours?"

"Nay."

"That sits ill with me," Sin said. "I have a feeling we haven't heard the last of them."

"Most likely not," Lochlan concurred.

"So what should we do?" Alexander asked. "I've notified my cousin what they've done, and he has issued an order of execution for them, but until they're caught . . ."

"There's not much we can do," Braden said.

Sin finished off his tankard of ale and poured more. "Sure there is."

"What?" Braden asked.

"Marry Lochlan off."

Lochlan shoved playfully at Sin's arm. "You're drunk."

"Is he?" a feminine voice asked.

They looked up to see Sin's wife, Caledonia, approaching the table.

She moved around the side of the table until she was behind Sin's chair. Looking down at her husband, she gave him a chiding, gentle smile. "I had a feeling my wayward husband was spending far too much time down here."

Sin looked a bit sheepish.

"Come, my lord," she said, taking Sin's hand. "We have a long journey home tomorrow, and I promised my brother Jamie that we would be back in time for his birthday."

Sin kissed her hand, then rubbed it against his cheek.

Lochlan was amazed by the gesture that was so alien to Sin. He was glad to see his brother so well suited with his wife.

Sin was another one he had never expected to see happy. It did him good to know life had finally treated his elder brother kindly.

"Good night, gentlemen," Sin said, rising to follow after his wife.

They passed Maggie in the entranceway.

Lochlan smiled as she came forward, eyeing the three of them suspiciously. He remembered a time when he had contemplated her death and had wished many vile things upon her.

Now he was glad he had refrained from the urge to kill her.

"Look lively, Braden," he said to his youngest brother. " 'Tis your turn to have your ears boxed."

Braden scoffed, "My sweet Maggie knows

better than to box my ear, eh, love?"

There was a saucy sway to her hips as she approached the table. "It depends on if you've done anything to have them boxed for."

She smiled sweetly at Alexander and Lochlan. "Do you mind if I steal him away from you?"

"Not at all," Alexander said.

Braden got up, swept her up in his arms and headed for the stairs at almost a dead run.

Lochlan watched them leave, his heart light at his brother's antics. No doubt Maggie would be gifting him with another niece or nephew soon.

"So," Alexander said once they were alone. "Have you any plans to take a bride?"

Lochlan swirled the ale around in his cup as he considered that. In truth, there was no woman in his heart. He doubted if there ever would be. But still, his duty commanded him to take a bride.

There was only so long he could put off that particular responsibility.

"Mayhap one day," he said quietly.

Alexander arched a brow at him. "Aren't you a little old now not to be looking?"

Perhaps he was. But Lochlan had too many things that demanded his time, and marrying a woman sight unseen wasn't something he relished.

"To everything there is a season."

Alexander laughed at that.

Footsteps sounded outside the room, followed by the main door opening and closing.

Lochlan and Alexander exchanged puzzled frowns.

It was far too late for company.

An old servant entered the hall with a youth behind him. The boy hadn't quite reached his majority.

Dressed in rags, the boy carried a weathered satchel.

"Forgive me, my lord," the old servant said to Alexander. "The lad said he had news of Lysander."

Alexander motioned the boy to come forward. "Is there a problem?"

The boy hesitated, then shrank back. He looked warily at the servant, then to Lochlan.

"Speak, lad," Alexander said patiently. "No one will harm you."

Still the boy looked doubtful. "I have word, my lord. This man came to our village and he told me I was to bring this to you."

The boy rushed forward, dropped the satchel on the table, then ran back to a safe distance as if he expected the wrath of hell to fall down upon his young head.

Lochlan frowned at his fearful actions.

Alexander ran his hand over the worn leather. "Is this Lysander's?"

The boy swallowed. "I know not, my lord.

I was only told to give it you and to not open it."

By the pallor of the boy's face, Lochlan could surmise the child hadn't listened.

"Who gave you this?" Lochlan asked.

The youth scratched his neck nervously. "He said there was a letter for Lord Alexander inside and . . . and to tell his lordship that next time you should hire yourself someone better than a French knight." The boy was shaking. "Can I go home now, please, my lord?"

Alexander nodded.

The boy shot from the room as if Lucifer's hounds were after him.

Lochlan's frown deepened.

Alexander studied the bag. "How very strange."

"Aye," Lochlan said, leaning forward to look at it as well. "It is indeed."

Alexander opened the satchel and dumped its contents onto the table.

Lochlan stood up the instant he saw the green and black plaid that their father had commissioned years ago for his sons. He'd never known anyone other than he and his brothers to have it.

His blood went cold as he stared at it in disbelief.

Alexander opened a small piece of parchment while Lochlan pulled the plaid closer to examine it.

"Canmore," he read aloud, "I don't like being made a fool of by anyone. You can tell the gypsies that they are next on our list. You should have never told the king about us. Had you stayed quiet, your daughter might have lived. Now we'll be coming for her and the rest of the MacAllisters. Guard your backs carefully."

Alexander's hands shook and his face turned dark red with rage. "It's signed Graham MacKaid."

Lochlan barely heard the words. He was too fixated by the initials embroidered in the corner of the tattered and worn plaid.

K.M.

Kieran MacAllister.

But how?

Who would have had his brother's plaid? No one outside their clan would have access to it.

Seeking more clues, Lochlan unfolded the material and cursed as a disembodied hand fell to the floor.

Alexander's own curse rang out as he saw it and the strange brand that was on the back of the hand.

"So help me," he growled. "I'll kill every one of those bastards for this."

Lochlan found it hard to breathe. Hard to focus. He ran through his mind the man whom he had met briefly. A man he had paid all too little attention to.

"Who was Lysander?" he asked Alexander.

"I don't know, to be honest. I found him in France about five years ago when I went to visit a friend. He had just come back from Outremer and refused to speak of it."

"And this plaid?"

Alexander shrugged. "It was wrapped around him when he asked for work. Does it mean something to you?"

It meant more to him than his own life. "Did he say how he came by it?"

He shook his head. "I only know it was very dear to him. My wife's maid tried to take it from him once to clean it and he almost tore her arm for the trouble. He was rather feral in the early days of his employment."

Alexander retrieved the hand and went to find the priest to dispose of it.

Lochlan ran the monogrammed corner of the plaid through his long fingers as he stared at the initials his mother had placed there.

How had a Frenchman found Kieran's plaid?

None of the brothers had ever journeyed farther than England except for Sin, and Sin had never taken a plaid with him.

If not for the initials, he might think that perhaps the weaver had created more of the design and sold it.

But those initials matched the one for his plaid, Braden's and Ewan's.

Nay, this was Kieran's. He knew it. There was no doubt in his mind that it was his brother's, and by the looks of it, it was quite old.

A souvenir of Outremer.

Which meant that Kieran hadn't died that day when he'd gone out to the loch on his own.

For some unknown reason, his brother had faked his own death and then left Scotland.

But why?

Why would Kieran not send word to them. Why would he allow them to believe he was dead all these years?

Lochlan sat down as the news sank in.

No doubt the MacKaids had found the plaid after they killed Lysander and had sent it back to them.

They would have known exactly who this belonged to and what it meant.

Lochlan drained his ale in one gulp.

Somewhere out there, Kieran MacAllister might still be alive.

And God have mercy on his brother should he ever find him.

Epilogue

A month later

Ewan held Nora's hand as they walked through the framework that would one day soon be their new home. It would be a fine manor home fit for his lady wife and their new babe, whose arrival was now confirmed.

His heart light, he watched Nora tell the steward exactly what she wanted the great hall to look like while his own thoughts drifted.

He still couldn't believe what Lochlan had told him about Kieran.

None of them could.

Kieran was alive.

If he ever got his hands on him, Ewan would kill him for it.

Damn his brother for his selfishness that had cost all of them untold years of suffering.

But it was hard to hate Kieran, for it when all he had to do was look at his wife and think of the joy she gave him. For her, he would gladly suffer all over again.

Ewan was still wary that the MacKaids would make good their threats against them.

So far no trace of them had been found.

Not that he was worried. It would take more than them to come between him and his wife. Not to mention that Pagan had sworn to see them dead over what they'd done to Lysander.

Ewan held little doubt the man would make good on his promise. Something about Pagan said that he would make a formidable enemy.

Surely the man would make them regret the very day they had been born.

"Ewan?"

Looking up at Nora's call, he went over to her side.

She stood in the center of what would one day soon be their own hall, where they would entertain and live out a life he had never dared hope for.

"Think you this will be finished by the time the baby comes?"

Ewan nodded. "Aye, my love. I'll make sure of it."

He cast a meaningful look to the steward, who quickly assured him all would be done in plenty of time.

Nora smiled at her husband as the steward rushed away and told the workmen to hurry their labors.

These had been the happiest months of her life. She couldn't imagine anything better than the life they had now.

Well, except that she still wanted to travel.

But Ewan had promised her that as soon as the baby was old enough, he would take them to Aquitaine to visit her mother's family.

She took his hand and laced his fingers with hers. "You know, my lord, I am suddenly feeling very tired."

He cocked a brow at that. "Are you?"

She tried to keep her face straight as she frowned, but couldn't quite manage it.

Instead, she feigned a yawn. "Aye, you needs get me home soon or else I could fall asleep where I stand."

Ewan laughed and scooped her up in his arms. "In that case, love, I'd best be on my way."

Nora laughed as he sprinted with her toward their horses.

Once he had her astride her own, she leaned down and whispered in his ear.

"You know, Cat sent me a package."

A deep, lustful glint came to his eyes. Every time a package arrived from Cat it always heralded something that made her husband extremely happy.

"Did she now?" he asked.

"Aye," she said, thinking of the sheer gown that awaited them. The material was so thin that it would scarce cover her. "This time, it's a *red* one."

She saw the fire in his eyes as he leaped

onto his own horse. He set his heels into the flanks and tore off at a breakneck speed.

Nora followed along at her slower speed.

"Nora!" he called, urging her on.

How she loved this man, impatience and all.

But then when taming a bear, one could only do so much.

Author's Note

Please note that in *Taming the Scotsman* you will find the term gypsy, which modern readers will most likely attribute to the wandering bands of Romany who traversed Europe at a much later date.

As with most terms, the word had an earlier meaning that has been lost in "modern" English. During early- mid-medieval times, gypsies or gipsies took their name from gipser, the medieval term for a man's purse.

Since thieves were known to cut "gipser" strings, they were referred to as gipsies or gypsies. Most gypsies were thought to be of the peasant class, but not all were. To Ewan and Nora, a gypsy would just be someone who traveled about and was up to no good. They would be similar to a wandering outlaw band.

It's not until the very end of the medieval period that this term is associated with the Romany.

And please note, too, that many things in my series aren't what they appear. If this book leaves you with questions, they will be answered; watch carefully for clues about Kieran and the Brotherhood of the Sword.

Was Kieran's plaid really left with his sword by the loch? Could he still be alive even now?

Perhaps Lochlan will find the answers one day soon . . .

About the Author

USA Today bestselling author Sherrilyn Kenyon knows men. She lives outside of Nashville, Tennessee, with her husband and three sons. Raised in the middle of eight boys, and currently outnumbered by the Y chromosome in her home, she realizes the most valuable asset a woman has for coping with men is a sense of humor. Not to mention a large trash bag and a pair of tongs.

Writing as Kinley MacGregor and Sherrilyn Kenyon, she is the bestselling author of several series including *The Dark-Hunters*, *Brotherhood of the Sword*, *The MacAllisters*, and *The Sex Camp Diaries*. Her novel, *Fantasy Lover*, was voted one of the Top Ten Romances of 2002 by Romance Writers of America.

The employees of Thorndike Press hope you have enjoyed this Large Print book. All our Thorndike and Wheeler Large Print titles are designed for easy reading, and all our books are made to last. Other Thorndike Press Large Print books are available at your library, through selected bookstores, or directly from us.

For information about titles, please call:

(800) 223-1244

or visit our Web site at:

www.gale.com/thorndike
www.gale.com/wheeler

To share your comments, please write:

Publisher
Thorndike Press
295 Kennedy Memorial Drive
Waterville, ME   04901